AGENT OF VENGEANCE

By Scott M. Neuman

To my wife, Gila.

*Without her help, this novel would
never have seen the light of day.*

1

The ominous night sky almost seemed to reach down and touch the Wailing Wall as the Jews of the City of David trembled in silence. The State of Israel was on a level five security alert, meaning imminent war, and Jerusalem had become a ghost town. Many of its residents had already been called up for reserve duty in the Israel Defense Forces, and the remainder were huddling in bomb shelters, awaiting the unknown. *Mishmar Hagavul,* Israel's Border Police, was vigilant in keeping the hostiles among the Arab population inside under a strict curfew. Not one soul could be seen among the ancient streets and corridors of the Old City.

A feeling of doom had swept over the city. The midnight deadline was drawing closer. In a land famous for its prophets, no one could predict what would happen after the clock struck twelve. The following twenty-four hours had been given a name in the spirit of the Bible: Armageddon Day.

Nervous mothers, young children, and elderly grandparents whispered to each other in the darkness. Their statements of comfort echoed the old phrases that had often been used on the eve of countless tragic events in Jewish history. "Everything will be just fine." "Surely God will protect us." "Do not fear, the Messiah is about to arrive." "We Jews have always outlived our enemies."

Strangely, there was no mention of disaster. However, in their hearts they knew that there was only one logical outcome: the complete annihilation of their beloved country. Every citizen of Israel, save one, was sure that the dawn would bring a terrible holocaust ending the dream of the modern State of Israel.

The one citizen that knew better was the Prime Minister. The leader of the nation of the Jews that night was making a very different prediction: "Israel will not only survive, but will be victorious against all odds."

This Prime Minister knew that God's chosen people would not suffer. The leader of the Jewish nation was holding a key that would open up the gates of Hell. This key was to be used only when it was determined that there was no other option to protect the People of Israel. Now, Israel's enemies were gathered at the border and waiting to attack without mercy. The Prime Minister understood that Israel had no choice but to do to these invaders what they were planning to do to the Jewish people.

A single low-watt bulb suspended by a twisted black electric cord was the only source of light in Shelter R-4. The bulb cast long shadows as it slowly swayed above an aging olive-green metal utility desk with a lone black rotary phone and 1950s era swivel chair. The shelter was located over one hundred feet below Israel's parliament building, the Knesset. With its Brutalist rectangular shape, concrete and stone construction, and narrow slits for windows, the Knesset resembled a giant military pillbox. It had been designed to be the most secure building in the world. Its security system was so elaborate that experts had deemed it better protected than the U.S. gold reserves at Fort Knox.

Shelter R-4 was small, just twelve by fourteen feet, and only minimally furnished. There was only one entrance, on the east wall, a four-inch-thick door made of solid steel. It was opened by way of a unique cylindrical key that was passed directly from each outgoing Prime Minister to the incoming Prime Minister. There was no other copy of this key. Every Prime Minister was required to wear the key around his or her neck twenty-four hours a day, 365 days a year.

Located along the north wall was a metal cot with a thin blue foam mattress. There was no sheet. A striped pillow without a case was laying on the bed along with a gray wool army-issue blanket. Along the south wall rested two steel boxes of different sizes. From the larger box one could barely hear the low humming of a machine. An electrical cord connected the machine within the box to a special generator which was designed to provide a practically indefinite source of electricity. The

Prime Minister felt chills looking at this box, which emanated a foreboding aura. It contained, in a concrete sense, the essence of evil.

This was the first time the Prime Minister had entered R-4. In fact, none of Israel's Prime Ministers had ever entered the room. The leader of the Jewish nation, who had been a combat soldier and fought courageously in more than one war, had been overcome by a feeling of dread upon entering. It was time to make a decision that would affect millions of lives and alter the course of history, and the clock was ticking.

The Prime Minister reflected on the course of events that had led to the need to open Shelter R-4. Less than a year ago, the Supreme Leader of Iran, the Grand Ayatollah, stunned the world by announcing that his county had completed a multi-billion-dollar project to replace the United Nations. He called the complex the "New United Nations." This action, the result of a pact to undermine U.S. dominance in world affairs, was secretly backed by Russia and China. In less than a week, nearly every country in the world withdrew from the U.N. The only countries that remained were the United States, England, France, Australia, Brazil, Chad, Fiji, Canada and Israel.

One hundred and eighty-five countries gathered in Teheran a month later for the inauguration of the New United Nations. After a lavish opening-day ceremony, the first meeting was held. At the top of the legislative agenda was "Liberation Resolution One: A Permanent Solution to the Palestinian Problem." A working committee formed earlier in the month, made up of delegates from Libya, Syria, Iran, South Yemen, and chaired by a Palestinian Arab who was referred to as the Ambassador from Canaan, had created the proposal. The resolution stated that Israel would be ordered to dismantle its government and military forces and surrender its sovereignty to the New United Nations. This body would then install a new government made up solely of Palestinians and a new country called Canaan would take its place among the nations of the world.

Liberation Resolution One was unanimously approved by both the General Assembly and the Security Council. To implement the resolution, the Security Council ordered the formation of a multinational force so overwhelming that the Jewish State would have no alternative but to submit to its will. In the event that the State of Israel refused to disband its government and open its borders to the army, it would be subject to invasion in which every one of its citizens, regardless of age or gender, would be declared a hostile combatant and eligible for summary execution under the rules of the New Geneva Convention. The Grand Ayatollah called this strategy "the Ultimatum."

Over the past few weeks, the largest army in the history of the world, comprising over forty million soldiers representing most of the nations on Earth, were deployed along Israel's 624 miles of borders adjoining Lebanon, Syria, Jordan, and Egypt. In the Mediterranean and the Red Sea a massive naval force which included over a thousand warships were waiting to unleash a barrage of cannon and missile fire on the tiny county. In airfields located in the Sinai Peninsula, Saudi Arabia, Lebanon, and Jordan, a combined air force consisting of well over 40,000 jet fighters and bombers readied for the coming air strikes. At 22.00 Greenwich Mean Time, midnight Israel time, the multinational military force flying under the flag of the New United Nations would invade the State of Israel.

Earlier in the day, the President of the United States had called the Prime Minister of Israel to apologize that all diplomatic efforts including threats of sanctions had failed. The President sincerely expressed his dismay and confusion on how to respond in a world where insanity seemed to reign supreme as the forces of darkness had taken over much of the planet.

The President surprisingly offered the services of the United States Rapid Deployment Force to stand in solidarity with Israel. The force consisted of two airborne divisions that could be fully deployed in Israel in less than eight hours. CIA analysts predicted that the invasion would last less than two days. Therefore, these two divisions were the only support that the United States could offer in such a time frame. Moreover, the President's power was limited without Congress voting to declare war on practically the entire world.

The Prime Minister thanked the President for this true offer of friendship, but told him in no uncertain terms that modern-day Israel

7

has never asked another county to defend it, and even now, in the face of insurmountable odds, Israel preferred to handle the situation alone. "Besides," the Prime Minister added, "two divisions, more or less, would not change the course of events."

What the Prime Minister did not discuss with the President was the dramatic recommendation made by the Chief of Staff of the Israel Defense Forces earlier in the day. After delivering a lengthy report regarding Israel's ability to defend itself against a massive multinational force, he had concluded: "That there is no possibility that our military, neither alone, nor combined with others sympathetic to our plight, can repel an attack of the magnitude that will be delivered by the so-called New United Nations Freedom Expeditionary Force. Therefore, with no other options or alternatives, it is recommended that the Prime Minister implement the "Fletcher Option."

Surprisingly, the Chief of Staff had no idea what the Fletcher Option was or what it entailed. He knew that it was connected to the legendary American hero, Ronald Fletcher, who was affectionately referred to in Israel as the "Gentile Giant." Fletcher had been awarded Israel's most distinguished medal for bravery. This military option was referred to only in a single directive called "*Ain Brierah*," meaning "no choice."

The directive dated back several years. It listed the conditions necessary for the Chief of Staff to recommend implementation of the Fletcher Option. It was clear from the directive that its use could open a Pandora's box that might result in a worldwide apocalypse. But now Israel was truly facing the Armageddon.

After speaking with President, the Prime Minister descended to Shelter R-4, opened the special lock, and approached the smaller of the two boxes. Pulling open the box's front panel revealed a keypad. Every Prime Minister since the institution of the Fletcher Option had been required upon taking office to memorize the 48 numbers needed to open the smaller box. Strangely, the larger box had no keyhole, no panel, and no keypad. It was as if the contents had been sealed forever.

Inside the smaller box was a thick file, which the Prime Minister placed on the green utility desk and began to read. The file began with a brief chapter called "Introduction to the Fletcher Option." This chapter explained how the Fletcher Option came into existence and Ronald Fletcher's role in its creation. Reading the introduction brought back old memories of the Prime Minister's own personal relationship with Ronald Fletcher, and the role the leader of the nation of Israel personally played in the development of the protocol about to be implemented.

Following the introduction was the bulk of the file, which detailed over two hundred possible scenarios Israel might face and ways the Fletcher Option might be utilized. The Prime Minister scrutinized every option to determine which one contained the best solution to Israel's crisis. Finally, the Prime Minister selected Protocol XXVII, which described a scenario eerily similar to that which that Israel was facing and a strategic response that could be implemented.

Now that the decision was made, the Prime Minister opened the heavy steel door of Shelter R-4 and walked slowly down the long hall to a room labeled "Tactical Operations." Inside was a brightly lit command center containing all the equipment necessary to execute any of the protocols detailed in the Fletcher Option. The Prime Minister handed the selected protocol to the lone soldier in the room, who immediately set about carrying out its detailed instructions.

The Prime Minister then returned to Shelter R-4 and sat down on the cot. With eyes closed, the Prime Minister thought about the significance of handing such a file to an ordinary soldier and the catastrophic consequences that would soon be unleashed. Then the Prime Minister smiled, remembering Ronald Fletcher and the events that took place years ago, and warm memories slowly replaced the cold reality of Israel's current crisis and the burdens of leadership and responsibility.

2

Herr Professor Werner Broder was a perfectionist par
excellence. He had been working on the same experiment since the end
of World War II. Every day, without a moment's break, he would spend
fourteen straight hours in his laboratory. Broder had not taken a
vacation in years. He was living up to his pledge not to rest until the
program he had created would end in success.

Physically, Broder reminded his colleagues of a small, mole-like
creature not accustomed to life above ground. His oval face and
completely bald head were accentuated by thick, wire-rimmed glasses. It
was often joked that Broder was wearing two of his microscopes. He
had no discernible neck to separate between his head and his short,
chubby body. He also only had one outfit: an ancient lab coat, long
turned gray, which appeared as if it had not been sent to the laundry in
decades. Broder's assistants would whisper that with his disheveled
appearance he would eventually be mistaken for one of the Jewish
subjects of his laboratory experiments.

Broder had only one project on his agenda. All his efforts were
directed toward developing a stable delivery system for a certain deadly
biological agent. For years he had slowly and methodically tried to solve
the last step holding him back. Overcoming this obstacle was his only
goal in life.

Broder carefully noted in lab book 3328 on the "Strain
Program" that experiment 738,065 had been a failure. He took it in
stride. After all these years, Broder had begun to anticipate failure.
However, he still felt that he would eventually find the solution.

"Luck plays no role in scientific research," he often lectured his
assistants, "and only strict adherence to the rules of experimentation can
produce positive results."

During the final stages of World War II, Adolf Hitler spoke passionately of miracle weapons in development that would save Germany. The Allies thought that he was referring to V2 rockets or nuclear weapons. However, after the war, the Allies searched in vain for signs of the revolutionary military technology that they were sure Germany had been pursuing. Instead they found a half-hearted attempt by a poorly staffed and inadequately funded research facility that had barely succeeded in completing the initial steps needed to construct an atomic device.

Broder, however, knew the Fuhrer had been referring to a weapon of an entirely different nature. He understood why so little of Germany's vast resources were directed to the production of an atomic bomb. The reason was simple: all scientific efforts had been focused exclusively on the Strain Program. Both Adolf Hitler and Werner Broder agreed that the Strain was the most powerful weapon ever conceived.

Werner, a solitary man in his youth, had reacted with uncharacteristic enthusiasm when Hitler became the head of the Nazi Party. In fact, he idolized Hitler. Broder had the distinction of being the first faculty member at the University of Berlin to join the Nazi Party. Universally recognized as a brilliant scientist, he became a full professor of microbiology at the age of thirty. However, no matter how busy he was in his lab, Broder was always among the first in line to hear Hitler speak. He saw in Hitler a strong leader capable of reclaiming the lost glory of Germany.

Werner's fondest memory was his first private meeting with the Fuhrer. "Speak up, don't be bashful!" Hitler said, with a warm smile on his face. "I have been told that you have some information you will only tell me."

Broder was standing in front of Hitler's large mahogany desk. The year was 1944. Werner was visibly trembling. Last week, in the National Biological Research Center in Munich, Werner came upon a discovery so startling that he insisted on reporting it directly to Adolf Hitler. After much debate among Broder's superiors, following Werner's persistent refusals to discuss his finding with anyone other than the

Fuhrer, it was decided to allow Werner to, in their words, to "hang himself."

Though Martin Bormann, Hitler's personal secretary, was initially skeptical, he eventually consented to allow the meeting given Broder's long history with the Nazi Party. He scheduled Broder four minutes to speak with Hitler.

Entering Hitler's office, Werner was beyond himself. "My Fuhrer, I am a specialist in microbiology. For the past week I have been analyzing soil samples from an open gravesite at the extermination camp Treblinka. About ten days ago, all the Jewish laborers and two camp guards assigned to a marked-off area suddenly died of an unknown cause. Normally, this would be a matter of little consequence at Treblinka. However, two facts caused the camp authorities to call our center for assistance. First, they died suddenly. None showed any signs of any illness prior to their demise. Second, and more importantly, the report stated that after their sudden deaths, their skin and bone tissues broke down within minutes, turning the bodies into dust.

"Of course, when I reviewed the report, I must say that I did not believe it. As far as I know, such a phenomenon has never been described in any scientific journal. So I decided that I must go to the site personally to investigate. When I arrived, I told the Commandant of the camp that I would like to observe what had been reported. He ordered twenty Jewish inmates into the cordoned-off area. Before my eyes they all died almost instantaneously, just as the report described! All that remained was a gray, dust-like material.

"For the past week I have been running tests on the soil samples on site using our field laboratory, with Jewish inmates from the camp as the subjects. This agent is different in structure than any other known to science. It is unable to replicate outside of a host like a virus, but it does not seem to be affected by any substance known to kill viruses. It is also unusually resistant to heat, and continues to be lethal even when heated to extreme temperatures. It is also quite unusual in that it only affects humans and causes no harm to any animal or plant species. This agent is by far the most lethal substance I have ever come across. I call it the 'Strain.'

12

"I believe that a significant quantity of this substance could theoretically wipe out the human population of a country the size of Poland in less than a day. What makes this agent ideal for warfare, if it can be weaponized, is that after extraction from the soil it is no longer virulent after twenty-four hours. Meaning that after a day, the area in which it was released becomes completely safe for human rehabitation."

Broder concluded, "I hypothesize that if I can successfully weaponize this substance, it could be developed into the world's most effective weapon. After releasing it into a targeted area, after twenty-four hours we can occupy the country which will be free of its prior inhabitants. The land, industry, and wealth would be ours, intact!"

Up until Werner completed his speech, Hitler had sat quietly in concentration behind his desk. When Werner finished, Hitler rose from his chair as if possessed by the devil. The Fuhrer's steely blue eyes glowed as he exploded like a madman.

"Eureka! How many years have I been waiting for someone to walk through my doors and tell me of this kind of possibility? Why was I not informed that the potential for such a weapon could be made?"

Hitler returned to his seat, staring out the window in deep contemplation.

Werner was taken aback by Hitler's sudden outburst. He said, sheepishly, ""Until now, no such substance was known to science. It is impossible to determine how it was initially formed. Perhaps it emerged because this particular gravesite was used for bodies that had undergone unusual medical experiments at Treblinka involving radiation and noxious gases. In any case, I ordered that the entire site be sealed off, and I am bringing in the most state-of-the-art equipment from my former laboratory at the University of Berlin. We will not rest until we have developed the Strain for the service of Germany."

"With your help, Herr Professor, I can turn the war around!" Hitler said with a glimmer in his eyes.

"Mein Fuhrer," Broder said, "Unfortunately, I have only scratched the surface with my analysis of the Strain. It will be a tremendous undertaking to transform it into a weapon of war."

Hitler turned his gaze to the ceiling. Twenty-five minutes had passed. Outside, Bormann tried in vain to comfort the Ambassador of Japan who considered the delay a personal insult and an affront to his country.

Broder had been standing at attention the whole time. He was sweating profusely, and his glasses were slipping down his nose.

Hitler turned, looked into the cowered eyes of Broder, and smiled.

"Herr Professor, you will be provided with everything you need to make this weapon. All of Germany's resources are at your disposal. Next to me, you will be the most powerful man in Nazi Germany. All I ask is that you give me your personal pledge that you will not fail me."

Broder nodded as Hitler continued.

"This project must be executed in total secrecy. Only the two of us will know the true purpose of your work. I will instruct Bormann, my secretary, that you have free access to meet with me for any reason at any time. Professor Broder, you will not let me down!"

Hitler turned to a large map on the wall behind his desk. He studied it for several minutes. Hitler then picked up a pointer from his desk and waved it in the direction of the map. He placed the tip over a small island off the coast of Greece. Then he changed his mind.

"You will build your laboratory on Crete." Hitler ordered. He gave a parting nod to Werner. "Please wait outside."

Hitler then called in Martin Bormann. Ten minutes later, Bormann emerged with a letter in his hand. He handed it to Broder without saying a word.

Werner stared at the official letter from Adolf Hitler. It stated that Werner has essentially unlimited access to all of the resources of Germany's treasury and military. The letter granted Broder the power to requisition any funds and personnel that he needed for the completion of his project.

Werner staggered out of the Reich Chancellery. Meeting Adolf Hitler in person was a dream come true. Now, Hitler had made him his partner to save Nazi Germany. He told himself, "I have now only one goal in life: to fulfill my promise to my Fuhrer."

From the Chancellery, Broder went straight to Berlin Airport and entered its administrative offices. He showed the letter to the director of the airport and demanded a plane and a pilot. After reading the letter, the director cancelled a scheduled flight to Switzerland and ordered that Broder be taken anywhere he wished. When he arrived in Crete, he found that with Hitler's letter, all doors were open to him.

It took Broder less than a week to find a suitable site for his facility. Mount Kedros was isolated enough for a top-secret laboratory, and its rugged terrain answered the need for security. Due to local resistance, most of the villages in the area had been razed to the ground by German troops, and therefore the remaining locals were likely to keep their distance from Nazi activities.

In order to bring in the necessary supplies, Broder set up offices in the names of fictitious companies in Athens, Barcelona, Budapest, and Prague. Each office operated independently, and were unaware of the operations or even existence of other offices. He randomly distributed orders of building materials and equipment so that it would be impossible to discern what he was constructing.

Hitler, an amateur architect, decided that he alone would design the laboratory and the surrounding facility. His plan was to maintain total security and at the same disguise the facility's true purpose.

The laboratory was located in the center of the base and surrounded by three concentric concrete walls. The outer wall was fifteen feet high and was guarded by an elite SS brigade. The middle wall, twenty feet high, was located one kilometer inside the outer wall. The terrain was highest at this point. The area between the outer and middle walls was cleared of all rocks, plants, and trees, leaving a flat surface where a minefield was laid. The innermost wall, three hundred feet from the middle wall, was thirty feet high, making it the tallest structure on the mountain. Between the inner wall and the middle wall a twenty-foot-wide moat was dug and filled with a think synthetic oil manufactured to have the same characteristics as quicksand. Anything that fell into the moat was immediately swallowed up by this sticky substance.

There were no guards between the three walls. Securing the area were nests of automatic machine guns set off by weight-sensitive plates placed at random throughout the areas between the walls. Any movement detected by the plates would also trigger high-intensity search lights.

The buildings above ground level were disguised to look like weather monitoring facilities. All administrative offices, housing, security, and supplies were located on the upper level. One building at the end of the complex housed hundreds of Jews to be used as test subjects. The lower level, located twenty meters below ground, consisted of several different research laboratories connected by underground tunnels.

Soil and debris from the contaminated areas of Treblinka were excavated by Jewish slave laborers and shipped to the site in triple layered zinc barrels. Hundreds of Jews were killed by the Strain during the excavation. The barrels were stored in a large underground warehouse and accessible only by passing several layers of security and a specially designed airlock.

An elaborate security protocol assured absolute secrecy. No one, including Broder, ever left the area behind the inner wall. All materials and supplies entered the base via an automated rail line. Flatcars entered a gate in the SS command center adjacent to the outer wall and passed through gates in the middle and inner walls without any human assistance. When they arrived to the central complex, the flatcars were unloaded and stored. Any waste products created by the project staff or laboratory were burned in a special facility within the complex. In this way nothing from the inside complex ever reached the outside.

The guards in the SS security station in the inner complex were selected specifically because they were orphans and would have no need to contact family members on the outside. In the inner security office, there was a single landline and radio transmitter which was fully disassembled when not in use. The landline connected to only one phone, that of the chief officer of the outer security center, Oberst Kropp. Kropp was responsible for fulfilling all needs of the inner compound.

With these arrangements, no information concerning the workings of the project ever left the base, thus ensuring total secrecy. The facility was manned by Professor Broder's staff from the National Biological Laboratory. After helping transfer all the materials excavated from gravesite area containing the Strain, the overseeing staff from Treblinka were transported to the facility, and the Jewish slave laborers were killed off with Zyklon-B gas. Therefore, the only person outside of the facility who knew of the Strain Program was Adolf Hitler.

Werner Broder had two objectives in developing the Strain into an effective weapon of war. First, to isolate the strain from the soil and stabilize it in order that it would maintain its lethality. Second, to develop a reliable delivery system.

After two years of work, the delivery system was ready. It consisted of a tempered steel cylinder the size of a tennis ball. The cylinder contained a receiver capable of processing long-wave radio signals. When the cylinder received a correctly coded transmission it would open, releasing its contents. A specially designed radio transmitter, similar to the German code machine known as Ultra, complete with Enigma ciphers, was developed. The Strain transmitter was capable of sending coded signals around the world. Broder was especially pleased with the construction of the delivery cylinder. Durability testing confirmed that it was capable of lasting indefinitely, even in the most hostile environments.

Professor Broder was also successful in isolating the Strain from the soil samples. However, whenever the Strain was removed from the original soil sample, it would die within twenty-four hours. No media proved capable of retaining the stability of the Strain, and every effort to prevent its breakdown was a failure. Finding an appropriate medium was critical because Broder's experiments showed that even in the soil from Treblinka the Strain was slowly losing viability. Additionally, the Strain was present in the soil diffusely and needed to be isolated and concentrated to make an effective weapon of war. The problem was that there was an infinite variety of potential media to choose from. Broder knew eventually that he would come upon the solution, but time was not on his side.

There was also the question of distribution. Cylinders could be placed strategically to cover all populated land areas of Earth. However, Hitler had realized that many countries had naval assets at sea that would be out of reach of the Strain. He sent an urgent message to Broder to address the issue. Broder sent back a message stating that large cylinders, the size of naval mines, would be produced to be strategically placed in rivers, lakes and oceans. Upon "Judgement Day," the Strain in these cylinders would be released upon all the waterways on Earth infecting any humans at sea.

The war situation had become catastrophic for the Germans. The Allies were closing in on Germany's borders from both the East and the West. Crete itself was under nearly constant bombardment from American and British forces. In December of 1944, mainland Greece was liberated by the Allies. However, the German garrison on Crete tenaciously held out due to Hitler's insistence on sending heavy reinforcements to the island. The German High Command did not understand this obvious waste of manpower and resources, but Hitler overruled them. What the High Command did not know was that Germany's last hope of winning the war was the ongoing efforts of the Broder Laboratory.

Professor Broder, realizing the desperate situation, worked his team of scientists and technicians to exhaustion. Each was required to fill a minimum of four twelve-hour and three sixteen-hour shifts per week. Broder himself only slept four hours a day. This grueling work schedule continued until about three months before the end of the war.

On February 3, 1945, Allied bombers on a routine mission struck a coastal ammunition depot in Crete about one hundred miles from Broder's facility.

"Hey Jack, great job!" Tom the co-pilot called out to Captain Armstrong, the squadron flight leader. "Lenny's B-52 must have hit a munitions dump. Man, it went up like a match box!"

"Probably tripped some sort of chain reaction," Captain Armstrong called back.

"We have a major problem now, though. The rest of the plane's racks are full."

"What's the problem? We still have plenty of fuel to return to base," shot back the Captain.

"Roger. But that means we'll have to stick around for unloading. That and all the paperwork will cut a half-day off our weekend pass." Tom groaned.

"OK, gotcha. Good thinking. What's our secondary target, Tom?"

"K-5. Looks like a weather station, but the boys at intel think it's a relay station for Kraut signals."

"Great - let's show 'em what a Kansas tornado looks like!" the Captain said with a smile. "And if you Germans are listening, we got enough bombs left to teach you peeping Nazi bastards the whole English language."

With that, Captain Jack Armstrong's squadron of B-17 Flying Fortresses turned to the direction of Broder's base.

3

"Ronnie, are you sure you're going to meet us at the beach?" Mary asked from behind the steering wheel. She was parked on Hayarkon Street in front of the U.S. Embassy in Tel Aviv, Israel.

"Don't worry, I just have to give a quick report. Maximum one hour. Honest. Then I'll join you and the kids at the beach in Netanya, and then we'll all go for dinner, O.K.?"

"Fine," Mary said, with a look of disbelief. "Anyway, I have to go, the kids are waiting for me at home."

Ron bent over and stuck his head into the open diver-side window. He gave Mary a long kiss. Then she drove off.

Ronald Fletcher was enjoying his current assignment in Israel. As the son of the famed General George Fletcher, he had been an army brat as long as he could remember, growing up on bases in more than fifteen countries. When his father retired, the family settled down in Kenosha, Wisconsin where Ron's grandparents lived.

On his first day at Kenosha High School, Ron, then a junior, met Mary, a freshman, as they both reached for a straw in the cafeteria. It was love at first sight.

As Ron walked in the direction of the United States Embassy, he thought about how lucky he was. He had married the first and only woman he had ever loved. She was still, in his eyes, the same beautiful freshman at Kenosha High School. Mary was five foot five and very petite. Her button nose perfectly complimented her glowing green eyes and thin, delicate lips. Mary still wore her glistening black hair with the same simple flip from her high school days. Then, as now, she was every boy's dream, but from that very first meeting, she only had eyes for one boy, Ronald Fletcher.

And why not? Ron was a local celebrity. Years of scrimmaging on far-flung military installations at Stuttgart, Okinawa, and Daegu had honed Ron's skills, and he had been starting quarterback for the last two years at his old high school in Washington State. Tryouts at Kenosha were a breeze, and within a few weeks he was both first-string quarterback and Captain of the Kenosha High School football team.

Ron was six foot five and weighed around two hundred pounds. He had the squared jaw look of a movie star. Though he spoke quietly, if he lost his temper it was best to stay clear. With Ron, it was one punch and lights out.

Upon graduation, Ronald Fletcher received a full scholarship to the University of Chicago, not for his athleticism, but rather for his academic achievements. While he worked on his B.A. in U.S. History, he was constantly shuttling back and from Kenosha to spend time with Mary. At graduation he asked Mary to marry him and she joyfully accepted. The wedding took place at the Quadrangle Club. After Mary graduated high school, she joined Ron at the University of Chicago and studied psychology while Ron began his post-graduate studies.

After completing a P.H.D. in International Relations and Diplomacy in four years, Fletcher shocked Mary and his family by suddenly announcing he was leaving academia to serve in the U.S. Army. After recovering from the initial shock, Mary realized that Ron needed to serve not only because of his own patriotism, but also because he felt a family obligation to serve.

Ron had a natural knack for picking up languages and had practiced his skills all over the world. He could speak fluent German and Japanese without an accent, and had a working knowledge of several other languages. Even though he joined the army as a mere recruit, his intellectual abilities and top physical condition set him apart from the crowd. After basic training he was sent to Officer Candidate School in Fort Benning, and then completed the Special Forces training program at Fort Bragg.

From there Fletcher has sent to Fort Holabird, Maryland where he completed further courses at the United States Army Intelligence Center. By that time the Vietnam War had begun, and he was deployed to active duty. Ron was made a liaison officer to a Vietnamese brigade, and completed a series of in tours in which he rose to the rank of lieutenant colonel and was appointed chief liaison officer for the Green Berets. During his time in Vietnam, Ron earned just about every medal the United States Army could award.

Fletcher gained a reputation as a fearless commando as the leader of an elite unit of American and South Vietnamese joint unit known as the Lion's Pack. Their official mission was to cause fear and panic among the Viet Cong leadership. Operating behind enemy lines in North Vietnam, and sometimes in neighboring Cambodia and Laos, Ron and his men averaged capturing or killing at least five Viet Cong officers a week.

Ron's coup de maître was the capture of Major Ho Lin. Ho had the reputation of being the most proficient interrogator, i.e. torturer, in the Far East. He had developed his sadistic skills to perfection. Lin described his techniques as "the art of obtaining information through prolonged agony." By the time of his capture, Ho had become the Viet Cong's top interrogator of Vietnamese agents caught spying for U.S. Intelligence.

Fletcher offered Ho Lin the choice of death or working for the South Vietnamese. Lin chose the latter and began to employ his talents for Fletcher's purposes. When the Viet Cong learned that Lin had joined the South Vietnamese interrogation unit, terror ran rampant among their leaders. Often Ron would only have to mention Lin's name and his prisoner would break down and "volunteer" any information Fletcher requested.

Over time, Lin and Fletcher developed an unlikely friendship, and Lin offered to tutor Fletcher in the use of his techniques. Ron proved to be an excellent student, finding a mystical harmony in the oriental philosophy as applied to both physical and mental torture. Ron became proficient in the use of a tool that Lin had designed called the "Vu Khi," meaning "weapon" in Vietnamese. This was a six-inch long collapsible steel needle made with a hollow center into which various instruments could be introduced. Ron's favorite accessory was a quartet of titanium microblades that would could be twisted under the skin to dramatic effect. Lin taught Fletcher how the Vu Khi could be used either as a weapon or as an aid for extracting information from noncooperative subjects. Over time, Fletcher made the Vu Khi his trademark instrument.

When Fletcher ended his military service he was recruited by the National Security Agency, a clandestine intelligence organization which was established in 1952 by the Department of Defense. He quickly rose through its ranks. His current cover in Israel was that of Director of Education at the U.S. Embassy in Tel Aviv Embassy. His real assignment, however, was to accompany Israel commando teams on their raids into Lebanon. This was in keeping with an undisclosed pact between the United States and Israel to help ensure intelligence regarding emerging terrorist organizations was quickly disseminated to all interested parties.

It was a demanding position, since many of the Israeli operations were unusually risky. In fact, the previous four agents who had held Ron's assignment had been grated transfer requests on the basis of "immediate danger to personal safety." Fletcher, however, enjoyed the raids, and when an operation seemed to be nosediving out of control, he would unofficially drop his observer status and join in.

Two months earlier, the unit Fletcher was accompanying had been ambushed by a company of Hezbollah terrorists on maneuvers. All nine of the Israeli commandos were hit with fire. They were surrounded and outgunned. Ron, the tenth man, was the only one who had not been injured. Eventually, the Hezbollah terrorists moved in to capture the commandos. Ron noticed that they were not checking the severity of their wounds, so he acted as if he, too, had sustained a serious injury. As a result, he was included when they bound the Israelis' hands and tossed them in the back of a truck with a canvas roof to take them back to Hezbollah's base camp.

One terrorist armed with an AK-47 assault rifle was stationed in the back of the truck to guard the Israelis. Fletcher saw that the guard, exhausted from the maneuvers and the gunfight, kept glancing out of the truck to keep awake. He covertly removed the Vu Khi from a hidden compartment in the side of his right boot and used it to cut off his bonds. When the terrorist again turned his head, Ron jumped on him and stabbed the Vu Khi into his right ear, penetrating deep into his brain. The terrorist died instantly.

Fletcher then grabbed the terrorist's assault rifle, climbed out from under the canvas roof, and clinging to the side of the truck worked his way toward the passenger-side door. He smashed the passenger window with the stock of the AK-47, and then flipped it around and held down the trigger, emptying an entire magazine into the front compartment. As the truck veered out of control, he jumped through the broken window and grabbed the wheel. After a quick stop to kick out the bullet-ridden bodies of the terrorists in the cab, he drove the truck to the unit's pickup point, ramming through two roadblocks on the way. Thanks to Fletcher's actions, all the soldiers survived. Ron was subsequently awarded Israel's highest medal for valor in a secret ceremony.

Fletcher entered the U.S. Embassy through a side door. Waiting next to the security guard was Mike Barnes, the Assistant Director of Education for the Embassy and Ron's assistant. Barnes, an African American, was a former college all-American linebacker with Alabama's Crimson Tide. He had joined the Navy after graduation and trained as an underwater demolition expert. From there he was transferred the then-newly created Navy Seals. He was trained in hand-to-hand combat, high altitude parachute jumping, and even foreign languages. In Vietnam he had been part of the Phoenix Program, and had been recruited by the NSA after discharge. He had recently been assigned to the Tel Aviv Embassy to be Fletcher's assistant and eventual replacement.

"Sir," Barnes said, "the Ambassador just called. He wants you to drive down to the Ministry of Defense in Jerusalem."

"What for?" Ron asked.

"He says you need to give an official statement about Israel's flights over Southern Lebanon yesterday. There are reports circulating that the Israelis bombed targets with American-made ordinances."

"Mike, didn't you tell him that those are just rumors? We've checked this out at least a dozen times!" Ron said, frustrated.

"I tried, but he didn't want to listen. He said he's flying stateside this week and has a meeting with the Secretary of State. If the subject comes up, he wants to show that he investigated."

"Between you and me, this more about his career than diplomacy. You know he wants the Ambassadorship to England. I guess he has to show that he cares about protocol," Ron complained. "What time is my appointment?"

"Noon."

"Oh, that's just great. There goes family day at the beach. Mary's going to have a fit! This is the second time this month I promised and didn't show up."

4

As the Strain facility was being bombarded by Captain Jack Armstrong's Rowdy 52s, Werner was sleeping soundly on the lower level. In order to maximize the number of experiments he could run, he had long ago moved his quarters from the upper dormitories to a simple cot in a storage room near the main lab, just a few hundred yards from the sealed warehouse holding the soil samples containing the Strain.

The lower level, boasting fourteen-foot thick concrete walls made at the same grade that had been used to fortify the Fuhrerbunker, had been designed to insulate the main lab and storage room from any disturbance of the upper levels up to and including intense bombing. It was deafeningly silent, save a faint hum from the ventilation system.

At 6:10 a.m., Professor Werner Broder's assistant knocked on his door to tell him the day shift was ten minutes late. He rose and walked to the intercom to chastise the team leader responsible. When there was no answer, he angrily hurried to the elevator to investigate the delay. As Werner had not left the lower level for over a week, he felt it was in any case a good opportunity to "go topside" and inspect the facility. After waiting five minutes for the elevator he realized that something was very wrong. Broder headed to the staircase and began to climb the two hundred and twenty-four steps to the surface in double-time.

When Broder finally reached the steel security door sealing the lower level from the surface, he was completely out of breath. With great difficulty he pulled down on the grey handle and pushed open the heavy door. He looked out and was stunned by the sight of mangled steel beams and fallen concrete blocks. The upper level had been completely demolished. Seeing his life's work now destroyed, he turned grey and collapsed. Later that day, Nazi soldiers investigating the site found him sitting in a pile of rubble, mumbling to himself. Broder was immediately evacuated to the island's main army hospital in Heraklion. There he was diagnosed as suffering from a severe nervous breakdown.

It was a tremendous blow to Hitler when he received the news of the bombing of the facility and Werner Broder's condition. Until that time, his belief that Broder could help turn the tide of the war in Germany's favor had been his only solace. Now, all hope had vanished.

Hitler dispatched an elite SS battalion led by his most loyal officer, Gruppenfuhrer Rudolf Kempler, to Crete to take command of the Strain Facility. Kempler was a natural cold-blooded killer. Hitler's first order to Kempler was to shoot Oberst Kropp for his failure to adequately protect the facility. Kempler had no compunction to carry out the order. Immediately upon arrival, as he was being warmly greeted by Kropp, Kempler coolly removed his Luger from its holster and shot Kropp between the eyes.

Kempler inspected the facility and sent a detailed report to Hitler. It stated that though the lower level of the facility had remained intact, Professor Broder was in no mental condition to continue his efforts to develop the Strain. This news completely shattered Hitler. The Russian forces, led by Stalin's most talented general, Konstantinovich Zhukov, were by then less than one hundred kilometers from Berlin. With no other option, Hitler ordered that Broder should be airlifted to Berlin and treated at Germany's top sanatorium.

Hitler was now totally despondent about his fate and that of Nazi Germany. Now facing ultimate defeat, in a moment of weakness he confided the details of the Strain Program with his most trusted follower, Doctor Joseph Goebbels, Minister of Propaganda. Goebbels listened carefully to the details. As he listened, he, too, was crushed as he realized his personal dream of universal Nazi Socialism was dying.

When Hitler finished, Goebbels comforted his Fuhrer and told him that all was not lost. Again, he repeated the mantra that just as Fredrick the Great was able to bring Germany to victory from inevitable defeat in the Seven Year War, so too would the Fuhrer. Goebbels asked Hitler to give him a few hours and he would return with a surprise.

Several hours later, Hitler met with Goebbels in the conference room of the Fuhrerbunker. Hitler was in a bitter mood.

"The lion," Hitler began, "is under siege by a gang of idiotic, rock-slinging baboons. And even my own people are turning on me now that the enemy has the upper hand. If it was in my power, I would wipe out the whole unjust world!"

Goebbels nodded in agreement. He began to speak, slowly and cautiously. "My Fuhrer, you told me that Professor Broder was positive the Strain could be prepared into a weapon of war."

Hitler nodded, then said sullenly, "But there is no time! We will consider ourselves lucky if Germany lasts another two weeks!"

"Perhaps consider this, my Fuhrer. We could send Broder, with all his staff, to a remote location where he would finish his weapon. When it is complete, he can execute your final order and destroy the entire non-Aryan world. At that time you will have your final victory."

Hitler frowned. "That's not enough! I have to personally give the order when it is the right time. I must be there!"

"Then why not go into hiding with him?" Goebbels asked.

"You know as well as I do that if I accompany Broder into exile, the world would never rest until I am found. They would search the ends of the earth. And if they find me, Stalin will put me on display in the Moscow Zoo. Look what they did to our Italian friend, Mussolini. His own people hung him from a meat hook in the town square. No Josef, I must die here in the Bunker."

Goebbels had been waiting for this declaration. "Well, mein Fuhrer, what if I tell you that you can die here in the bunker and still be able to order Broder to use the weapon any way you deem fit?"

Hitler laughed. "My dear Josef, you are starting to believe your own fairy tales. Have you gone mad?"

"Perhaps, but not about this." Goebbels answered. "Please bear with me for just a moment and hear what I am about to say."

Hitler nodded.

As you know, Himmler, Goering, and Bormann have become enormously rich by looting the nations we conquered."

"Of course I know. I turned a blind eye to this. I was never interested in collecting money or trinkets."

"Well, for many years I was offered a cut of the booty, but I always refused. But eventually I realized that I could use the wealth for a greater good. Like the Medici family used their wealth to patronize Michelangelo and Leonardo Da Vinci, I decided I would use my share to further the pursuits of geniuses aligned with our own interests."

Hitler looked at Goebbels impatiently. "Yes, go on."

"About a year ago, Himmler introduced me to a Dr. Julius Schreiber. He is the Chairman of Medicine at the University Hospital in Hamburg, as well as the Chief of the Department of Eugenics. A man completely devoted to the vision of a pure Aryan nation. He explained that the Government had stopped his funding in order to cover military expenses. I decided I would personally fund his research, and met with him periodically to discuss his progress.

"Mein Fuhrer, after the terrible Generals Plot, I realized that without you Nazism is but a shell. Knowing that Dr. Schreiber was an expert in medical research, I asked him off-hand one day if there was a way to keep you alive forever. I was just musing, but Dr. Schreiber said he would accept it as a challenge. He told me that he would give me an answer at our next meeting.

"A few weeks later, I had already forgotten the conversation, but when we sat down, the first words out of his mouth was that yes, he knew how to keep you alive forever.

"Obviously, I was flabbergasted by such an outrageous claim, but Dr. Schreiber displayed only the utmost confidence. He insisted that I come down to his lab and he would prove it. So we went straight to his Institute. He showed me the proof. And, I tell you, he was speaking the truth. I wasn't sure how to approach you with this, but after our conversation this morning, I realized the time had come."

Hitler was dumbfounded. "Is this another one of your fantastic tall tales to comfort me?" Hitler sighed. Then he said, resigned, "I suppose I could meet this Dr. Schreiber."

"If I may so bold," Goebbels announced, "The good doctor is waiting outside."

Hitler glared at Goebbels. "Oh, of course he would be. Bring him in to my private quarters."

Hitler called Bormann and ordered him to bring both Goebbels and a Dr. Julius Schreiber to his personal quarters. When Hitler entered a few moments later, they stood up and gave the Nazi salute with an emphatic, "Heil Hitler!" Hitler half-heartedly returned the salute and shuffled toward his chair. He looked confused and perplexed.

Dr. Julius Schreiber, a tall, thin man with the build of a praying mantis, had shown an unusual interest for medicine from his earliest days. At six years old, he performed his first medical procedure, exploratory abdominal surgery, on a calico cat which he had received as a birthday present. When his mother discovered the mutilated creature, he explained simply that he "just wanted to see how it works."

Schreiber continued his grotesque "experiments" throughout primary and secondary school, but was otherwise a model student. Upon graduation, he received a full scholarship to the Medical University of Vienna, and completed his studies two full years early with honors.

Dr. Schreiber, however, had shown little interest in treating patients, and was determined to dedicate his career to academic medicine. A prolific researcher, he was made full professor in record time. However, despite many early successes, he was often reprimanded by his superiors for unethical conduct. He was finally punished with a one-year suspension after publishing an article about brain surgery to cure "rebellious urges" that had been performed on "volunteers" from a local mental institution. At the hearing he had inherited a nickname that stuck with him for the rest of his career, "Dr. Frankenstein."

During his suspension, Dr. Schreiber sought to pursue his research outside of the university. One of his proposals regarding a eugenics project found its way into the hands of Heinrich Himmler, who was enthusiastic about the idea.

The proposal was to create a step-by-step protocol for producing pure Aryans. Schreiber proposed selecting existing male and female Aryans, based on his own criteria, and breed them like horses. Those selected would be Germans that were eighteen years old and were tall, strong, and intelligent. Only candidates with blond hair and blue eyes were to be considered.

Himmler, the black-haired, balding former schoolteacher, was enthralled with the concept of breeding pure Germans to create "Super Aryans." The thought of using eugenics to produce the "Master Race" would be, in his mind, the ultimate achievement of the Third Reich. After a two-hour meeting Himmler decided to sponsor the project.

Months later, during the initial stages of the Super Aryan Project, at an informal dinner party, Himmler introduced Dr. Schreiber to Goebbels. Immediately the two Nazi fanatics hit it off. They spent the entire party talking about different ways science might help in furthering the goals of the Third Reich. At the end of the night, Goebbels approached Himmler and asked if he could steal away Dr. Schreiber to work on some his own ideas. Himmler was delighted to grant this favor, knowing that this would create some good will with the Minister of Propaganda.

Hitler stared at Dr. Schreiber, trying to size him up. After a moment, Goebbels asked Schreiber directly, "Can you make the Fuhrer live forever?"

Schreiber answered slowly and carefully. "If you are asking whether I can maintain the Fuhrer's consciousness, memories, and ability to communicate indefinitely, then yes, I can, absolutely."

Schreiber turned towards Hitler and continued, "May I be so bold, my Further, to address you directly."

Hitler, arms folded, nodded.

"At first, when Doctor Goebbels asked if there was a way to prologue life eternally, I was fascinated by the idea. However, all organic structures inevitably break down. The brain, the most important organ and the seat of consciousness, is the most fragile of organs. Without adequate blood flow, it begins to break down within three minutes.

"In the course of my research, however, I had encountered a very unusual case of a young woman with cancer of the blood which seemed to break all the rules of organic matter. This young woman, who we called Patient Y, had in her blood a cell with an unusual shape which, when isolated, never seemed to lose any vitality over time. These cells were not only immortal themselves, they seemed influence the vitality of adjacent cells. When put in a medium, we were able to keep many different tissues, including bone, skin, and internal organs vital for years, without any signs of breakdown.

"So I had an idea that we could use Patient Y's immortal cancer cells as a way to keep tissues alive indefinitely. However, these cells could note propagate complex mechanical processes, such as keep the heart pumping or the intestines digesting food. We would have to isolate just the most essential part of the human brain that contained the essence of life.

"This brought me to the pioneering work of Heinrich Kluver and Paul Bucy, who discovered the area of the brain that holds emotions. Bucy named it the 'Limbic System.' It is a semicircular area of dense tissue at the center of the brain. I decided to run a serious of experiments to see if I could isolate that area of the brain and keep it functioning outside of the human body. In order to do so, I needed human 'volunteers.' Fortunately, Herr Goebbels was able to supply me with an endless number of Jews for experimentation. After many failures, I developed a procedure in which the entire limbic system was removed intact and placed in the Patient Y medium, with electrodes attached to the brain tissue to provide a continuous low-voltage current. In this way I was able to keep this brain tissue alive for much longer than three minutes. I called this device 'Das Maschine.'

"The next step was to determine whether this dissected section maintained its identity and consciousness. Through countless hours of sending electrical signals to the tissue and receiving electrical pulses in return, I was eventually able to 'decode' the messages and achieve basic communication. To test whether this device actually worked, one of my staff members would make one of the 'volunteers' memorize a long number of at least eight digits. After surgery and dissection, I would send signals that represented the first two digits. To my amazement, the dissected section would send back the last six digits as a response.

"But one problem remained. My experiments found that transplanting the Limbic System alone did not result in a full consciousness, but rather merely a type of primitive computation device, like an adding machine. It had the ability to take the information it was sent and perform basic processing functions. But it had no actual identity or being, no soul, if you will.

"I searched desperately throughout the other areas of the brain to locate the section which controlled upper-order thought and communication. Sadly, for a long period of time, I was unsuccessful.

"But I had a moment of luck. One of my lab assistants once offhandedly mentioned something he had seen in the works of 17th century philosopher Rene Descartes. In discussing the immortality of the soul, Descartes suggested that there was a tiny organ in the center of the brain called the 'pineal gland' that served as a control center. He identified the gland as the location of the soul.

"With this in mind, I went to work. Our earlier experiments involving the limbic system had not included the pineal gland. My experiment proved Descartes' theory was correct. With the pineal gland included, the subjects in Das Maschine retained capacity for higher thought, memory, emotion, and communication.

"After months of painstaking work, we were able to achieve advanced communication. The first step was to train the subjects before dissection. After 'planting' them in Das Maschine, they were able to understand messages transmitted one letter at a time and send back intelligible responses."

Hitler was fascinated. "What about the rest of the body?"

"Superfluous. The body is not what a human being is. It is more or less a vehicle for transportation. Granted, it allows certain sensory functions such as touch, sight, smell and hearing. But a person's true essence is his intellect, while human senses are transitory and illusory. Do we really need to smell a flower? Taste food? Hear an opera, or see the sky? My answer is no. These are mere distractions that actually hamper the ability of the brain to reach its full potential.

"In the last few weeks, we have perfected a communication device, a simple keyboard, for sending messages to Das Maschine. The individual in Das Maschine sends back information that is printed from a teletype machine. We have achieved success beyond anything I could have ever dreamed of, and all in your service, mein Fuhrer!"

The room was silent as Hitler and Goebbels tried to grasp the implications of Schreiber's words. Then Goebbels spoke up. "What about pain? Is it painful?"

Schreiber answered. "No, quite the opposite. The surgery is done under general anesthesia. Once the brain tissue is connected to a system of electrodes, pain and pleasure are controlled by a simple dial on Das Maschine.

"I have developed a method to manually control the brain tissue responsible for sensations of pain and pleasure. In fact, the dial allows for these sensations to be incrementally adjusted. It is clearly marked on the control panel of Das Maschine. At one extreme, the being inhabiting Das Maschine will experience ultimate pleasure, and at the other extreme, ultimate pain."

Hitler frowned. "You are saying that I won't be able to walk, talk, eat, feel a gentle breeze in my face, or experience any other sensual pleasure. It will feel like prison!"

Schreiber responded, "On the contrary, with proper calibration you will feel wonderful. Of course, we could leave the machine on its ultimate pleasure setting, however, the experience on this setting is so overwhelming you will not want to even maintain contact with the outside world, and may even be too much for an extended period of time. We will find the setting in which you feel fantastic, but are still able to function at an optimal level.

"In any case, as you are well aware, ordinary physical pleasures are fleeting. I understand your current medical condition only allows you to walk short distances. Goebbels told me that one of your greatest pleasures in life had been your long walks at Berchtesgaden. They are no longer possible. Nor are the pleasures you had experienced speaking in front of giant rallies at Nuremberg. What I am offering with Das Maschine is both eternal life and eternal pleasure. If anything, it will be totally liberating, a worldly Garden of Eden."

Hitler responded. "But what will I be without my ability to speak?"

Schreiber paused for a moment. "This may be a possibility in the future. The American corporation 'Bell Labs' has developed what they call a vocoder, which can make sounds approximate to vocalizations in response to input from a keyboard. We should be able to take recordings of your speeches and integrate them with Das Maschine, however, this will take time."

"What about vision, and hearing?"

"We have not yet perfected inputs from a camera and microphone, however, we have learned from our experiments that some processing is necessary from the occipital lobe in the back of the brain. We will make sure to include tissue from that area so that when we have perfected this technology, we will introduce it as a separate module."

Hitler sighed. Ever since the German army's defeat at Stalingrad, he knew the war would eventually be lost. Furthermore, his physical condition had deteriorated since the assassination plot at Wolf's Lair which he miraculously survived. He was, in short, a wreck of a man. His tremors and shuffling gait made it clear to even his most loyal followers that he was living on borrowed time. Now that the German Army was losing battle after battle, the war front was approaching his doorstep. Soon, the Russian Army would be in Berlin. He faced the terrible prospect of capture and disgrace by his most hated enemy, Stalin.

Hitler thought to himself. "How could it be that after achieving the impossible I would have such a horrible end? I nearly conquered the world. But now I am cornered like a rat by enemies approaching from all sides!"

For some time, Hitler had resigned himself to fact that only suicide could save him from utter humiliation. But Dr. Schreiber's breakthrough offered a second chance. He would have the power to shape his own fate, and could yet live to see his dream of the Nazi Party ruling the world. And through Broder's Strain program he would enjoy wreaking sweet revenge on his enemies. There would be a Fourth Reich. A world populated by Super-Aryans and ruled forever by him. All of his achievements to date seemed miniscule compared to this new vision.

Hitler said to Dr. Schreiber, "Still, how can I condemn myself to prison in a box?"

Dr. Schreiber smiled. "Just the opposite. You will not even realize that you are part of Das Maschine. You will have total vitality and clarity, without the weakness of a physical form which will ultimately break down and return to the dust. You will have the strength of your youth and the wisdom you have gained building Germany into a Juggernaut. You will truly be God-like, living in a constant heavenly state of existence."

With these words, Hitler's decision was made. Hitler told Goebbels he had authority to do whatever was needed. Then he turned and dismissed Dr. Schreiber, swearing him to absolute secrecy.

Goebbels and Hitler spent the next two weeks developing a plan. Hitler named it "Project Valhalla," after the Norse myth that described the kind of heaven Hitler planned to create for himself. In the Nordic version of heaven, when heroes die in battle, they are gathered to a great hall ruled by the king of the pantheon of gods, Odin. There, the heroes dine with him and the other gods forever.

The plan was perfect, except for one detail. In order for it to work, Goebbels and his family would not be able to accompany Hitler into exile. Goebbels would have to sacrifice himself and his family for the greater cause of Nazism. Hitler knew that of all his followers, only Goebbels could be trusted to supervise the staged suicide of Hitler in the Fuhrerbunker and its subsequent cover-up. If all went according to plan, there would be no endless search for Hitler by his numerous enemies.

Fortunately for Hitler, Goebbels was completely on board. When he discussed the plan with his wife Magda, she readily agreed. Magda told her husband that this final sacrifice was the ultimate honor they could receive, and would immortalize them in the history of Nazism as the greatest disciples of the Fuhrer, having died to ensure the escape and rebirth of their great leader, Adolf Hitler.

5

It was an unusually humid day as Mary Fletcher and her two children, Bobby and Jane Elizabeth, approached the clear blue waters of the Mediterranean Sea. With miles of sandy beaches and a sprawling boardwalk lined with restaurants, cafes, and video arcades, Netanya was a tourist trap that drew giant crowds all summer.

Mary loved Israeli beaches, but, as on this day, the bustle at the center of the beach could be overwhelming. She had once described the scene in a letter to her best friend in Wisconsin.

"The Israelis play a beach game called *Makklot*. Two players are armed with enormous ping pong paddles, though there is no table or net. In this vicious game they use a black ball, a bit larger than a golf ball and made of extremely hard rubber. I don't know what the rules are, but one thing is for sure, every few minutes the ball goes astray and hits an innocent bystander, like me, on the head. Why, it is my impression that the object of the game is to hit sunbathers."

As they moved their way through the mass of beachgoers, Mary told her children, "I think we'd better set our blanket on the other side of the beach, away from the crowd."

Bobby, the older sibling, complained. "Do we have to? Those boys already asked me to join them in beach soccer!"

Mary stared back at Bobby with an admonishing look. "Well, young man, I thought you promised your sister you would play with her first?"

Bobby looked toward his little sister, who adored her older brother, and nodded in agreement.

He shouted to the boys, "*Yotar meuchar*," meaning "later" in Hebrew. Bobby, like his father, had a knack for quickly picking up languages.

Mary decided she would do some reading and sunbathing while her children played in the sand. Bobby announced that, as Americans, it was their patriotic duty to build a sand model of Washington D.C. on the Israeli shore.

Mary put sunscreen on Bobby and Jane and sent them off closer to the sea where the sand was more suitable for building. She then laid down on a blanket with a book and lemonade with mint she had bought from a kiosk on the boardwalk. All were having a wonderful time as a moist breeze rose up from the sea to provide some cool relief from the sun.

About an hour later, the loudspeakers from the lifeguard station began rumbling. Mary was half asleep. Knowing very little Hebrew, she assumed that a lifeguard was warning a child to stay within the zone marked for swimming. Bobby was nearly fluent in Hebrew; however, he was too engrossed in the construction of the Washington Monument to pay any attention to the warning.

The other sunbathers nervously retreated from the shore and toward the beach parking lot. In the distance, a small black rubber boat with five men landed on the beach. The men wore black-and-white patterned keffiyehs, Arab headscarves, that hid all but their eyes. They were dressed in worn green khakis with black combat boots. Each carried an AK-74 assault rifle.

Mary was woken by a blast of automatic rifle fire. Rising, she saw one of the terrorists running in the direction of her children.

Mary screamed out to Bobby, "Take Jane and get behind the boat! Hurry!"

About one hundred feet from the newly constructed sand city laid the wreck of an ancient wooden rowboat. Following his mother's command, Bobby grabbed Jane and made a mad dash. They nearly reached the boat as the terrorist opened fire. A cloud of sand was kicked up into the air and rained down on the children. Luckily, the spray of bullets fell short of their mark.

Mary instinctively shouted at the terrorist to distract him. He turned and looked in her direction, giving the children a few vital seconds to slip behind the hull.

Seeing that the children had found refuge behind the boat, the terrorist decided that Mary, being completely exposed, was now an easier target. He took careful aim with his AK-74. This assault rifle, the successor to the legendary AK-47, was known for its remarkable accuracy over long distances. A rarity in the Middle East, it had been acquired covertly from a corrupt Afghani intelligence officer.

As Mary turned to escape, three bullets ripped through her back. She fell to the ground, writhing in pain. With her remaining strength, she managed to crawl a short distance away from her children, hoping to create a further distraction.

The terrorist broke into a run toward Mary, shouting *"Allahu Akbar!"* As he approached his victim, Mary was near her last breath. He stood towering over her. Mary looked at him. Her eyes seemed to scream, "Haven't you done enough?"

The terrorist raised his AK-74 and shouted, "Jewish whore! *Allahu Akbar!*" He then brought the gun's stock down with all his strength onto her head, crushing her skull. After staring with much satisfaction at his handiwork, he remembered the children behind the boat. He turned and ran in their direction.

From behind the boat, Bobby and Jane had watched the violent murder of their mother. Bobby thought to himself angrily, "Where is my father? He could have done something!" Jane, on the other hand, was hysterical. She could only think over and over again about the brutal attack on her beloved mother she had just witnessed.

As the first terrorist, apparently the leader of the group, approached the boat, the other four terrorists followed his lead. The beachgoers, now a relatively safe distance from the attack, had watched Mary's death by bludgeoning in abject horror. Now, hearing the cries of her innocent children, they felt helpless.

Shlomo Mizrachi was watching the events unfold from the parking area. A short, stocky, middle-aged man, he had run the beach's most popular ice cream stand for the last decade. Born in Morocco, Shlomo had moved to Israel in 1943 and fought in Italy as part of the British-organized Jewish Brigade in World War II and later in Israel's War of Independence. Upon discharge he got married and worked menial jobs. After being called up to fight the 1956 Sinai Campaign, he moved to Netanya and set up an ice cream stand near the beach. Later he saw action in the Six Day War. In the Yom Kippur war, Israel's most recent conflict with the Arabs, he served in the *Hagah* or Civil Defense.

Though out of shape and hardly combat-ready, Shlomo was not the kind of person to stand by and watch children being harmed. He pulled out from underneath his popsicle freezer the WWII-issue Enfield No. 2 Mk I revolver which he had kept as a memento. Though he never envisioned himself as a warrior, watching the terrorists approach the beach had given Shlomo a rush of adrenaline which he had not experienced since his army service. He knew that he would never shy away from fighting Israel's enemies, no matter what the odds. With reckless abandon, the stocky grandfather of three dashed in the direction of the terrorists. As Shlomo ran he shouted to the crowd with desperation, "There are children behind the boat!"

Not far from Shlomo's ice cream stand, Zelda Steiner reached for the pistol in her purse, a .25 caliber, eight-shot Beretta Jetfire. She had just celebrated her seventieth birthday. Having grown up in Radziejow, a small town in Poland, she was twenty-two years old when the Nazis invaded her country. Within four years, the Nazis had murdered her entire family, including her husband, an accountant from the nearby village of Alexandrow, and her two children. She survived Auschwitz and made her way to Israel after the war, marrying Yitzhak, a *sabra*, or native-born Israeli. She became a mother again and eventually had three sons, two daughters, and eight grandchildren. As a member of Kibbutz Lavi, she ran the cooperative dairy for over thirty years. After her husband passed away, she retired to a small apartment near the Netanya beach to be closer to her grown-up children and grandchildren.

Zelda Steiner understood that the terrorists intended to butcher the two children hiding behind the boat. In her mind, these Jihadists were no different than the Nazis. Zelda knew what she had to do. She took the Barretta from her purse and followed closely near Shlomo.

While the lead terrorist was far ahead and closing in on the boat, Zelda and Shlomo were only about a hundred yards behind the four terrorists following him. The two fired a few rounds, causing the terrorists to drop to the sand and return fire. The lead terrorist spun around and spotted Zelda and Shlomo. He screamed in Arabic, "Jewish scum!" and changed directions, charging the two courageous Israelis.

Yoram Cohen, long since retired and living off his pension and German reparation checks had been taking his daily stroll along the shore collecting seashells when the warning came from the loudspeakers. At first, he turned to escape. When he heard the screams of Bobby and Jane, however, he froze in place. Yoram wasn't armed, but he felt he couldn't just leave the children alone. Against all his common sense he ran towards the boat.

As Yoram approached the children Bobby cried out, "They killed my mother!" Jane was curled up next to the rotted hull repeatedly mumbling, "Mommy, mommy."

Yoram spoke practically no English, however, he understood the meaning of these words all too well. At the age of eight he had witnessed both his parents slaughtered by sword-wielding Cossacks during a pogrom in his native city of Kiev, Russia. He too, like Zelda, was a survivor of the Nazi extermination camps. Yoram knew their position was hopeless. The four terrorists were now approaching the boat and strafing it with automatic fire. He could hear the clattering of the bullets hitting the side of the boat. There was no place to run.

Yoram grabbed Bobby and Jane and laid them down. He crouched over them and tried to shield them with his body. He kept repeating to them *khrabryye deti*, meaning "brave children" in Russian.

Then he started to pray in Hebrew. "Shema Yisroel, Hear O' Israel, the Lord is our God, the Lord is One." This passage, perhaps the most sacred prayer in Judaism, is traditionally recited by a Jew who is facing imminent death.

As round after round fired from the terrorists' AK-74 assault rifles hit the boat, the leader shouted an order in Arabic: "Leave them for now, let's finish off these Zionist pigs."

The five now began to spray bullets at Zelda and Shlomo. Zelda, about twenty yards from Shlomo, was hit in her left shoulder. As the leader charged in her direction, Shlomo tried to cover her. However, with only three bullets remaining in his revolver, and the other four terrorists heading towards him, he was in a bad situation.

The leader decided to finish off Zelda the way he had killed Mary Fletcher. As he raised his assault rifle to bludgeon her, Zelda lifted her gun and fired. The bullet pierced the terrorist's neck and he fell to the ground, gasping for air. His blood formed a crimson pool in the sand around them.

Shlomo, seeing the fallen terrorist, crawled in the direction of Zelda. When he reached her, he said to Zelda, gently, "Please stay still." The elderly grandmother was in terrible pain, but her face revealed a distinct glow of satisfaction.

Shlomo picked up the now-bloody AK-74 as he glanced with the disgust at the terrorist leader, who was drowning in his own blood. But he had no time or inclination to put the murderer out of his misery. It had been many years since he had operated an automatic rifle, and he was trying to remember his training.

Shlomo grabbed a magazine from the belt of the gasping leader and stuffed it into his pocket. In order to conserve ammunition, he switched the rifle from automatic to semi-automatic mode. He then opened fire.

The four remaining terrorists were now faced with a new situation, leaderless and facing a veteran with an AK-74. Laying in the sand, they argued about their next move.

Two miles to the south, Aryeh Glickstein and Shmuel Roth, both former Golani infantrymen, were serving in reserve duty. Every year for the past six years they had been assigned to the same job, patrolling the beach between Herzliya and Netanya eight hours a day. In six years of patrolling they had not once spotted anything even remotely suspicious, save the occasional lost suitcase. But as Aryeh often told Shmuel, "It beats manning a roadblock in the middle of the Negev Desert."

Nearing the end of their shift they were approaching Netanya when suddenly a voice came over the jeep radio. "Patrol Aleph-3, proceed immediately to Sector 28. Snakes have been spotted."

Aryeh hit the gas and the two sped to the public beach in Netanya. Within two minutes they arrived at the boat, where they saw Yoram lying motionless on top of two children. One, a young girl, was screaming in hysterics, while the other, an older boy, was trying to comfort her.

Shmuel jumped from the jeep as Aryeh slowed down. Holding his Uzi submachine gun firmly at his waist, he began firing rapidly in the direction of the terrorists. With its distinctive boxy shape and legendary reliability, the Israeli-produced Uzi had become a favorite of both Israeli Special Forces and Hollywood producers. Now caught in a crossfire between Shmuel's Uzi and Shlomo's requisitioned AK-74, the terrorists were in a bind.

Aryeh stopped the jeep and went to check on the old man and two children hiding behind the boat. He pulled Yoram's lifeless body off the children, and was relieved to see that they appeared to be unharmed.

Aryeh told them firmly in Hebrew, "Everything is going to be O.K., just stay behind me." He then went back to the jeep and hopped onto the back, where a Browning M2 .50 caliber heavy machine gun was mounted. The machine gun's awesome firepower was overwhelming, and Aryeh's barrage of bullets created a barrier that prevented the terrorists from approaching Shmuel or Shlomo.

The terrorists soon realized that they were caught in a deadly crossfire. There were only two options. One was to make a break for their assault boat. However, they would be an easy target for Israeli patrol boats and aircraft, making escape impossible. The other option was to charge the entrance to the beach and kill as many Israelis as possible until they were martyred. A crowd of beachgoers had remained to watch the firefight at what they thought was a safe distance. In unison, the terrorists began to rush toward them.

For a moment, panic struck the crowd. The terrorists successfully dodged the bullets fired by Shmuel, Aryeh, and Shlomo. A massacre seemed inevitable.

Suddenly, the crowd became quiet. The panic-stricken beachgoers turned to look in the direction of an Army truck that had just skidded to a halt twenty feet away. Out jumped a unit of soldiers wearing green fatigues and red combat boots, signifying to that they were paratroopers, Israel's top combat soldiers. This was Unit 269, *Sayeret Matkal* or General Reconnaissance, often considered to be Israel's most elite commando unit. They had been on training maneuvers just eight miles away on the Green Line when Captain Motti Golan had picked up news of the attack over the truck's radio transmitter. Golan. Always the maverick, knew his men were needed and fast, so without awaiting orders they had headed immediately to the site.

Upon arriving, Golan ordered his unit to split into two groups. The first group was ordered to defend the crowd and close off the entrance to the beach. The second group was directed to engage the terrorists. Half took a position near Shlomo and Zelda, with the unit's medic attending to Zelda's wounds. The other half moved into position at the north side of the beach, effectively cutting off thee directions for the terrorists, leaving only the sea open.

Golan raised his arm, signaling the soldiers to open up with heavy automatic fire. The commandos were equipped with Israeli-made Galil assault rifles, which were more than a match for the terrorists' AK-74s. At the same time, Shmuel continued to strafe the beach with Uzi fire alongside Aryeh manning the jeep's mounted heavy machine gun.

Having no cover on the beach, the terrorists were left with their faces in the sand. With no choice, they crawled toward their assault boat floating in the shallow waters.

Golan was not interested in a prolonged chase that could put more civilians at risk. He gave a signal to his unit, raising up one hand with his palm facing upward. This let his soldiers know to raise the elevation of their aim seven feet above the heads of their terrorists. He then picked up the radio, instructing Shmuel and Aryeh to cease fire, as they were not familiar with his planned maneuver. He then ordered a group of four soldiers at Shlomo's position to strap their Galils to their backs and take out their bayonets.

The terrorists slithering towards the sea with their faces in the sand did not notice the change in elevation of the fire. All they heard was the sound of bullets whizzing above their heads.

Captain Golan then gave the signal to the four commandos to charge. They ran in a crouched position at full speed under the umbrella of bullets. Within seconds they pounced on the terrorists. Three of the commandos, with cold precision, cut the throats of their assigned terrorists. The fourth, as ordered, pressed his knife firmly against the Adam's apple of his terrorist, drawing blood, but making sure not to kill him.

Golan gave the signal to cease fire. Then he walked over and stood above the trembling, lone subdued terrorist. Speaking calmly in Arabic, he said in a commanding voice, "Please give me a reason to cut your throat." The terrorist, already feeling the blood soaking the collar of his khakis, gave no reason, and Motti took him prisoner.

6

Hitler considered his new project, "Valhalla," to be his greatest achievement. Now he would finally be able to fulfill his vision of a pure Aryan society, built from the ground up and planned to the last detail. While the whole world was awaiting the military defeat and collapse of Nazi Germany, Hitler delighted in knowing that he would get the last laugh.

Three elements were necessary for the successful execution of his plan. First, a suitable location must be found. Then, transportation of personnel and supplies would have to be arranged in total secrecy. Finally, Hitler himself would have to vanish in a way that would prevent his enemies from searching for him after hostilities ended.

Hitler meticulously scrutinized dozens of relief maps provided to him by Goebbels until he settled on his ideal site for the project. In the winter of 1941, a team of geologists tasked with identifying potential oil reserves had accompanied Rommel's Tank Corp during their campaign in Northern Libya. During a survey, they had discovered a cluster of underground caverns resembling a four-leafed clover, hundreds of feet below the earth's surface. Knowing that this type of geological formation could potentially contain oil deposits, the geologists sent down a drilling team to explore the interior. Though no oil reserves were discovered, the team noted substantial coal deposits that ran along the perimeter of the cave. Though the depth and the remoteness of the site made coal mining economically unfeasible, the details of the survey were reported and filed, gathering dust on a shelf until it was retrieved for Hitler's perusal.

The reasons that made the site unfeasible for mining were, in fact, exactly why it was ideal for the Valhalla project. The site was located fifty miles from the coast of Libya, in the Sirte Basin of the Sahara Desert, one of the most remote and desolate places on Earth.

The average temperature was over one hundred thirty degrees Fahrenheit. It was constantly plagued with sandstorms. Even desert nomads steered clear of this part of the Sahara. Furthermore, Hitler believed that the Allies would never search for him in an area that had been under their control for over two years.

What made the nearly ten-square-kilometer cave complex perfect for Hitler's project, however, was a feature discovered by the exploration team that was completely unexpected. Natural springs at one edge of the cave fed a sizable underground river of potable water. This reliable water source was critical for long-term human habitation. Adding to the site's appeal was the unusually high ceilings reaching nearly two hundred feet above the floor of the cave. As he read the report, Hitler thought to himself that the descriptions of cavern complex could easily have described legendary Valhalla of Norse mythology.

The second part of Hitler's plan was so complex it would seem to be a logistical nightmare. In order to build Valhalla, enormous amounts of building materials and supplies would have to be transported to the remote site in secret. As Hitler's plans called for an underground city with a projected population of fifty to one hundred thousand inhabitants that would be able to live in total isolation from the outside world for a minimum of fifty years, all equipment would need to be in place from day one.

Valhalla was more than just a fortress from which Hitler would rein destruction on his enemies. It would also be the birthplace of the Fourth Reich, which would bring to fruition Hitler's dream of conquering of the world and repopulating it with a "Master Race." In Hitler's vision of Valhalla, he would play the role of Odin at the head of the banquet attended by his Super-Aryans as his valiant warriors. Hitler envisioned that one day, after sanitizing the Earth from its present inhabitants, his Super-Aryans would emerge from their underground sanctuary at Valhalla to repopulate the planet.

Hitler worked with Dr. Julius Schreiber to conform his breeding program to Alfred Eydt's study of Aryan morphology. In Hitler's vision, continents would be populated according to Eydt's classification. Europe would be populated with the Nordic Aryan, Asia with the Falian Aryan, Africa with the Eastern Baltic Aryan, North America with the Western Baltic Aryan, South America with the Dinaric Aryan, and Oceania with the Eastern German Aryan.

To this end, Dr. Schreiber organized the selection of six hundred young women and sixty men between the ages of fifteen and eighteen. This seed group was flown from Berlin's Institute for Research of Heredity to the remains of the Strain facility in Crete, which would serve as a staging ground before the final move to Valhalla. At the same time, Hitler ordered Professor Broder, who had by then recovered from his nervous breakdown, to make up a list of the necessary equipment, supplies, and manpower he would need to complete the Strain Program.

Hitler understood that in order to build Valhalla, skilled manpower was essential. Hitler tasked Goebbels to identify one hundred unmarried SS engineering officers and bring them to a training seminar in Berlin. Upon their arrival, the engineers were housed in a hangar at the Berlin Military Airfield, one of the few buildings that remained after many Allied bombing runs. Instead of a seminar, the officers found themselves at an impromptu award ceremony. Hitler arrived at the hangar and pinned on each officer's uniform an Iron Cross, Second Class. Once a highly coveted metal, after 1943 it was freely awarded in order to maintain loyalty. Upon the conclusion of the ceremony, the engineers were boarded onto transport planes and flown directly to the airfield near the Strain facility on Cyprus.

Heinrich Mueller, head of the Gestapo, was alerted to the unusual movements of the engineering officers as well as vast amounts of vital war material being sent to Cyprus. It was his duty to report suspicious activity regarding SS personnel to his direct superior, Himmler, but his intuition suggested that perhaps the Fuhrer was directly involved and might not want the information publicized. Therefore, he decided to bypass Himmler and go directly to the Fuhrer to inquire.

When Mueller scheduled to meet with Hitler to discuss the matter, Hitler was placed in a precarious position. Hitler had intended from the beginning to maintain total secrecy from the Nazi bureaucracy which he had come to distrust. He realized that even if he denied everything and ordered Mueller to drop the matter, Mueller was likely to discover Valhalla and put the entire project at risk, especially if he was captured and interrogated by the Allies after the war. Initially, Hitler decided he would have Mueller executed by the Fuhrerbunker guards on some pretext. However, he changed his mind, concluding that Mueller's mysterious disappearance would likely create even more exposure.

Hitler personally liked Mueller, so he decided to include Mueller in his plans. This turned out to be a shrewd decision. Mueller, a ferociously sadistic Nazi, would be able to utilize his position as the head of the Gestapo to procure tens of thousands of tons of supplies without anyone daring to question his purpose.

After an hour-long meeting with his Fuhrer, Mueller knew everything there was to know about the Strain and Project Valhalla. Hitler put him right to work overseeing the procurement program.

Mueller knew exactly what to do. He first concentrated all financial resources at his disposal, including over ten thousand kilograms of gold Jewish dental work which was smelted into bullion and sold for cash. He also collected a vast fortune of cash reserves that had been confiscated from hundreds of banks throughout conquered Europe. The money was deposited in Swiss bank accounts by Nazi sympathizers.

He then ordered agents around the world to purchase materials and goods from a list provided to him by Hitler. The purchases were made at black markets in many different countries by locally stationed Gestapo agents. Such transactions were not unusual during the closing stages of World War II, in fact, there was an unwritten rule that cash payments for supplies meant no questions asked. Mueller coordinated the shipment and delivery of these purchases by assembling a private merchant fleet which would pick up and deliver these supplies to a makeshift port on the coast of Crete.

Mueller was also able to secretly order the transfer of thousands of Jews who were being evacuated by way of forced death marches from Poland's extermination camps and boarded them on to his merchant fleet. These Jews served three purposes. First, he needed "volunteers" for Schreiber's experiments to develop additional modules to Das Maschine. Second, Broder needed Jews as test subjects for the

Strain program. Finally, slave labor was necessary for the back-breaking work required to build and maintain Project Valhalla.

On February 1, 1945, the first phase began. All supplies and initial manpower were loaded onto cargo ships docked in the port in Crete. The convoy of ships were under top secret orders to head toward a designated spot off the Libyan coast. In order to prevent Allied naval forces from intervening, Hitler arranged a distraction. Two groups of U-boats were sent to engage larger British vessels at Malta and Sicily. Though there was some initial resistance by senior naval officers to what seemed to be a completely futile suicide mission, a brief and violent visit by Gestapo agents quickly dissolved the opposition.

As the vessels departed for Libya, Heinrich Mueller flew to Crete for a meeting with SS Gruppenfuhrer Otto Kempler, the official in charge of Hitler's security team for the project, at the mountaintop ruins of the former Strain facility. Mueller handed Kempler a mahogany box that held twenty sealed envelopes. Each one contained the handwritten orders of the Fuhrer. Mueller instructed Kempler to open the first envelope which was marked with a handwritten Roman numeral I and bore the signature of the Fuhrer.

The first envelope contained a short note on linen paper signed by Hitler stating that Kempler was to open each envelope in numerical order and execute its orders completely before opening the next envelope. It then instructed Kempler that his first orders were that as the ships left port, he was to destroy the port and adjacent town, leaving no witnesses.

On February 3, 1945, Kempler executed Hitler's orders with unparalleled ruthlessness. The Gruppenfuhrer and a full battalion of 800 Waffen SS struck at three in the morning. They killed every moving creature from the hills surrounding the Strain facility to the port. By 5:00 a.m. all civilians were dead. The death toll included the original crews of the cargo ships, who Kempler executed by locking them in a warehouse full of dynamite and then personally lighting the fuse. The crews were replaced with Nazi *Kriegsmarine* officers and their subordinates.

After Kempler determined there were no potential witnesses left, the entire lower level of the Strain Laboratory was transported to the port area and loaded on cargo boats. The Jews of the facility were placed aboard a prisoner ship. Dr. Broder and his staff of scientists, along with Kempler's troops, were boarded on the last remaining freighter containing the drums holding the soil from the open gravesite of Treblinka. These ships joined the convoy that was gathered about five miles at sea and ready to set sail as per the schedule in Hitler's second directive. As the ships left port, timed explosives destroyed both the Strain facility and the port area.

Every ship in the convoy flew flags of neutral countries. Halfway to their destination, the convey split into two groups and sailed separate courses, avoiding areas patrolled by Allied warships and, for that matter, German U-boats. On February 6, all ships rendezvoused in the Gulf of Sirte off the Libyan coast.

According to the instructions in envelope five, Kempler ordered a SS platoon to row to shore and scout the landing area described in the enclosed map. At the same time, prefabricated barges were assembled to transfer the supplies and passengers to the shores of the secluded beach that was rarely, if ever, patrolled by the closest British garrison located over one hundred miles away. It took less than a day to transport all supplies and personnel to the shore. On the beach, over three hundred trucks were fueled and loaded with the supplies and equipment.

Kempler then ordered the now skeleton crews still manning the ships to sail to an area in the Gulf where the waters were deepest. Upon arrival, the sailors sent dynamite charges in every freighter and boarded landing crafts. Once they were approximately one mile away from the ships, the SS officer in charge turned the red knob of a remote detonation device which caused the entire flotilla to sink in unison. Fifteen minutes later there was no trace of the ships, which had disappeared 4,000 meters below the surface of the water.

When the crews returned, the giant caravan of trucks began their trek into the vast Sahara Desert. Over three thousand Jewish prisoners followed behind on a forced march. Gruppenfuhrer Kempler ordered his SS soldiers to viciously beat any Jew that was lagging behind.

Upon arriving at the designated site, a salt marsh ten miles southeast of Mount Haruj, Kempler instructed his officers to make camp. He handed the chief engineering officer a list of instructions contained in envelope twelve. The officer and his team quickly located one of the drilling holes from the 1941 geological survey. Using specially designed boring equipment, the engineers expanded the hole, which was located above the southern cavern of the clover-shaped complex, into a wide shaft. Then the engineers installed a heavy-duty traction elevator comprised of a steel cage suspended by wires. A large desert camouflaged tent was hastily erected to hide the elevator shaft. A gas-powered generator was then set up to provide electricity.

The first team of engineers, donning masks attached to large cylindrical oxygen tanks, entered the elevator and were lowered over three hundred feet beneath the surface to the cavern floor. They brought down powerful search lights which were connected to the generator on the desert surface.

After testing the quality of the air of the cavern, they removed their oxygen masks. Testing had demonstrated that the air was safe to breathe and had no traces of methane gas. The temperature inside the cavern was a moderate 23 degrees Celsius, 73.4 degrees Fahrenheit. The team did a brief survey and identified the coal deposits near the entrance of the western cavern as described in the survey. An additional substantial coal deposit was found in the far corner of the cavern. The team then headed to the underground river. Water analysis demonstrated that the water of the river was potable and had a surprisingly low bacterial count.

With habitability established, the team returned to the surface to organize construction crews. Two hundred Jewish prisoners were attached to the crews to provide manual labor. At the same time, preparations for a permanent elevator and control room were initiated in the area of the shaft.

The first task at hand was to assemble a coal power plant in the western cavern. Tons of specialized equipment were transported to the floor of the Valhalla complex to build the plant. Teams of Jewish prisoners were immediately put to work to perform the backbreaking job of mining the coal to fuel the generators. At the same time, SS engineers began to install hundreds of light fixtures along the ceiling of the cavern complex, along with an enormous HVAC system to regulate the environment. One week later, on the eighteenth of February, Gruppenfuhrer Kempler threw a large switch located in the control room, turning on the lights throughout the caverns. This act informally proclaimed Project Valhalla as the new Germany, birthplace of the Fourth Reich.

Kempler organized each of the complex's four caverns according to Hitler's instructions. The Northern Clover, by far the largest of the four caverns, was set aside for Dr. Schreiber's Aryan repopulation project. An entire city was to be constructed to house the "seed population," with architecture and layout designed to resemble the streets of Berlin. There were plans for a hospital, schools, and a park complete with its own pond. A dock was constructed for recreational rowboats to be used both on the soon-to-be-dug lake and the river. According to the master plan of the city, each of the six Aryan communities would have its own neighborhood. Schreiber projected that the population from his breeding program would be over sixty thousand within forty years.

In the far corner of the Northern Clover was a tunnel that led to a cave which would house the new Strain Research Facility. Professor Broder and his team of scientists were housed in an enclave of villas just outside the entrance. The cave was hermetically sealed with a ventilation system separate from the rest of the complex. After the construction of the lab was completed, the steel drums containing the contaminated soil from Treblinka was moved into a specially designed storage facility. The barrels were stacked seven-high in rows of thirty. Three sealed security doors were installed in the tunnel leading to the lab in order to ensure that the Strain was adequately quarantined from the rest of Valhalla.

The Eastern Clover was established as a giant warehouse where hundreds of thousands of tons of supplies were categorized and stored. Food, clothing, and equipment were organized in long rows of crates that towered high up into the cavern. The SS logistics officer in charge of East Clover boasted to Kempler that the supplies under his management could easily support a population of one hundred thousand for over a hundred years.

This area also contained the Project's hydroponic farms. This new technology was essential for food production at Valhalla, with its artificial lighting and poor soil. In the end stages of the war, Hitler had German agents at the University of California in Berkley steal seeds and research protocols from American scientist William Fredrick Gerickes, who had pioneered the growing of crops without soil. A laboratory was set up at Valhalla for developing hybrid seeds to create cultivars of different plants that could thrive in the low light environment. After a short time, a steady supply of fresh vegetables and some fruits were available in large quantities to assist in the feeding of Valhalla's growing population.

In addition to containing the coal mine and power plant, the Western Clover also contained what the complex's Aryan inhabitants called Holle, or Hell. With its three-to-a-bed and five-high wooden bunks, barbed wire and guard towers, it had been designed to resemble a concentration camp. The Jews were slave laborers and assigned the most undesirable jobs in Valhalla. They were the manual labor for all building projects, collected garbage, and did every job that the Nazis felt were inappropriate for Aryans to perform.

Most of the Jews were assigned to fourteen-hour shifts mining coal to fuel the furnaces that powered Valhalla. The heat in the mines and around the furnaces, combined with the stifling air, made work conditions unbearable. It was common for Jews to simply pass out, sometimes multiple times, during their shift. Jews that were unable to keep pace were handed over to Broder and Schreiber to be subjects in their nefarious experiments.

The South Clover contained the entrance and exit to the surface, as well as the control room with all of the equipment needed for maintaining Valhalla's environment. The surface entrance of the elevator shaft was sealed with a fortified steel door which was camouflaged to match perfectly the desert terrain. The doors could only be opened and closed electronically from the control room.

The headquarters of the SS and Gestapo were also located in separate bases in South Clover. Each military branch had its own barracks and ammunition warehouse and conducted its own training exercises. The area between the bases and the control room and elevator entrance were separated by two layers of electrified fences with guard dogs in between the fences.

A rivalry began between the SS and Gestapo forces in Valhalla while they were still both technically under the authority of Heinrich Himmler. In continuing with his long-adopted leadership strategy to encourage competition and animosity among his underlings, Hitler ordered that Kempler be overall commander of Project Valhalla with one exception: Mueller would retain sole authority over Gestapo forces in the project. As a result, Mueller only paid lip service to Kempler's authority.

Mueller was not present during the setup of Valhalla. At the meeting in Crete he had cryptically told Kempler, "Don't worry, I'll be joining you after I complete one last important mission." Before leaving his Gestapo troops, Mueller had assured them that Hitler had given him far-reaching authority, and the near future he alone would dictate who would be in charge of Valhalla.

The instructions in envelope nineteen were brief. It ordered Kempler to set aside the central area that connected all four clovers for "future instructions." The orders also stated that the final occupants of the project would be arriving in the very near future.

Ronald Fletcher was at a conference attended by a number of senior IDF officers, diplomats from Israel's Foreign Service, and Defense Minister Yigal Rosen when the news of the terrorist attack arrived. An aide grimly handed Minister Rosen a note informing him that the Prime Minister of Israel was requesting to discuss an emerging situation with him over the phone.

When Rosen returned, he told the group, "There's a terror attack in progress at the Netanya beach. I'll be going there now."

Fletcher's face turned ash gray. Minster Rosen saw his reaction. He asked, "Is something wrong, Mr. Fletcher?"

Fletcher hesitated, trying to gather his thoughts. "My wife and children are there." Realizing that the evening commuter traffic between Jerusalem and Netanya would make the trip take hours, he then added, "Can I accompany you?"

The Minister suddenly recognized the look he had seen on Fletcher's face. It was the look he had seen on the faces of countless families when he, as a junior officer, had informed them that their loved ones had been the victims of a terror attack.

Rosen wanted to let Fletcher come with him, but it was against protocol to let a foreigner be present on what was officially a military operation. It was likely that Fletcher would be exposed to classified or even top-secret information. On the other hand, Rosen understood the anxiety Fletcher must be experiencing. Especially because he knew Fletcher outside of his official capacity, and his own children had become friends with Bobby and Jane.

The Defense Minister finally told Fletcher, "You can come. My helicopter is waiting on the landing pad."

Fletcher knew Rosen was breaking the rules. He was the kind of man who rarely asked for favors. However, when he did, he made sure that he repaid the favor many times over.

Within minutes they were soaring high above the Judean Hills surrounding Jerusalem. As the helicopter sped to Netanya, a radio linkup to Golan's paratrooper unit provided live updates of the firefight taking place on the beach.

Fletcher began to blame himself for putting his family in danger. "Why didn't I just cancel the meeting and go with them?" he asked himself over and over. He had told himself many times that, statistically, Israel was safer than New York City. Still, wouldn't a good father do more do to keep his children safe? Attacks in Israel were infrequent, but they were catastrophes when they happened, and terrorists don't distinguish between soldiers and civilians, adults and children. Why did he have to put his family at risk?

By the time Rosen's helicopter landed in the parking lot of the beach, the fighting was over. Fletcher exited the helicopter and watched as the army and police tried to restore order. He pushed his way to a restricted area where relief activities were being coordinated. The Defense Minister and his aides remained close to the helicopter while a canopy was erected to form a temporary military command post.

Fletcher approached the cordoned-off area and was stopped by a soldier. He looked into the crowd and spotted Rachel Bronot, the head of Nekama, meaning vengeance in Hebrew, the anti-terrorist department of Israel's secret service, the Mossad.

Bronot was known throughout the international intelligence community as being smart, beautiful, and lethal. She was about five-foot seven inches, and had long, black, silky hair that fell to the center of her back. Her olive-shaped green eyes were accentuated by long, flowing eyelashes and thin, pursed lips. She was known for being strictly business, unapproachable in a social setting. Her parents, born in Yemen, were strictly orthodox, and she followed the strict moral traditions of her community.

Fletcher knew Bronot on a professional basis. She had given briefings on several cross-border missions in which he had participated.

He called out to her for assistance. Bronot immediately recognized him. She nodded to the soldier to let Fletcher pass.

Fletcher walked directly up to Bronot, asking, "Have you seen my wife and children?"

Bronot had preliminary information that one of those killed in the incident was Fletcher's wife. Given her investigative training, she immediately recognized that the wedding band on Fletcher's finger matched the victim's ring. She was also aware that Fletcher's children were currently being treated by medical personnel.

Bronot didn't want to be the one to inform Fletcher of the catastrophic news, but, given the situation, she had no choice. "Your children are safe," she told him. "The doctor is now examining them. I have been told that they were not injured in the attack."

Fletcher looked back, awaiting the worst.

Having no alternative, Bronot blurted out, "I'm so sorry, Ron. Your wife..."

Fletcher's eyes became moist. His stomach felt as if it had just caught a cannonball. His body began to shake from his shoulders to his ankles.

Trying to collect himself, he demanded with a whisper, "Where is she?"

Picturing Mary's mutilated body, Bronot responded, "Ron, I don't think it's a good time to see her. She's not in good shape right now."

"Where is she?" he repeated, louder. His intense tone sent a chill down Bronot's spine.

She knew that there was no stopping him. Bronot pointed towards a Mogen David Adom ambulance parked about thirty feet away.

Fletcher broke into a sprint, pushing an approaching security guard out of the way as he headed to the ambulance. Bronot managed to signal the guard before he drew his firearm.

Fletcher entered the back of the ambulance and saw a body on a stretcher covered by a long white sheet. Kneeling beside the stretcher, he slowly lifted the sheet, revealing Mary's bloody and mangled face. But Fletcher only saw the beautiful face of his childhood sweetheart staring out into space. Time stood still as memories from their earliest days together flooded his mind. It was if they were in the eye of a hurricane, where the world stood still and existed only for them.

After a brief moment that seemed like eons, the reality of the situation fell suddenly on Fletcher, and the full weight of Mary's untimely death and her departure from the world forever shook him to his core.

An emotion Ronald Fletcher had never before experienced began to envelop him. It was a rage that was bitter cold and overwhelming. "What monsters could murder such an innocent soul?" he asked himself. "How could they cause such suffering?" An evil like this, he told himself, must be stomped out of the world.

Fletcher tried to fight the hate. He had avoided it his entire career, having witnessed personally how it had ruined the lives of friends and colleagues alike. But he knew that the only antidote to his rage would be the sweet revenge he would personally wreak against anyone who had lifted a finger to enable the tragedy before him.

Looking at Mary, he said, "I swear that I will not rest until I have hunted down and killed every last person who did this to you."

Fletcher knew that he was no longer in control of himself, but it did not matter. Nothing mattered but the all-encompassing thought of revenge. He left the ambulance and saw Bronot, who was waiting to take him to his children. They walked together in complete silence.

When he reached the mobile care unit where the children were being treated, Jane caught sight of her father. She jumped off the cot and ran to him, crying hysterically. Fletcher picked her up and hugged her tightly to his chest. Her tears were dripping down his cheek as she kept repeating, "Where's Mommy, where's Mommy?"

Bobby, at first glance, seemed under control. He walked up to his father and announced, "Dad, I saw Mom get killed. He shot Mom and hit her with his gun. I couldn't do anything." Then he blurted out, "Why weren't you there, Dad! You would've stopped him! I know you would!" Then Bobby looked down at the floor and broke down in tears.

Bobby's stinging words and the taste of Jane's salty tears multiplied the feelings of rage brewing within him. It was as if a demon was tearing him apart from inside. Fletcher said to himself, "You're damn right, I would have killed every one of those bastards!"

He felt as if his blood was boiling within his veins. Even his natural fatherly instinct to comfort his children, at the time they needed him most, was clouded by this unstoppable force. He convinced himself that the only way to deal with Bobby and Jane's suffering would be to unleash his fury on their mother's killers. Fletcher had succumbed to this singularity of purpose, to bring the full force of his wrath against all those responsible.

Fletcher's racing thoughts were interrupted by a nurse, speaking in Hebrew, who told him that the children needed rest. She returned them to their cots as the physician in charge approached Fletcher. He spoke in English.

"Mr. Fletcher, I'm so sorry for your loss. Thankfully your children were not physically harmed. Mentally, however, they have just experienced a tremendous trauma. It will take some time until they recover."

"We have had a great deal of experience, unfortunately, with children whom have survived similar acts of terrorism. We have a program which may help decrease the risk of future psychological complications. We feel that it's in the best interest of your children to place them in this program."

Fletcher's thoughts were elsewhere. He was listening but not listening.

The doctor concluded, "That would mean placing your children in our inpatient facility for one week."

Fletcher thought to himself, "A week is about how much time I need." He finally looked directly at the doctor, answering, "Yes, of course, if you feel it's necessary. You have my permission."

Fletcher's mind quickly shifted back toward formulating a plan. He would need accurate intelligence, and fast. Being familiar with the operations of terrorist organizations, he understood that there was probably a complex hierarchy behind the attack. He suddenly recalled having heard in the Defense Minister's helicopter that one of the terrorists had been captured alive.

Fletcher thanked the doctor, then searched for Rachel Bronot. He found her sitting behind a folding desk, in an open tent, reading a report from Naval Intelligence.

Fletcher asked, "Who's the terrorist you caught?"

Bronot looked up. "We don't know. He's refusing to answer questions. He's arrogant and completely unrepentant. If it wasn't for the law, I would personally...well, you know."

"I understand. Is there any way that I might see him?"

Bronot hesitated for a moment, considering the legal implications.

"Well, we could walk over to that truck over there, maybe we'll see something," she said.

Bronot escorted Fletcher through a crowd of heavily armed soldiers. He recognized at least two of them who had been part of a large-scale mission into Syria in which he had been present as an observer. The reason for such heavy security was not only to prevent any attempt at escape, but also to deter citizens from vigilante justice.

The truck was a non-descript eighteen-wheeler with a uniquely designed semi-trailer unit. Within its thick steel walls were six interrogation cells. Due to an Israeli law which outlawed the use of physical torture in the interrogation of terrorist suspects, intelligence services had partnered with psychologists from Israel's top universities to develop alternative methods to extract information. The process which they developed began by immediately isolating the terrorist within the container. Through strict isolation and stimulation depravation, the terrorist eventually becomes detached from his former life, associating reality with only the four corners of the cell. Within weeks and sometimes months, the terrorists inevitably break down and cooperate with the investigators.

Fletcher was familiar with this method. He knew that it was effective, but he could not let precious minutes and hours slip away. He needed information now.

Fletcher and Bronot entered the back of the trailer and looked through the one-way reinforced mirror of the holding cell. As he stared at the terrorist, who looked perhaps no older than seventeen or eighteen years old, Fletcher realized that just minutes ago this punk was assisting in the murder of his wife and attempted murder of his children. He knew from his experiences in Vietnam, Africa, and Lebanon, that teenagers were often used as pawns in a deadly game of politics and terror, and could be just as cruel and cold-blooded as their superiors. Fletcher had no mercy for this so-called "freedom fighter."

Fletcher turned to Bronot. He asked in an innocent voice, "Rachel, could I have a few minutes with him alone? I just have a couple of questions."

Bronot had read Fletcher's dossier and was quite familiar with the expertise in interrogation that he had developed in Vietnam. On the one hand, she was bound by official policy of the State of Israel that under no circumstances was any form of physical torture to be employed to extract information. On the other hand, Bronot also wanted information fast. The coordinated tactics and advanced weaponry used in the attack suggested that a powerful organization, perhaps even with state support, was acting behind the scenes. Prompt intelligence could potentially thwart an even more deadly attack in the near future.

Moreover, Bronot had a gut feeling that something was different about this attack. First of all, the target location. There were more remote beaches nearby that would have had a slower security response. In fact, the attack was perhaps a bit too suicidal, with no real escape plan despite the otherwise sophisticated nature of the operation. Perhaps it was a smoke screen for something much worse to come? Whatever or whoever was behind it, Bronot knew she should act quickly to prevent a far worse catastrophe.

Bronot looked Fletcher in the eyes. He was a handsome man who in many ways reminded her of her former fiancée, Captain Rafi Alon. Rafi had also been well over six feet tall with light brown eyes and curly brown hair. He had been a fighter pilot who was shot down over the Gaza Strip during the Six Day War in 1967. Though he parachuted safely, a Palestinian Fedayeen company fighting alongside the Egyptians captured him before Special Forces could come in for the rescue. According to witnesses, the Palestinians tortured him by forcing his head into the engine compartment of their running jeep. A few hours later they decapitated him. It took Israel ten years of negotiations to recover his body.

After her fiancée's murder, Bronot vowed to dedicate her life to fighting terrorism. Over the course of a decade, she had worked her way up from the security detail of the Prime Minister to become the head of one of the most respected anti-terrorist agencies in the world.

Bronot was a veteran in the art of revenge. In keeping with Israel's policy of not allowing any terrorist with Israeli blood on their hands to go unpunished, she had personally tracked down every member of the Fedayeen Unit responsible for Rafi's death. One by one they were hunted down by her agents and assassinated.

After a long pause, she finally responded to Fletcher. "You know I don't have the authority to allow you to question him. But I could really use a coffee. Do you promise me you'll be on your best behavior if I leave you for a few minutes?"

Fletcher nodded. "Scout's honor, I'll behave."

With that, Bronot turned her back and exited the trailer.

Fletcher was now alone with the terrorist. He entered the cell and closed the shutters behind the one-way mirror. The terrorist was sitting shackled to a metal stool which was bolted to the floor of the container. He wore only a sleeveless white undershirt and boxers. He was tall and thin, with a hint of an adolescent mustache.

Ron evaluated the young man. In his mind, he saw one of the dozens of Vietnamese youth that he had so skillfully interrogated. They too, had sold their souls to follow in the footsteps of killers.

Fletcher thought to himself, "He has no idea about what he is about to face. Now he'll get to know what it's like to be terrorized."

Fletcher addressed the Palestinian in flawless Arabic, without even a hint of an accent. "What's your name?" he demanded.

The teenager looked at him with disdain. "I will tell you nothing, Yehud!" He then spat on the floor in a show of defiance.

In a flash, Fletcher sprung on the terrorist. He maneuvered behind the chair and placed the thin neck of the young terrorist in a vice grip with his forearms. He then pushed his knee into the terrorist's back while simultaneously squeezing his arms together, emptying his lungs. Within a fraction of a second, the terrorist was unconscious.

Moving around to the interrogator's chair, Ron sat the terrorist upright and pulled down on his jaw, opening his mouth. He then pulled out his tongue.

Fletcher removed from the lapel of his gray sports coat the collapsible needle he had brought from Vietnam known as the "Vu Khi." With an uppercut motion he stabbed the steel needle through the tongue of the unconscious terrorist. The needle was fully extended, reaching from the terrorist's Adam's apple to between his eyes. He then twisted the needle, waking him. With the point of the needle inching toward his forehead, the terrorist tried desperately to move his tongue to avoid being cut by the needle.

The terrorist watched intently as Fletcher slowly removed a butane lighter from his front shirt pocket. He flicked it open, using the flame to heat the shaft of the Vu Khi. The terrorist's eyes were frozen in fear watching the base of the needle turn red while feeling a sensation of intense burning envelop his tongue.

Moving the flame from the shaft of the Vu Khi to in front of the terrorist's terror-stricken eyes, Fletcher began to speak slowly.

"Soon you will face a death that only a few unfortunate men have experienced. First, you will experience such intense pain that you will empty your bowels all over yourself. Then you will beg me to kill you, but I won't. I want to enjoy watching you die in agony. Your only chance to stop this is to answer all my questions."

The terrorist sat with his mouth open wide, trying to move his lips away from the glowing needle as Fletcher returned the flame to its base. The cherry glow of the tip of the needle became orange as an incredible wave of pain shot through the terrorist's tongue.

Fletcher calmly asked, "Let's try again. What is your name?"

Without hesitation the terrorist answered, "Muhammed Fellah." With his tongue trapped by the needle, it came out as a mumble. Fletcher had long ago developed the ability to understand what was said with the Vu Khi in a suspect's tongue.

"What was the purpose of your mission?"

"To kill as many Jews as possible."

"What is the name of your organization?"

"The Palestinian Liberation Guerilla Army."

"Was there anyone else involved in your attack who didn't come to the beach?"

"Yes, our leader, Ali Rajad."

"Where is he now?" Ron asked.

"I don't know. He got off the ship early, near the Lebanese border."

"What ship?"

"A Liberian freighter. The Banju." The terrorist winced. He was ready to answer any question that might help end the pain.

"Why did your leader come along?" Ron asked.

"He didn't say. Maybe something to do with three canisters he was playing with on the freighter. He put them into a suitcase when he got into a rubber boat like ours."

Fletcher took out a blue handkerchief and used it to remove the burning hot Vu Khi. Immediately the pain dissipated. A moment later, Rachel Bronot returned.

"I got you a cup of coffee, Ron, let's drink it outside."

The crowd had begun to thin out. Bronot and Fletcher made their way to the shore. The two walked slowly south in the direction of Tel Aviv.

"Well, did he volunteer anything?" Bronot asked. She already knew the answer, having watched a live video feed of the interview from her car.

"Actually, he was talking so fast, he bit his tongue." Fletcher remarked with a smile.

Fletcher reviewed with Bronot the information he had obtained from the terrorist. Then it was his turn for questions.

"Who is Ali Rajad?" Fletcher asked.

"He's the head of a small but vicious terrorist organization called the PLGA, Palestinian Liberation Guerilla Army. We simply call it, the 'Plague,' for short."

She continued, "Rashid is probably responsible for at least a hundred deaths in Israel in the past few years. His organization makes Black September look humane in comparison. I understand that lately he has been running a sort of terrorist-for-hire agency. Rashid's clients want various operations done but want to keep their involvement a secret. Rashid will do almost any kind of operation anywhere in the world for the right price. In the process, he has made a small fortune for himself."

"I don't remember any operation against the PLGA recently," Fletcher said.

"Unfortunately, you're right. He keeps his base of operations deep inside Lebanon, near the Syrian border, too deep for our commando raids. We've bombed it in the past, but a few months later it just sprouts up again." Bronot said, with obvious disappointment in her voice.

As they turned back toward the relief area they walked in silence. Fletcher was thinking about how best to investigate the PLGA, while Bronot could not stop wondering about the three mysterious cylinders of Ali Rajad.

8

In April of 1945, the final stage of Hitler's plan for the birth of the Fourth Reich was initiated. Hitler was obsessed with the fear that Stalin would scour the ends of the earth until he was found. Therefore, he realized that in order to disappear he would have to make sure that Stalin found the dead body of Adolf Hitler. If his plan was successful, there would be no endless search for him after the war.

Hitler had spent the last days of the war in the reinforced underground compound known the Fuhrerbunker. He was there day and night, with the exception of brief military conferences in the Reich Chancellery. In order to get to the conferences, he would ascend to an upper bunker known as the Vorbunker which was connected to the Chancellery by a tunnel. Due to air attacks and Soviet artillery bombardment, Hitler eventually changed the location of the military conferences to the Vorbunker.

The Vorbunker contained conference rooms, a kitchen, storage space, living space for Hitler's personal guard, and a room used to board the Goebbels' children. The lower Fuhrerbunker was approximately 28 feet beneath the garden of the Chancellery. Its concrete roof was 9.8 feet thick, and its walls were 13 feet thick. Down the middle ran a wide corridor that was used as a lounge and conference room. On the east end of the corridor was a stairway leading up to the Vorbunker, and on the west a stairway that connected to an emergency exit. South of the corridor was Hitler's private quarters, study, and a guest room that would eventually become Eva Braun's bedroom. Next to Hitler's bedroom was a room for his dog, Blondi, and a concealed entrance to a passageway that lead up to an unfinished ventilation tower located in the Chancellery garden.

To the north of the corridor were the Goebbels' bedroom, Hitler's doctor's office and quarters, a telephone switchboard center, electrical generators, and a ventilation control room. Hitler lived in the Fuhrerbunker for 105 days, until the end of the war.

On April 29, shortly after midnight, Hitler married Eva Braun in a surprise ceremony. The wedding festivities continued late into the night. By the following morning, Hitler had turned his attention back to his plan.

The first step was to kill his beloved German Shepherd, Blondi. Though Hitler had developed a reputation as an animal lover, having owned several dogs prior to Blondi, he had no compunction in ordering his personal physician Dr. Werner Haase to feed Blondi a cyanide tablet. He told Dr. Haase that he wanted to test its potency in case it would be needed for any of the human occupants of the Fuhrerbunker. However, Hitler had two completely different reasons for killing Blondi. The first was in order to suggest to the inhabitants of the bunker that Hitler himself was contemplating suicide. The second was that he needed to vacate Blondi's room to allow Dr. Schreiber to prepare his equipment.

After Blondi's body was removed from the room, Dr. Schreiber and an assistant began to bring in boxes containing Das Maschine and its modules, as well as the necessary surgical equipment. In short order, Schreiber and his assistant established a makeshift surgical theater in Blondi's room.

In the early afternoon of April 30, a farewell gathering for the Further was attended by about twenty members of Hitler's staff. Goebbels had been spreading a rumor for the past several weeks that Hitler had decided to command the defense of Berlin from the Fuhrerbunker until the very end, and, if Germany lost the war, he would commit suicide. For the past few days, senior Nazis such as Bormann, Himmler, and Goring had attempted to persuade Hitler to abandon Berlin for Ploem where German forces were still in control. When confronted, Hitler would defend his patriotism and refuse to abandon Berlin. This drama continued until the farewell party.

At approximately 2:00 p.m., Hitler ate lunch with his two secretaries and his personal cook. Afterwards, he attended yet another farewell ceremony. At 2:45, Hitler and Eva entered his study. After sitting on the couch for a few minutes, Hitler gave his new wife a parting kiss. She then swallowed a vial of poison. As soon as Eva lost consciousness, Hitler was brought into Blondi's room for the operation. Dr. Schreiber had spent the past few weeks perfecting his surgical technique on dozens of Jewish "volunteers." Upon Hitler's entry, Dr. Schreiber administered a powerful, fast-acting anesthetic. Within twenty minutes he had successfully removed the necessary brain tissue needed for Das Maschine as well as those to be used in future planned modules. As per Hitler's instructions, Dr. Schreiber kept the incisions on his scalp to a bare minimum, suturing them carefully after the extraction.

Following the surgery, two of Mueller's Gestapo agents returned Hitler's body to the couch, placing it next to Eva's corpse. One of the agents picked up the Walther PPK 7.65 pistol that was lying on the sofa and fired it directly at the area of the primary surgical incision at a distance of about three inches. The sutured area was now completely obliterated by the bullet wound and gunpowder burns. The agents then returned to Blondi's room. They locked the door and barricaded the recently constructed concealed door to the unfinished ventilation tower. Schreiber spent the next several hours connecting the electrodes to the brain tissue which was now immersed in a suspension of immortal cancerous cells within Das Maschine. Finally, he connected the electrodes to a specially designed pulse generator that mimicked a heartbeat of 70 beats per minute. By 1:00 a.m., Dr. Schreiber had finished the procedure, exhausted but satisfied with his work.

To test whether Das Maschine was properly connected. Schreiber typed into the attached teletype device, "The operation was a success."

Within seconds, the teletype printer began clicking and a response appeared. "Thank you, Doctor Schreiber. Sincerely, Adolf Hitler".

At around 3:30 pm, several of those present in the Fuhrerbunker thought they heard gunshots. Hitler's personal aide Otto Gunsche rushed into the study and discovered the bodies of Hitler and Eva Braun. A few seconds later, Goebbels entered with a blanket and covered the heads of the couple. He told the shocked onlookers, "We must ensure our Fuhrer will be remembered as he truly looked, and not in such an unseemly state." The two bodies were taken above ground for cremation. Goebbels explained that Hitler had chosen to be cremated because he did not want to be put on display for his enemies' gratification, which would be a disgrace for the entire German people. The real intention, of course, was to avoid any examination of Hitler's wounds.

That night there was total confusion in the Fuhrerbunker. Martin Bormann tried to ready a plan for the escape of the bunker's occupants to Ploem, where Admiral Karl Donitz was now the official head of Germany.

At 2:30 a.m., a truck arrived at the exit of the secret passage in the unfinished ventilation tower. Gestapo agents loaded Das Maschine and the boxes of surgical equipment into the back of the truck. Then Dr. Schreiber, Mueller, and the remaining Gestapo agents boarded the trunk and left Berlin. With their departure, all of those associated with the plan, save Goebbels and his wife, were on their way to Project Valhalla.

At 4:00 a.m., the truck arrived at the Havel River near Pichelsdorf, where two French Bréguet 521 Bizerte seaplanes were waiting. Each plane had room for a crew of eight and ample space for cargo. After transferring to the planes, a brick was placed on the gas pedal of the truck which subsequently sank into the river. The seaplanes took off and successfully avoided Russian patrols of the area. They first flew northwest to avoid areas of battle, then turned south, maintaining a cruising speed of 124 miles per hour.

The next morning, Goebbels' wife Magda anesthetized their six children, and, while they were unconscious, placed cyanide capsules into their mouths, murdering them. Then Goebbels and his wife emerged from the Fuhrerbunker into the bombed-out ruins of the Chancellery garden. There they ordered Goebbels' assistant to shoot then both and burn their bodies.

This phase of the operation was a complete success. With the death of Goebbels there was not a single individual, outside of those in the seaplanes, that knew of Hitler's escape. Everyone who remained alive in the Fuhrerbunker would testify that Hitler committed suicide.

Backing up their testimony were the bodies of Adolf Hitler, Eva Braun, Joseph and Magda Goebbels, and their six children, whose identities were later confirmed through dental records obtained by Russian Army investigators.

The seaplanes crossed over Southern Europe and made their way to the Mediterranean Sea. The planes finally touched down on the coordinates of Project Valhalla in Libya. The pilot transporting Das Machine adjusted the plane's radio to the predetermined frequency and announced their arrival with the code words, "Fourth Reich." Immediately a pair of perfectly camouflaged giant steel doors opened from a small sand dune to admit the final inhabitants.

As Mueller and Dr. Schreiber, along with Gestapo agents carrying Das Maschine and its modules boarded the elevator, SS forces dismantled the French planes and placed the parts into crates to be stored in the East Clover. With that final act, the earth swallowed up the last traces of the operation.

The residents of the Valhalla Project were curious. Since the opening ceremony, it was the first time that the mechanical clatter of the elevator had echoed throughout the caverns. Gruppenfuhrer Kempler and his staff waited at the bottom of the shaft for the project's new residents.

As the elevator gate opened, Heinrich Mueller was the first to step out. Kempler looked past him and stared at the strange grey steel cube with a teletype device affixed to its side. Above the teletype machine there were hundreds of small switches and knobs with numerous flashing lights.

Mueller addressed Kempler with his usual contempt.

"You are now to open envelope twenty," Mueller ordered Kempler.

With no small measure of anxiety Kempler reached into his briefcase and removed envelope twenty. The color in his face drained when he read the contents to himself, written in Hitler's own handwriting.

"Das Maschine contains my entire being. I, your Fuhrer, am indeed still very much alive. I remain in complete control of the destiny of the Aryan Race. You will execute all orders which I will communicate by means of the teletype device."

"I know that you may harbor some skepticism. In order to remove any doubt, I will offer you an opportunity to prove that the soul of Adolf Hitler is contained within the box that you see before you. I grant you permission to ask a question that only I could know the answer."

Kempler hesitated. Having made a personal oath to Hitler pledging total obedience, he had always been completely loyal and unquestioning. He had complied with all orders regarding the Strain program and Project Valhalla, despite his many personal doubts. He had even complied with orders to mercilessly execute Jewish children, on Hitler's insistence that they represented a moral danger to Nazi Germany, even though he felt it was utter nonsense. However, now he was being asked to believe the impossible. But with Mueller standing behind him and breathing down his neck, he had no choice but to play along.

Kempler did not have to think long to come up with a question. Kempler told the Gestapo agents guarding Das Maschine to step aside. They didn't move. Mueller smiled, enjoying the display of loyalty, and then ordered them to comply. Kempler then crouched into a position where he could comfortably type.

" During our final meeting this year on the sixth of January you scolded me. What for?"

Within seconds the staccato of the teletype printer revealed the answer: "I pointed out that you were missing a button on your topcoat. And judging by the deep color of red that your face turned, you were quite embarrassed."

Kempler swallowed. Only the Fuhrer with his phenomenal memory and his pedantic demand for perfection would remember something so trivial. That was enough proof for the Gruppenfuhrer.

From that day, Project Valhalla changed from a military installation to a complex city-state. Hitler, fully functioning in Dr. Schreiber's apparatus, was free of all the physical ailments that had plagued him since the failed assassination plot. Within Das Maschine he was in a constant state of what could only be described as euphoria. Hitler's diabolical mind was now blissfully free to churn out endless decrees, keeping the cavern complex constantly buzzing with activity.

Hitler's first major project was the construction of a giant coliseum in the center of the four-clover complex. It was adorned with Roman and Renaissance sculptures and priceless works of art, all the Nazi spoils of Europe, which had been transported to the caverns. Its most striking feature was the backdrop to the stadium's main stage. Looted from the Catherine Palace near St. Petersburg, from what was known as the Amber Room, it was composed of a wall of ornate panels made of gold leaf and amber and adorned with statues of golden cherubs. Hitler made one addition to the decor: a giant Nazi eagle made of solid gold holding a swastika in its claws.

Upon the stadium's completion, Hitler proclaimed it the "Reich Temple." He declared that from this temple a new, fully Aryan religion would emerge, based on the paganism of ancient Germany but with one twist: the deity of the religion was Hitler himself. From then on, he would be referred to not as Hitler but as the "Reich Gott." Mueller was ordained as the religion's High Priest, and Kempler was declared Angel of War. The religion, named "Fuhrerism" by Mueller, would be practiced by all of Project Valhalla's inhabitants, save the Jews.

Some of the SS officers and Broder's scientists were believing Christians and complained about the new decree. They were quickly arrested and sacrificed by beheading at the Reich Temple's inaugural services. High Priest Mueller proclaimed to the shocked attendees that this was necessary to atone for the sins of the people and appease the Reich Gott. Afterward Mueller ordered each and every citizen of Valhalla to kneel and recite an oath of obedience to the Reich Gott and Fuhrerism.

"I believe with all my heart that the Reich Gott is the Master of the Universe, and Fuhrerism is the only true religion. I solemnly pledge to fulfill the will of the Reich Gott and will joyously sacrifice my life if called upon to confirm my belief."

All the project's residents, looking at the headless bodies of the original protesters, affirmed the oath. There was little dissent against the new religion afterward, and anyone who even hinted at disbelief was quickly arrested by Gestapo agents and executed during the weekly Sunday service. High Priest Mueller would say before the beheadings, "Only by sacrifice may a soul be purified from the grave sin of apostasy."

Over time, even those residents that began as skeptics transformed to be among the most fervent followers of the Fuhrerism.

The next major proclamation of the Reich Gott was that only designated breeders in Dr. Schreiber's Super Aryan Project would be allowed to produce children, so as not to pollute the future population with the mixed blood of average Germans. The only exception would be for Jews living in Hell, who were allowed to reproduce under strict quotas to maintain a population necessary for labor and experiments. When an SS corporal was caught with a female breeder two weeks later, they were burned together alive at the stake at Sunday services. The smell of their burning flesh was enough to deter the residents of Valhalla from considering such a sin in the future.

Aryan babies were placed immediately after birth in government dormitories and raised according to Nazi ideals as expounded by the Reich Gott. They were never to know who their birth parents were. They were given a spartan education that included reading, writing, science, and mathematics.

Upon graduation at age sixteen, all females, save those who were especially gifted, joined the breeding program. Male students that showed particular promise were sent to the recently inaugurated institution of higher learning, Heydrich University. There, Dr. Schreiber and his staff taught them biology, engineering, higher mathematics, physics, and other subjects needed to maintain Valhalla. The remaining boys were drafted into one of the three military branches. There they would remain until retirement at age 60.

The SS was the largest branch. Most of their time was spend in combat training and drills, with their main mission being defense of the compound.

The second branch, the Gestapo, was in charge of internal security. Their duties included guarding the Jews of the West Clover, investigating crimes such as heresy and blood pollution, and spying on the leaders of the other divisions. In practice their role was primarily to terrorize the population into perfect compliance with the decrees of the Reich Gott.

The third branch, the Messengers, was an elite paramilitary intelligence organization whose function was to operate in the outside world to implement the revenge of the Reich Gott. Recruits were hand-picked and trained by Mueller himself along with his top agents. They were taught foreign languages, intelligence gathering techniques, the use of conventional and unconventional weapons, and hand-to-hand combat.

The Messengers were of the few in the complex that had the privilege of listening to short-wave radios tuned to the broadcasts of various countries in the outside world. Mueller, as the Minister of Propaganda, limited listening to classical music, news, and sporting events. It was prohibited for the rest of Valhalla's residents to listen to broadcasts from the outside.

By 1970, most of the personnel in the three branches of service were Super Aryans. Hitler, upon Mueller's urging, ordered a purge of everyone in the compound above the age of forty-five. By eliminating these inferior Aryans, Mueller argued, the danger of ethnic pollution would be greatly reduced. Also, vital resources and supplies could be saved. Hitler agreed but made exemptions for Mueller, Kempler, senior Gestapo agents, Messengers, and Dr. Schreiber and his staff. The purge was announced by High Priest Mueller during the mandatory Sunday religious service. This prevented the possibility that Kempler might order a military revolt to protect his veteran soldiers. The older residents were lined up on the stage of the stadium and each was handed a cyanide pill. After raising their arm in a Nazi salute and together proclaiming, "Heil the Reich Gott!" they swallowed their pills.

Subsequent decrees demoted the status of those exempted, save Mueller and Kempler, to that of second-class citizens. They were barred from contact with the other residents of the complex. Kempler, always the loyal Nazi, understood the "wisdom" of Hitler's decision. He continued to train the SS into a formidable force against any intruders.

Dr. Schreiber and Professor Broder were still held in high standing, but were too busy with their scientific pursuits to notice the transformation that was happening in Valhalla. Mueller, of course, exulted in his status as the High Priest and second-in-command to Hitler. His Gestapo agents ensured total obedience among the populace.

As a result of the purge, almost all the residents of Valhalla had been born in the project and raised to believe in the omnipotence of the Reich Gott. Hitler had accomplished his goal of becoming a deity of ultimate authority with a legion of Super Aryan warriors at his command. From within Das Maschine, he had achieved a level of loyalty from his subjects constituting total subservience. To the residents of Project Valhalla, Hitler had become the Lord of the Universe.

9

A few hours before the attack on the beach in Netanya, Ali Rajad descended from the Liberian freighter MV Banju into a small rubber boat and paddled toward an isolated rocky beach about four miles south of Israel's border with Lebanon. There, two Arab terrorists from Qalqilya in the West Bank were waiting for him. He ordered one of them to wade out into the water and assist him in disposing of the boat by deflating it and cutting it into pieces which they submerged underwater.

He then told the pair to wait near their cars, which as per his earlier instructions had been parked 100 meters apart in the sand. Approaching one of them, Rajad handed over a map of Tel Aviv highlighting the Yarkon River. Opening his leather satchel, he removed a glimmering steel cylinder. He then pointed to a marked area on the Yarkon where the cylinder should be tossed.

Rajad then approached the second terrorist. This time, the map illustrated the path of *HaMovil HaArtzi*, the National Water Carrier of Israel, an 81-mile-long channel that distributes fresh water to cities and farms in central Israel. Again, he removed a cylinder and handed it to the terrorist, pointing out its intended destination.

The two terrorists got in their cars and drove off. Rajad walked up a dusty path leading inland and saw a third car which had been left for him, a late model blue Fiat 127. It had yellow license plates, indicating that it was registered to a citizen of Israel. In reality it was a stolen vehicle, and the plates had been switched with those of a car that had entered long-term parking at Ben Gurion Airport the previous day.

Rajad entered the car and removed the keys from under the driver's seat. He had instructions to place the third cylinder in the Sea of Galilee, which provided water to all of the major population areas of

Northern Israel. He restricted his route to back roads, avoiding highways.

After a few hours, he arrived at his destination. There he tossed the cylinder precisely at the spot marked on the map. With great satisfaction he took out his cigarette lighter and turned the friction wheel. He placed the map into the flame and scattered the ashes into the wind.

Now that his mission was complete, he had time for a leisurely drive. As he passed the many Arab hamlets in the Northern Galilee region of Israel, a broad smile broke out on his face. He knew the Israelis were tough opponents; however, Rajad had proved that the State of Israel could be vulnerable. And today he had an additional reason to celebrate: it had been his biggest payday ever.

Ali Rajad was born on June 4, 1954 in Jerash, a United Nations Relief and Rehabilitation Administration camp just north of the Jordanian capital of Amman. It was first set up as a temporary refuge for those Arabs that fled Israel during Israel's Independence War in 1948. After the war, the leaders of the Arab world made a calculated decision to refuse to resettle the refugees. This left the residents of Jerash permanently stateless, condemned forever to be political pawns for the greater struggle against the Jewish State.

Rajad was raised in an atmosphere of hatred and frustration, one of thousands of refugees living in squalor. As a child, he was indoctrinated into the belief that the blame for their current status rested exclusively on the State of Israel. Some of the older refugees were aware that rather than being driven out of their homes, they had been urged by the leaders of neighboring Arab countries to temporarily vacate in order to allow the unfettered slaughter of Jews. In fact, those Arabs who did not heed the call and remained in Israel had retained their property and many were prospering. The ones that had left, however, lived in a continuous state of despair. However, knowing what retribution one might face in the camp for expressing such unpopular views, these older refugees prudently kept such thoughts to themselves.

Rajad learned to hate Jews and the State of Israel from his parents, his teachers, and his mullah. By the age of sixteen, Ali had a burning desire for revenge against the Jews. He longed for an opportunity to kill Israelis. And recruiters from a myriad of terrorist groups would often come to Jerash to seek volunteers. Rajad was eventually recruited by the largest Palestinian underground organization, Fatah, the Movement for the Liberation of Palestine. Rajad said goodbye to his parents, explaining that it was his duty to dedicate his life to fighting the Zionist enemy. His mother was supportive, telling Ali that she hoped he would one day become a martyr for the liberation of Palestine. His father, on the other hand, was reticent. He remembered the false promises of Arab leaders, and could not believe that their current state, however unfortunate, could justify the murder of innocents.

Rajad was sent to a training camp about one hundred miles south of Jerash. Though of average build, he quickly demonstrated his superiority to the other participants due to his intellect and determination. After six months he graduated from the course and was singled out as an outstanding recruit by his trainers. His reward was the privilege of being sent out on a mission.

The base commander, Abu Jamal, told Ali that the assignment would be easy. It would also help him gain experience which would prepare him for even more important missions. Rajad was tasked to smuggle a small amount of explosive material into Israel. He would pass off the material to another Fatah terrorist who would prime it in a device that would be planted at Machane Yehuda, the sprawling open-air fruit and vegetable market in central Jerusalem.

Rajad crossed into Israel along with hundreds of day laborers by way of the Allenby Bridge, known to Arabs as the Al-Karameh Bridge, located just north of the Dead Sea. In his green duffle bag was a cardboard box that contained twelve large Catholic prayer candles in glass containers decorated with hand-painted religious images. One the candles contained not wax but actually gelignite, a highly explosive material made of nitroglycerine and wood pulp.

When it was Rajad's turn to pass security, the naive youth placed the bag on a table manned by a veteran Israeli customs agent.

The inspector asked Rajad in Arabic to remove the bag's contents. Ali then laid each item on the table.

The Israeli focused on the cardboard box and asked Rajad, "What's in the box?"

Rajad said, "It contains candles for my family in Jerusalem."

The agent asked, "What are the candles for?"

Ali answered, "For their mosque."

The inspector opened the box and looked at the twelve decorative candles. He could not understand why a mosque would need candles decorated with pictures of Catholic saints.

The inspector told Ali to take the box to another table. There, an explosives expert noticed the slight difference in color and texture of the gelignite "candle." He tested it and found that the candle was, in fact, made of explosive material. Rajad was arrested on the spot.

Rajad had a short trial where in lieu of presenting a legal argument he shouted Fatah slogans and repeatedly claimed that a Zionist court had no authority to judge him. He was found guilty of smuggling explosives and was sentenced by a military tribunal to three years in prison.

Rajad was interred at a prison near the ancient ruins of the biblical city Megiddo, just north of Nazareth. The prison housed mostly Palestinians that had committed acts of terrorism. His initial enthusiasm for the Palestinian cause and allegiance with his fellow freedom fighters was shattered by an incident that took place during his first week of incarceration. Ali's youth and good looks led him to be raped by his fellow prisoners. The next day, the humiliated Ali contemplated suicide.

Ali's fortunes abruptly changed for the better after he ran into his old friend, Ishmael Kalem, in the prison yard. Ishmael was a giant of a man, six-foot-five and weighing nearly 320 pounds. Ali and Ishmael had met at the Jerash camp, where both of them had hustled odd jobs in the market. Ishmael had been working for a fish salesman, who, despite being much smaller physically, would beat Ishmael when he felt he was working too slowly. One day Ishmael couldn't restrain himself and threw a punch which fractured the fishmonger's skull, killing him. Ali, having witnessed the incident, devised a cover-up which caused the authorities to recognize the death as having resulted from a slip-and-fall accident. From then on, Kalem felt forever in Ali's debt. The two became inseparable. Together, they formed a gang specializing in petty theft and extortion. With Rajad's brains and Ishmael's brawn, the gang soon ruled supreme over the rough streets of Jerash.

The two went their separate ways after an incident that led to Ishmael's arrest and imprisonment. His cousin had been a member of a ring that stole cars in Israel and smuggled them over the green line into the West Bank. There, "chop shops" cannibalized the cars for parts that were resold back to crooked Israeli mechanics. Two years ago, his cousin was short one crew member for a night raid, and he approached Ishmael for some help. Unfortunately for Ishmael, the gang was caught in a police trap along the border and he received a four-year sentence. After his friend was sentenced, Ali decided to disband his gang and join Fatah.

In the prison yard, the two were ecstatic to have been reunited. After some small talk, Ali told Ishmael what had occurred the previous night. Ishmael's blood boiled as Ali poured out all the sordid details. The two agreed that in order to save Ali's honor there would need to be extreme retribution. Ishmael happened to have a few blades stashed away that he had smuggled in via visiting relatives. That night after light's out, Rajad and Kalem left their beds, slit the throats two of Ali's assailants, and castrated the third. Prison authorities investigating the situation found that all potential witnesses were substantially less than cooperative, and in the official report the attack was ascribed to "unknown parties."

From that day, on Ali and Ishmael were feared by all the prisoners. Rajad formed a gang that quickly grew to be the most powerful at Megiddo prison. In fact, he was so successful that any illegal activity among the inmates became subject to his personal approval. That meant that anyone planning to sell drugs or other contraband had to give him a large share of the proceeds. Furthermore, if there was a conflict between prisoners, the "litigants" were brought before Rajad for his ruling, which was zealously enforced by Ishmael and their gang.

Rajad, however, had his sights set beyond his interment at Megiddo prison. He was formulating extensive plans for the day he would be released. This included founding his own terrorist organization dedicated to the liberation of Palestine. He felt that the leadership of the currently active resistance groups were inherently corrupt and could never be a match for the Israelis. At the same time, he had plans to make himself rich, powerful, and universally feared.

Part of his strategy was to form a cell of dedicated loyalists on the outside of the prison from his gang members who had been released. That way, when he left prison, there would already be an infrastructure for his new organization. As his gang on the outside grew, Rajad ordered them to corner the heroin and ecstasy markets in the West Bank, which would fund the group's activities. Rajad had no qualms about providing drugs to his own people. He rationalized to himself that the addicts had to buy their drugs from someone, so why not him? Soon, Ali's coffers were overflowing with cash. Ali told Ishmael that the funds were needed as seed money to fund their true goal, the liberation of the Palestinian people. Of course, no one would be hurt if they took for themselves reasonable "consultation fees."

By coincidence, the release date for both Rajad and Kalem fell on the same day. Israel prison authorities escorted the pair to the Allenby Bridge and warned them never to set foot in Israel again. They were greeted on the other side of the bridge by a cadre of gang members. The Palestinian Liberation Guerilla Army was ready to launch. Rajad's dream had become a reality.

In the first few months, members toured refugee camps across Jordan to recruit members for the PLGA. Rajad turned out to be an inspiring speaker, making passionate orations that brought in enthusiastic recruits by the dozens. His rallies were also a way to bring in donations. His donors were driven by disillusionment regarding the established organizations, hoping that Rajad was the real deal. Rajad used these funds to improve his standard of living, and soon he was being chauffeured around Jordan in a bulletproof Mercedes. At the same time, he opened up offices in Beirut, Lebanon, and Tripoli to help launder drug proceeds and manage imports of weapons and other equipment. When funds fell short, he would send Kalem along with other trusted associates to wealthy Palestinians whose contributions he felt were inadequate. Needless to say, Kalem persuaded these holdouts to be quite generous.

Finally, Rajad opened up a base camp in central Lebanon, where the PLGA indoctrinated the recruits in Ali's personal brand of mayhem. At the same time, Rajad put out the word that his organization of trained killers was for hire. He found that he had a special gift for negotiating lucrative contracts. While most of his terrorism was against Israel, Rajad accepted assignments from around the world. PLGA cells perpetrated acts of terror in Europe, South America, Asia, and Africa. After several successful missions, the Soviets took note and began to use Rajad to promote their interests in the Middle East. Though Rajad had no interest in communism, he was easily persuaded to comply with their requests in exchange for advanced military hardware and cash.

Rajad learned that the biggest paychecks came from the Saudis, Libyans, and other fanatical Muslim governments. Ali accepted contracts to send his men on suicide missions both into Israel and other targets chosen by his patrons. On one such raid into Israel, a nursery school was attacked by the PLGA resulting in the death of over twenty children. Although all the terrorists were ultimately killed by Israeli commandos, Rajad received two million dollars from the Libyans for this "successful" action to further the cause of liberating Palestine. This money was routed into personal bank accounts in Switzerland and Germany and used to import luxury vehicles and designer clothes for Ali and his top associates.

Rajad felt justified in this manner of obtaining personal wealth. He felt that he was making a strong contribution to the Palestinian cause and at the same time earning a handsome living. The PLGA expanded to a force of over six hundred fighters, all trained at his base of operations in central Lebanon.

The PLGA soon became the most notorious branch of the Palestinian Liberation Organization, with which they maintained a loose affiliation. Rajad's ability to plan and execute complex operations made him feared by his fellow terrorist leaders. He maintained an ostentatiously large staff of personal bodyguards. He also knew how to work his connections. Rajad sent a constant flow of women and drugs to the mad dictator in charge of Libya, as well as select government officials in many different Arab countries. As a result, Rajad and the PLGA were shielded from nosy foreign intelligence services.

He also knew how to use a combination of the stick and the carrot to keep the power brokers in Lebanon at bay. When they were his friends, they received gifts in the form of cash and jewelry. But if they dared question him, they knew their wives and children could quickly become PLGA targets.

Just three years ago, Rajad secured the most lucrative contract of his career. Three men of obvious German nationality had entered the large anteroom of his Tripoli office where Kalem, officially second in command at the PLGA and chief of Rajad's large personal security force, stopped them. Kalem asked the Germans to state their business. Their apparent leader removed from his pocket a small box, the size of a cigarette pack, and handed it to Kalem. He said in flawless Arabic that the box was to be given to Ali Rajad as a gift.

Kalem was skeptical and ordered his men to watch the Germans while he ran a test for explosives on the box. When he was satisfied that it was not dangerous, he entered Rajad's plush office and handed him the gift. Rajad was startled to find that the box contained about a half-dozen flawless diamonds. Having often received diamonds as payment for missions, he had acquired some skill in their evaluation. He removed a jeweler's loop from his desk drawer and was shocked by their quality. In his conservative estimation they appeared to be worth at least two to three million dollars. Very pleased, Ali ordered Kalem to usher the Germans into his office.

As they entered, Rajad was surprised to note that the three men looked like brothers. They were all over six-foot-three-inches tall, with blonde hair and similar facial characteristics. What was most striking was their matching sickly grayish-white skin tone.

Rajad opened the conversation by asking, "What have I done to deserve such a handsome gift?"

The leader answered, "It is not for what you have done for us, but rather it is a down payment on a mission that we wish you to carry out." His Arabic revealed only a hint of a German accent.

"And what would that be?"

"In this pouch I have three items that I would like you to place in specific locations in Israel." He opened his black leather briefcase, revealing three individual compartments, each containing a shining steel cylinder.

The German continued, "Please do not ask us what is in the containers. Just know that if you successfully complete this small task, you will receive twelve additional boxes of diamonds of similar size and quality."

Ali was delighted but somewhat skeptical. For such a payment the mission sounded too simple. The original box would be more than sufficient payment.

"I am sure we can come to an arrangement," Rajad said, "But I must ask, why the PLGA? I'm sure you could find someone else to do this task for much less."

The leader was prepared for this question. "You are correct. But we have determined your organization offers the highest probability of success. And if you are curious about the unusually large compensation we are offering, it has nothing to do with the difficulty of the mission. In fact, the containers are to be placed in areas open to the public, with easy access by motor transportation. However, we have unlimited resources, and we are requesting your personal involvement and oversight. A mission of such high importance cannot be doled out to amateurs."

Ali understood. He personally wouldn't trust any of his rivals in the PLO to deliver a cup of sugar.

"What are the terms?" Ali inquired.

"The cylinders must be in their designated locations by the eighteenth of this month. That is a strict deadline that must be kept."

"And how will I receive payment for my services?" Ali asked.

The leader handed Rajad a small key. "We will know the location of the cylinders by means of the radio signal they emit. The moment the cylinders are in their designated places we will simply mail you a letter that contains the address of the bank and the number of the safe deposit box that holds your payment."

"Don't be offended, but what keeps me from holding you here until my associates determine the location of the bank and retrieve the diamonds?" Rajad asked with a smile.

The Germans did not see the humor in Rajad's statement. "We know your reputation. That is not how you conduct business. Besides, the bank could be anywhere. And we have many friends. We are expected in another location within the hour. If we do not arrive, our associates will simply remove the contents from the safe deposit box. We ourselves, I'm sorry to say, are quite expendable."

Ali and his guards broke out into a laugh. "I was just joking. But thank you for acknowledging my integrity."

The Germans did not respond. In Valhalla, there was no laughter or humor. Seeing that they didn't get his joke, Rajad dismissed their behavior as a cultural difference. He shook hands with the leader and the three Germans departed. Rajad never saw them again.

As the Germans left, he remembered that he already had a contract to complete in Israel that month, a suicide mission on the Netanya beach. It occurred to him that the two operations could be combined, and the attack on the beach would provide a convenient distraction for his own activities.

Regarding the cylinders, Rajad was not the least bit curious regarding what they contained. He daydreamed about the day he would open the safe deposit box and hold the exquisite treasure trove of diamonds in his hands.

As he drove past the Sea of Galilee, Ali Rajad smiled to himself. From abject poverty to seemingly endless wealth and power. Life was getting better all the time.

10

Joshua 74575 lived in block L3 in the concentration camp of West Clover, known simply as Holle, or Hell in German. Joshua had lived there since he was born because he was a Jew, and according to the Aryans, all Jews belonged in Hell.

Joshua knew what being a Jew meant mostly from the SS education officers. Once a week, on what was known as the Jewish Sabbath, he and his fellow inmates stood at attention for twenty-four straight hours and listened to a series of German officers rant about the evils of Judaism. They said that Jews cheated in business, were communists, and controlled the banks. Joshua had no idea what business, a communist, or a bank were, but he did know that it didn't really seem like his fellow Jews controlled anything.

Each lecturer would usually finish with a variation on the mantra: "You Jews are filth, scum, subhuman and lower than dirt. You try to pretend you are human, when, in fact, you are the offspring of the Devil."

Joshua, being naturally intelligent and resourceful, didn't believe a word of it. Having closely observed the Aryans, he had long ago concluded that the main difference between an Aryan and a Jew was that the Aryans had the ability to speak, while Jews could only mumble. Joshua had noticed that unlike Jews, Aryans possessed a small red flap inside their mouths. He was convinced that if Jews had flaps in their mouths, they too would be able to speak just like the Aryans. Instead, Jews were forced to communicate through a combination of grunts, head motions, and hand signals. What Joshua did not know was that when Jewish babies were born in Valhalla, the first order of business was for an SS physician to surgically remove their tongues.

Joshua 74575 didn't really mind the Jewish Sabbath. In fact, he found it a nice rest from the week's back-breaking labor. Even if he was not allowed to eat or drink the entire time, Joshua was in any case accustomed to getting by with a minimal diet. He didn't even mind that he couldn't evacuate his bowels if the need arose. He, like his fellow Jews, would just relieve himself in his pants, and after the Sabbath he would clean himself up.

Just two things bothered Joshua about the Jewish Sabbath. One was watching what happened when one of the other Jews failed to stand at attention, usually because they fell from exhaustion. This was to be avoided at all costs, because the Germans would inevitably take them away for what they called "special treatment." Many Jews never returned from special treatment. Joshua didn't know what exactly special treatment was, but he could tell from the broken faces of the Jews that did return that it must have been horrible. As a result, Jews did their best to be compliant with the laws of the Sabbath.

The second thing that bothered Joshua was that the Sabbath was when Jews had their Bar Mitzvah. Joshua still had terrible nightmares about his own Bar Mitzvah. Until he was 13 years hold, like all Jewish children, Joshua had only been referred to by the number tattooed on his arm: 74575. On the week of his 13th birthday, in the middle of the Sabbath education program, his number had been called out and he was instructed to step on to the wooden platform in the middle of Holle from which services were led. The SS Chief Education Officer read a passage from the Old Testament which was customary for Bar Mitzvah ceremonies. He then stopped and opened an ornamental black box, placing it on the ceremonial altar which was a shipping crate.

The officer then removed from the ornamental box a large iron cleaver. He faced 74575 and ordered him to lower his pants and place his penis on the altar. With no alternative save immediate execution, 74575 complied.

The officer then raised the cleaver and shouted, "In the name of the Reich Gott, I name you 'Joshua 74575.'"

The cleaver dropped swiftly onto Joshua's penis. A few seconds later he passed out from the excruciating pain. This was expected, so no punishment was instituted. When he awoke, Joshua found that he had been extraordinarily fortunate. The education officer had managed to do it right this time, removing only the foreskin. Many of his fellow Jews had not been so lucky on their Bar Mitzvahs.

At the age of eighteen, Joshua was selected by the Department of Reproduction to become a breeder. A high mortality rate from work-related injuries along with Broder's and Schreiber's experiments created a continuous loss of manpower, and the breeding program was necessary to keep the Jewish population stable.

When male Jews turned eighteen, their medical files were reviewed by an SS physician. Those who were seen as potential candidates were sent to the medical facility in East Clover for physical examinations. Despite inadequate nutrition and years of hard labor, Joshua 74575 had grown into a strong young man. He was now six foot two inches tall, with wide shoulders and curly red hair. After his physical, Joshua was certified as a breeder.

Jewish female breeders were chosen at the age of sixteen. Those selected would be paired with a male breeder who they would remain with until the birth of their child. The reason for allowing the breeders to remain together was that scientists at the Department of Reproduction had determined that it significantly increased the rate of live births. They called this the "Happy Mother Effect." A short time after giving birth, however, these happy mothers were almost always sent to either the Broder Laboratory or Schreiber's Research Facility for their nefarious experiments.

Miriam was chosen as Joshua's breeding mate. She was five-foot-seven and weighed 110 pounds, with brown hair and brown eyes. It did not take many visits to Miriam before they fell deeply in love. Joshua tried hard to avoid thinking about what would happen after she gave birth and she was sent to be a test subject for Nazi experiments.

Now that Joshua had been given breeder status, he no longer had to work in the coal mine. There, Jews were constantly being carried out of the shafts on stretchers due to heat exhaustion or lack of oxygen during their 16-hour shifts. Those who were determined to be working with insufficient enthusiasm were used as examples at the closing of Sabbath services.

The SS Chief Education Officer would order them to enter a glass booth the size of a large van located at the side of the wooden stage. He would announce that everyone should observe carefully the fate of those who fail to contribute toward the welfare of Germany and the Fourth Reich. Then he would press a button releasing Zyklon B gas into the booth. The glass booth would fill with the poisonous gas while the crowd standing at attention were forced to watch the ghastly sight of their fellow Jews pound on the glass, scream out in agony, vomit, and finally die.

Joshua was fortunate because now was among the few privileged Jews who worked outside the West Clover. For a few months he worked the garbage detail in East Clover. Then, he was informed by loudspeaker that he had been reassigned to North Clover. His new job was called by the Nazis the "Jew Keeper."

11

Ronald Fletcher walked feverously up and down the Netanya beach, lost in thought, until well after midnight. During this time, his determination for vengeance in its most terrible form had solidified. There was no question in his mind that bitter retribution was the only appropriate response.

As he paced along the soft sand, Fletcher mumbled to himself.

"My wife was brutally murdered for absolutely no reason. Without Mary, my life has no meaning. My children are so traumatized they require psychiatric care. A selfless old man was ruthlessly killed for no other sin than trying to protect my innocent children."

"No one is more deserving of the fire and brimstone that I will personally rain down on the savages that killed my Mary. They will curse the day they were born, and their mothers that brought them into the world. I will drain their bodies of blood and stomp them into oblivion."

Fletcher knew the only cure for the burning poison in his veins was coldhearted revenge. But he also knew that in order to remain effective he would need a cool head. He called upon the considerable knowledge and expertise that he had gained over his many years of fighting evil in the world. Slowly, a plan of action emerged.

Once Fletcher had decided how best to proceed, he walked down the boardwalk toward the center of town to hail a cab. Thirty minutes later he was in his beachside apartment in downtown Tel Aviv, only a few blocks from the U.S. Embassy. He went directly to his bedroom, not bothering to undress, and fell onto the bed. Within seconds he was asleep. It was an unsatisfying sleep, plagued by visions of Mary's bloody, swollen face, crying, "Where were you? Why didn't you save me?"

Fletcher rose at seven. Driven by habit, he perfunctorily showered, shaved, and got dressed. Only upon entering the kitchen did he notice the dead silence. Mary was not cheerfully preparing his usual breakfast of toast with butter, freshly squeezed orange juice, and a piping hot cup of black coffee. The chairs where his children sat were empty. There was no smile and kiss on his cheek from Mary as he sat down to read the headlines of the International Herald Tribune.

The dull silence triggered a swift return of the hatred that quickly rushed over him. He realized in an instant that his entire world had been destroyed. This time the feeling was so powerful that he began shaking all over, as if he was withdrawing from a powerful sedative. He felt painful, writhing knots in his stomach. Fletcher recommitted himself to the one-way-path he had chosen the previous night. He returned to his bedroom and began to prepare an overnight bag.

When Fletcher finished packing, he called Mike Barnes and told him to meet him at the restaurant of the Dan Hotel in forty minutes. He grabbed his bag and went directly to the hotel's second floor dining area, ordering its world-famous Israeli breakfast. This smorgasbord, comprising over fifty dishes, included a variety of breads, fruits, vegetables, juices, hard and soft cheeses, and eggs of various preparations. Fletcher had little appetite. Still, he knew he was about to start a dangerous journey and it was best to do so on a full stomach. He filled his plate and took a seat at a window table overlooking the Mediterranean Sea. He ate his food but did not enjoy the taste. Fletcher's mind was focused on his singular goal of revenging Mary's death.

Fletcher glanced at his watch and noticed Mike Barnes enter the room. He liked and trusted Barnes. They had served in Vietnam and came from the same world of elite combat soldiers.

Barnes was the first to speak.

"Ron, there's nothing I can say. I am so sorry. If there's anything that I can do, you name it, I'll do it."

Barnes sensed what his boss was thinking. He knew that Fletcher could not and would not let such a grave personal attack go unpunished. Moreover, Barnes had also personally been affected by the tragedy. Fletcher's wife had made him feel like part of their family. All

Fletcher had to do is ask and Barnes would follow him to the gates of Hell.

"Thanks, Mike." Fletcher answered. "Listen carefully. I've got some things I have to take care of. I'm taking off for a few days. Exactly how much time, I don't know. Cover for me as long as you can. Don't ask me where I'm going or why. But while I'm away, I want you to look in on my kids at the hospital. Explain to them that their father is on assignment and that he'll come visit as soon as he can."

"Sure, of course," Barnes replied.

Fletcher handed Barnes a torn page from a notepad. As Barnes read it over Fletcher said, "I need you to get hold of those items and bring them to me at Ben Gurion Airport in three hours."

Barnes understood immediately what was being planned. "Ron, please let me go along. I really want to. And you could use me."

Fletcher knew how useful Barnes would be on this mission, but it was impossible. This mission would likely involve flagrant violations of international law and ethics, unacceptable levels of personal risk to life, and a probable lifelong blacklist from intelligence agencies if revealed. Still, he appreciated Barnes' willingness to put himself on the line for a friend.

"Thanks, Mike, but this is something I have to do alone. Besides, I need you on the inside for intel. No matter what happens, you don't know anything, got it?"

Fletcher hated to say these last words, knowing that Barnes was a man of loyalty and would never do anything to put him at risk. Still, he wanted to emphasize the importance of total secrecy.

As the two stood up to leave, Barnes, in a rare display of emotion, spontaneously hugged him. Afterwards, the two friends shook hands and parted.

Fletcher went directly to the bank and withdrew nine thousand dollars in cash. Then he boarded a bus to the Tel Aviv Central Bus Station. At the station, he took a bus to Tzafria, a farming village close to Ben Gurion Airport, and then a different bus to the airport. In this manner, he was able to ensure no one was following him or tracking his movements.

Upon arriving at the main terminal of Ben Gurion, Fletcher walked a random route to a restroom located near the exit of the customs area. There were two stalls in the bathroom. Fletcher put down the seat cover of the stall to the left and sat on it, placing a book on the floor next to the partition separating the two stalls. The book, a 1956 World Almanac, could be seen from the other stall because the partition did not reach the bottom of the floor.

Seven minutes later, Fletcher saw his almanac being switched with a bulging black envelope by the occupant of the other stall. Fletcher opened it and began perusing its contents. First, he removed a French passport in the name of Claude Marchand. Then he removed a business class ticket to Athens, Greece on British Airways. Finally, he found a slip of paper marked "parcel receipt." He placed all three items in the inner pocket of his suit jacket.

Fletcher then emptied the remainder of the contents of the envelope on to the floor of the stall. He shuffled through several intelligence reports and dossiers. There were a series of satellite images, air and ground reconnaissance photos, and three detailed topographical maps courtesy of Israeli Military Intelligence. Fletcher studied the material for nearly thirty minutes.

When he finished, he returned all of the documents to the envelope and sealed it. Fletcher stood up and held the envelope by means of a plastic strap at its top. He lifted the seat and positioned the envelope above the open toilet. Fletcher then pulled a small tab at the bottom of the envelope. Almost instantaneously the inside the envelope began to emit heat and Fletcher felt a bubbling sensation reverberating through the strap. After a few seconds, the bottom of the envelope opened up, pouring its completely dissolved contents into the toilet. Fletcher then dropped the envelope itself into the toilet, and it too broke down upon contact with the water. He then flushed the toilet.

Ten minutes later, Fletcher boarded a flight to Athens. Upon arrival at Hellinikon Airport at about 2:00 p.m., he walked directly to the Air France reservation counter and picked up his reserved ticket to Beirut, Lebanon. The flight was scheduled to depart in less than forty-five minutes. By five o'clock he was standing in the customs line at Beirut International Airport.

Under a special agreement, intelligence agencies in France and the United States occasionally exchange blank passports. The NSA issues these passports for special operations that require perfect security, and Barnes had authorized the issuance of an authentic passport with Fletcher's actual picture under a false identity which had been designed to facilitate international travel. Still, Fletcher was careful not to carry any illegal weapons or contraband in order to avoid any unnecessary attention. This was, of course, with the exception of the Vu Khi, which even if examined would pass inspection given its benign external appearance. After stamping Ron's passport, he was waved through customs.

Fletcher proceeded to the airport's hectic lobby where there was a row of car rental booths. He scanned the signs across the top of the booths until he saw Cedars of Lebanon Car Rental. After signing forms and paying two hundred dollars, he was told to exit the lobby and a shuttle would take him to a large concrete parking garage near the airport. There he picked up the car reserved for him by Barnes, a nondescript ash-gray Peugeot 205. From there he drove north on the Beirut-Saida Highway until he reached the capital. Fletcher was familiar with just about every street in downtown Beirut. He took side streets as a precaution against anyone who might be following him.

Fletcher felt apprehensive being back in one of the most lawless countries in the world. As he drove, he reviewed his plan for the mission, step by step. Passing the U.S. Embassy in Beirut, he remembered his assignment there years prior. He had completed his tour without a major incident against U.S. property or interests. During his time working in Lebanon's capital, he had always been cognizant of the danger his family faced and had acted accordingly. He had always ensured that at least two trusted Embassy guards accompanied his wife and children whenever they left their apartment. Fletcher's thoughts drifted to remorse as he blamed himself for not having taken precautions to ensure his family's safety in Israel in the same way he did when he was stationed in Beirut. He felt deeply depressed as he passed the Café de Paris where he had sat for hours drinking espressos with Mary.

Driving through a seedy section of the city next to the Port of Beirut, Fletcher finally arrived at a row of large, poorly maintained warehouses. Scanning the area, he spotted a small flickering sign which read "Middle East Storage Company." Ron parked the Peugeot next to a ramp that led up to a double-wide loading bay. He walked over to the aging door below the sign and tried the shaky handle. It was open.

Ron entered the building and walked up a short flight of stairs leading to a second-floor office. Behind the warped wood counter was a gray metal desk covered with stamping pads and official-looking forms in Arabic and French. The walls were covered with aluminum shelves holding empty cardboard boxes of various sizes.

Fletcher took out the receipt Barnes had included in the envelope and rang a bell on the counter. Out from the back emerged a middle-aged man dressed in a tan suit with a red clerk's vest. What struck Ron was his perfectly maintained and waxed handlebar mustache. After scrutinizing the parcel receipt, the clerk, speaking in French, demanded payment of one hundred and thirty U.S. dollars for seven months of storage. Since Lebanese currency was constantly being devalued, U.S. dollars, though technically illegal to possess, had become the standard currency.

Fletcher, who was fluent in French, handed three fifties to the clerk and told him to keep the difference. Appreciative of the tip, the clerk gave Fletcher a smile and instructed him to meet him in the loading area while he disappeared into the back to locate the parcel.

Minutes later the clerk rolled a rusty old dolly holding a large wooden crate down the loading ramp to the Peugeot. Fletcher used a UV light to examine the several hidden seals on the crates to determine whether it had been tampered with. Ron was relieved to find that the seals were intact.

This business, a favorite among international intelligence agencies, was not a typical shipping and storage facility. The proprietors, who were Syrian Christians, were specialists in the art of avoiding customs and security inspections. For the right price, any desired item could be safely imported into Lebanon or exported abroad without any questions asked.

Fletcher helped load it into the hatch on top of the folded-down back seat. The clerk then shook Fletcher's hand in parting, saying "God bless you" in Arabic.

Fletcher was daydreaming while he travelled westbound on Avenue de Paris, fixing his eyes on the destruction caused by the Lebanese civil war. This area had been beautiful when he was working in Beirut, and now it had become a war-torn wasteland. He thought to himself that the Palestinian Liberation Organization had destroyed Lebanon just as they had destroyed his family. As he passed the U.S. Embassy, he teared up thinking about how Mary picked him up after work with ice coffees and sandwiches. He turned south down General De Gaulle Highway, passing the city's most romantic landmark, Pigeons' Rock. There Mary and Ron had spent priceless moments gazing at the rocky formations jutting out of the Mediterranean Sea.

Fletcher loosened his tie and prepared for the dangerous journey southeast. He thought to himself how deceivingly peaceful the Central Bekaa Valley appeared. On both sides of the highway he observed vineyards, olive groves, and forests of cedar trees. About a thirty miles past Château Kefraya winery, he turned right and began heading south. After some time, he spotted a dirt road that he had noted on one of the maps supplied by Israeli intelligence. It was nearly midnight when he turned on to this road which led to a desolate area comprised of rocky hills. Eventually he stopped, parking the Peugeot behind a ring of bushes.

Fletcher got out and removed the crate from the back, dragging it a few feet from the Peugeot. He then took the tire iron out of the back of the car and used it to pry open the box. Systematically he removed each item and organized its contents into separate piles.

The crate was affectionately referred to in intelligence circles as a "Goodie Bag." It was one of many prepared by the CIA in Langley, Virginia and distributed throughout the world. The crate contained all that was needed for a single agent to complete a hostile mission.

He first removed a Colt Commando CAR-15 automatic rifle. The Commando, with its thirty-round magazines, was relatively light but extremely lethal at close and medium ranges. It included a barrel attachment known as the Rifleman's Assault Weapon, with six ball-shaped rocket-propelled grenades that could blast through tank armor or thick concrete. Next to the Commando was an Austrian Steyr SSG 69 sniper's rifle with a detachable silencer and a Star-Tron Image Intensifier scope. There was also a Colt .45 ACP M1911 pistol with eight clips.

Ron was surprised to find an Israeli air gun about the size of the Colt M1911 that he had heard about but never actually seen. The gun fired a glass dart which was filled with a mixture of Vietnamese centipede and Fer-de-lance snake venom. It was said that the mixture would cause immediate paralysis, followed by a slow, agonizing death. Fletcher quickly reviewed the instructions for the air gun that was attached to a box of twenty darts.

Ron then removed a knapsack containing an M72 LAW anti-tank weapon and an M2-series grenade launcher that had been modified to fit the SSG 69. These were accompanied by a half-dozen M34 smoke grenades, also known as "Willie Petes," fifteen M67 grenades, a dozen MK3 concussion grenades, and twenty pounds of plastic explosives complete with caps and radio-controlled electronic detonators.

He then organized the remainder of gear which included twenty flares, K-rations for a week, commando gloves, combat boots in three sizes, five pairs each of undershirts, underwear, and heavy-duty army socks, a sleeping bag, a Gerber Mark II combat knife, an army compass, a 10 foot by 12 foot waterproof tarp, and three black nylon jogging suits. As per regulations, the total weight for all weapons and equipment was eighty pounds.

"Heavy, but not too bad." Fletcher thought to himself. "A Roman infantry soldier was required to carry about eighty pounds of equipment into battle. I guess times haven't changed."

Fletcher removed his clothes and put on one of the jogging suits and size 13 boots. He then strapped the now-packed knapsack to his back, and slung the two rifles and grenade launcher over his right shoulder. For an average soldier it was a heavy load, but Fletcher was focused on his mission and didn't even notice the weight. He began his long hike through the hills toward the PLGA base near Aaita El Foukhar, not far from the Syrian border.

Ron, having memorized the base's coordinates, used the M-1950 U.S. Army Lensatic Compass for navigation. He stayed off the dirt road, preferring seldom-used goat paths. As he walked, he reviewed in his mind the intelligence reports regarding the layout and security protocols of the base he was approaching.

On the one hand, Fletcher knew that he was about to attempt a solo attack on a small battalion of armed combatants in a fortified compound. The odds of success appeared to be strongly against him. However, his experience over the past two years serving side-by-side with Israel's top commandos had taught him that these terrorists were not really soldiers. They lacked the necessary skills and training needed to defend against his plan. These killers, responsible for Mary's murder, were only trained in terrorism. Sure, they could kill unarmed civilians, women, children and elderly people, but when it came to fighting defensively against trained warriors, such as Israeli paratroopers, Golani infantry, and Navy frogmen, they just didn't have the training necessary to defend themselves. Fletcher knew that his skills in warfare could match the best of the best, and therefore he had formulated a plan based on the intelligence he had acquired regarding the enemy and the arms and equipment he had at his disposal.

The PLGA base was located in an abandoned Lebanese Army fort, which in itself was founded on the ruins of a crusader outpost. It consisted of a few administrative buildings, an ancient water cistern used as an armory, a mess hall, and barracks that housed three hundred PLGA terrorists.

According to the Israeli intelligence reports, there were three nightly guard shifts. Fletcher had chosen to assault the base at 4:30 a.m., near the end of the third shift and before daybreak. There were five guards, one in each of two of the base's four guard towers, and three at the main gate.

Fletcher arrived at a barren hill overlooking the entrance of the base at about 2:00 a.m. He set down the knapsack and placed the two rifles and grenade launcher against a tree. He opened the pack and removed three cans. Fletcher started with the goulash, which, according to the date on the can, had just celebrated its sixth birthday. He ate it cold. He then downed a can of sweet corn along with a large amount of "corn juice." Finally, he washed it all down with a liter of water.

Fletcher then turned to his weapons. He cleaned the packing grease from both rifles as thoroughly as possible. Then he checked the clips, making sure the springs were in proper working order and that each clip was full minus one round to prevent jamming.

When Fletcher completed his weapons check it was nearly 3:00 am. He decided to force himself to take a short nap to make sure he would be alert later. As he opened his sleeping bag, thunder rumbled in the distance. Weather reports had predicted a brief heavy shower followed by dense fog. By the time he had entered the mummy-type down sleeping bag, which was covered above and below by the tarp, a heavy downfall of rain had begun.

Fletcher wasn't sure whether he actually slept, but at 4:00 his watch alarm buzzed. He opened his eyes and extricated himself from the sleeping bag, finding that he was now in the middle of a shallow pool of water. It was still dark and there was a persistent light drizzle. As predicted, thick fog had set in. His gear was stowed in the waterproof knapsack about ten feet away on slightly elevated ground.

Fletcher removed the two rifles and grenade launcher and performed a final inspection. He then rolled up his sleeping bag and strapped it to the bottom of his backpack. Jogging halfway down the hill, he stopped behind a large boulder. He lifted the SSG 69 and gazed through the scope. With the help of the Star-Tron image enhancer, he spotted all five guards. He quickly worked out the order of elimination in his mind.

Fletcher placed the guard in the farthest tower in the crosshairs of the sniper rife. The silencer did its job, muffling the sound of the fire as the bullet found its target in the center of the unsuspecting guard's forehead. In rapid sequence, he proceeded to eliminate the guard in the other tower and the three half-asleep guards at the gate.

"I guess I haven't lost it," Fletcher thought to himself, as he stealthily descended the hill toward the main gate of the PLGA base.

12

Rachel Bronot sat behind her desk with her eyes closed in deep contemplation, trying to unravel the puzzle of the three cylinders. She opened her eyes and glanced around her no-frills office, which consisted of a gray metal desk with two folding chairs, a filing cabinet, and an electric teapot. The previous day, thanks to information elicited by American NSA liaison Ronald Fletcher, Israeli security forces had picked up two men that had in their possession steel cylinders. However, no information of any real import had yet been gleaned from them.

Bronot's office was located within Israel's equivalent to the Pentagon, known as HaKirya. This complex could best be described as an army base in the form of a densely packed city. It was comprised of a cluster of office buildings enclosed by fences, walls, and security gates. HaKirya held the headquarters of all branches of the Israel Defense Forces, and within its walls took place the most critical Israeli military logistics and planning. On any given day, one could find the IDF's highest ranking generals and their staff members walking around the campus or eating in the cafeteria. And while the political office of the Defense Minister was located in Jerusalem, his base of operations was in HaKirya.

For the past three years, Rachel had been in charge of coordinating intelligence between the Mossad, Israel's equivalent to the CIA, the Shin Bet, Israel's internal security organization, and Military Intelligence. The information they gathered was analyzed and often times acted upon by her anti-terrorist unit, Nekama. This was her brainchild. Having realized that a significant number of attacks on Israel had failed to be prevented because of a lack of adequate coordination of information, Bronot had spent years speaking to any politician that would listen about the importance of an independent department which would consolidate and coordinate all available intelligence. Bronot's agency became, in effect, the place where the dots were connected.

As a result of her efforts, Nekama was born. Bronot was given unparalleled access to all sources of available intelligence. Nekama proved to be highly effective in thwarting terrorist attacks. But more than just stop attacks, it had been extraordinarily successful in identifying and neutralizing dozens of senior terrorists who made up the upper echelons of different terrorist organizations.

As she reviewed the preliminary report, she had drafted to the Prime Minister regarding the attack on the Netanya beach, Bronot felt that it was lacking perhaps the most important piece of information: the connection between the attack and the mystery of the cylinders.

Instead of having the cylinders sent to the central police laboratory in Jerusalem, Bronot had ordered that they be examined by the top-secret Army Biological Warfare Division. The preliminary lab report had stated that the first cylinder contained an unusual unknown material of organic origin. This material had been tested on a large sample of animals and plants and found to be harmless. Rachel had ordered testing to continue while she continued to work to obtain additional information on Rajad and PLGA through her intelligence network.

This question of "why" was at the heart of Bronot's uncertainty. Why would PLGA go to the trouble of staging a suicidal raid to cover the entry of their chief, Ali Rajad? Why would Rajad, who generally managed his operations from a safe distance, be personally involved in transporting the cylinders? She was convinced that failure to determine the nature of this operation could be catastrophic to the security of the State of Israel.

As Bronot reviewed the information in her mind, her phone rang. It was Professor Ehud Levy, the Army's top microbiologist, now in charge of Israel's biological warfare facility near the Dead Sea. Levy was a distinguished tenured professor of world renown at the Hebrew University in Jerusalem. Included among his myriad honors and awards was not one but two Nobel Prizes, one in Chemistry and the other in Medicine.

Their conversation was brief.

Levy, in a somewhat restrained, yet unnerving low-pitched voice said just two words, "Come quickly."

Bronot understood that Levy had a revelation that could only be explained in person. She ordered her secretary to secure one of HaKirya's helicopters that was on standby at the complex's landing pad. Within forty minutes, Bronot was sitting in Ehud Levy's office.

Israel's biological warfare facility near the Dead Sea was one of the most sophisticated in the world. It was established in the early 1960s after Gamel Abdel Nasser, then President of Egypt, had hired former Nazi scientists to develop cultures of Bubonic Plague to be used against Israel. The Mossad had stopped this program by assassinating several of the scientists and blowing up their main research site. At that time, Israel decided to develop its own program as a deterrent to any Arab country contemplating to attack the Jewish State with chemical or biological weapons. Israel recruited top Jewish scientists from around the world. In a few years the Dead Sea facility was on par with similar facilities in the United States, England, and the Soviet Union.

While Professor Levy was usually meticulous in his appearance, today he appeared disheveled. He was not only a brilliant scientist, but also a very rich bachelor from the Nobel Prize money. As a result, he had developed a reputation as somewhat of an international playboy. Levy was constantly traveling the world, lecturing at top universities, speaking before think tanks, and consulting friendly governments seeking his insights regarding the most pressing dangers to international security. He was quite personable, and was inevitably the center of every party and gathering.

Though the world was at his fingertips, including some of the most sought-after women, Levy really had only one woman in mind, Rachel Bronot. Levy couldn't get over the fact that while Bronot was the most stunning women he had ever met, she stood toe-to-toe with him in intellect and was also Israel's top spy. Bronot, on the other hand, was not interested in Levy's advances or, for that matter, any other of the many would-be suitors pursuing her. Bronot had not even thought about even dating since the day her one true love was brutally murdered.

Levy understood the internal pain Bronot was still going through, so he had learned to back off. Today, he knew that the two must focus on the potentially apocalyptic situation. So, he said to himself, he would deal with his feelings for Rachel after the crisis had passed.

Levy addressed Bronot on a professional basis. "I'm glad you came so quickly. We have one very big problem."

Bronot was disturbed by Levy's attitude. On previous meetings he had always projected total confidence, showing that he was in complete control of the situation. If there was an impossible scientific problem needing a solution, Levy was your guy. Bronot also knew Levy had reputation for understating facts. That worried her. If Levy used the words "big problem," it could only mean a catastrophe.

"It couldn't be as bad as you think?" Bronot asked.

"Worse, I'm afraid. If zero means harmless and ten means extremely lethal, I would give these cylinders a hundred." Levy paused to let his words skin in.

"Let me go over with you what just happened. After completing our preliminary tests on the usual selection of animal, plant, fungal, and bacterial species, I wrote up my report and sent it to you. Every indication had shown that the material in the cylinders was not biologically active in any way. Then I went to the cafeteria for lunch. While I was out, my assistant, Dr. Dalia Tamron, took over. She called me and asked my permission to remove the cylinders from the isolation glove box to conduct further analysis. I gave her permission since our preliminary analysis had indicated that the material in the cylinders was completely benign in nature.

"After lunch, I came to my office and made a few phone calls. About an hour later, I returned to the lab to conduct further testing. Before entering, I glanced at the monitor above the security guard's station and could not see any activity in the lab. This was very unusual. By protocol, we always make sure there is at least one staffer in the laboratory during regular hours. I then picked up the log and saw that Dr. Tamron never checked out. That's when I knew there was a real problem."

"Perhaps she just stepped out for a moment and forgot to sign the log." Bronot suggested.

"Impossible! We are meticulous about protocol here, for obvious reasons. Our security officers are assigned from elite units of Army Internal Security. They would not leave their post unauthorized even if beckoned by the Angel of Death.

"Even though the lab is hermetically sealed, and there was no possibility of any accidental leakage into the environment outside of the laboratory, I ordered that the entire research area be put on lockdown until we have determined the best way to approach this."

Levy called his secretary via intercom. "Please have the security tapes brought in."

Within a minute two security guards rolled in a large monitor with an attached video player.

Levy then said to Rachel. "Cameras in this facility continuously record all laboratory activity. Let me show you what happened."

Levy ordered the two guards to leave. He put a tape into the player and pressed play.

On the video, Dr. Tamron is seen opening a side panel in the glove box to remove one of the cylinders which had been opened in isolation. Four other technicians are working in different parts of the laboratory. Suddenly the scientists' bodies appear to break down into particles of fine, gray dust. The air filtration system gradually absorbs the dust, leaving the scientists' clothing and lab coats intact.

Levy shut off the monitor. Then he sat behind his desk, deep in thought. Rachel, too, began to absorb the real possibility that the cylinder was, in fact, a weapon of mass destruction.

After a long moment of silence, Rachel was the first to speak. "What do you make of that?"

Professor Levy took a few moments to reply. "Your guess is as good as mine. I've never seen anything like it. This is most certainly a biological weapon, even though, to my knowledge, no pathogen known to mankind is as efficiently lethal as that which is contained in the cylinder. I believe the amount of pathogen floating around in the lab would likely be enough to wipe out the entire country!"

Rachel replayed the tape. This time, she focused not on the scientists but on the rest of the room. She noted that the different lab animals, including mice and various primates, remained alive and seemed to be unaffected. Also, there was no noticeable change in the various plants in the room.

"It seems to be the ultimate in ecological warfare." Levy commented. "You can kill every human in a country without upsetting the animal and plant ecosystem."

"You know, it is believed there is another cylinder in Israel that has not yet been accounted for. What can be done?" asked Bronot.

"I would strongly advise to look for it while it is still intact. In the meantime, we will proceed with installing robotic equipment so we can analyze the pathogen in the lab without putting anyone else at risk of contamination. It may take days or weeks before we are sure of what exactly we are dealing with or how to defend ourselves from it."

He then added, "Other than that, my personal advice for you would be to book a ticket to Europe and leave Israel today."

Bronot was unmoved. "The way things are going down at the office, I don't think my boss will give me any time off."

As Rachel walked down the corridor, she became nervous. There was little chance at this point of finding Ali Rajad or the cylinder. Most likely, Rajad had already planted the cylinder and was now either in hiding or already out of the country.

Furthermore, she couldn't understand how the PLGA obtained a previously unknown pathogen that was so deadly. And why would they be involved in an operation that could potentially be just as lethal to the millions of Muslims and Arabs living in Israel? She concluded that Rajad probably did not know what was contained in the cylinder. And Israel's only chance, however slim, was to locate him and the cylinder while it was still intact.

Bronot boarded the helicopter and began planning her next steps.

13

The New Berlin Zoo was a picturesque zoological park surrounded by a grove of trees meant to resemble a forest. Within it there were wide paths bordered by vendors selling drinks, candies, and even souvenirs. One could travel around the zoo using the miniature train or on a path designed for bicycles and roller skates. Since it bordered the river, there was a dock where one could rent paddleboats and canoes. Hitler had designed the zoo and its grounds personally, as part of his effort to integrate his most precious memories into the infrastructure of Project Valhalla.

There was one job at the New Berlin Zoo that the Jews of Holle prayed they would never be assigned. A single Jew was expected to clean the cages of over three hundred animals every day of the week except Saturday, the Jewish Sabbath. The work hours began after the zoo closed at 6:00 p.m. and ended the following day at 8:00 a.m. It was known to the Jews that whoever was assigned this job would often never be heard from again. What they didn't know was why. Having grown up without any familiarity of animals, Jews didn't know to stay away from the zoo's more aggressive species. Furthermore, the human instinct of fight or flight had been beaten out of the Jews by their Nazi tormentors. That meant that when an animal attacked, the Jewish worker would often choose to wait for the violence to end, which usually occurred only after the Jew was dead.

Still, there were fringe benefits to those workers who managed to survive their first few days. For instance, one could supplement their diet by stealing food from the animals. The Jews of Holle, being provided rations that comprised of less than 900 calories a day, were in a constant state of hunger. The animals in the zoo were given a far more substantial and nutritionally balanced diet. A Jewish worker who took food from the animals would therefore have adequate nutrition and sometimes even have enough left over to share with the other occupants in their barracks.

The other benefit was that since the job involved large amount of rancid animal feces, no Aryan guard was assigned to directly supervise the worker. Jews in Holle were under constant harassment by the guards. Even during the short time allocated to sleeping, guards would randomly overturn beds to create an atmosphere of terror. As long as there was an Aryan around, Jews were in constant fear that they were the next to be beaten or taken away, never to be seen again. The Jewish zoo worker, however, was on his own. As long as he showed up and did his job, nobody paid any notice to him.

When the loudspeaker ordered Joshua to report to the zoo, he chalked it up as fate and didn't let the reaction of sympathy from his fellow Jews bother him at all. Joshua had an innate confidence that he could overcome any obstacle the Nazis would throw at him. His quiet defiance gave him a sense of inner pride. This attitude, along with his natural intelligence, had kept him thus far alive.

On his first day at the zoo, Joshua instinctively understood that it might be dangerous to enter cages with animals. This was a remarkable deduction, especially given that the Aryan manager of the zoo was under specific orders not to inform the Jewish worker of this danger. It was joke among the Aryans that if the Jew started his cleaning duties at the lion's cage, he would never get to see the giraffe. The previous worker before Joshua had been lucky. His first cage was the Primate House, and therefore he only received a pelting of rocks from a troop of baboons.

Joshua, to his good fortune, was blessed with patience and keen intuition. Before jumping into the job, he took time to observe the animals and their environment. He realized that attached to each cage was a small holding pen where the animal could be held during the cleaning. Also next to each cage was a long stick with a hook at its end which could be used to prod the animal into the pen. Joshua realized that only when the animal was in the holding pen and the gate separating the two areas was secured would it be safe to clean the exhibit.

Joshua was fascinated by the variety of life forms present in the zoo. Until he began working in the zoo, his only impressions of life had been from the concentration camp, the coal mine, and his work in the Aryan neighborhoods collecting garbage. Joshua loved watching the peacocks roaming free and displaying their beautiful feathers. His favorite animal, however, was the orangutan. His sad face reminded Joshua what so many Jews looked like as a result of their demoralizing life in Project Valhalla.

As he progressed through his duties on his first day on the job, Joshua decided that he rather enjoyed the work, despite the unpleasant odor. Also, for the first time in his life, he felt liberated because he did not have an Aryan guard constantly harassing him. After the first few cages, Joshua hoped that he would be permanently assigned to zoo duties.

One late night, Joshua had completed his work and was exploring the back areas of the zoo when he came upon a locked building. There was a large sign on the door marked "Untermenschen." Had Joshua been taught to read, he would have been familiar with the word, since he and his fellow Jews were constantly referred to by the Nazis as untermenschen, or subhuman.

Joshua was curious, so he looked around the building and found a window that was unlocked. Peeking through the window, he saw that there were no Germans inside, so he decided to sneak in. The viewing hall was dimly lit, but he could make out a row of cages. Upon closer examination the animals inside were old men. Each had a sign below the cage that explained something about its inhabitant. There was a Russian soldier, American pilot, Italian businessman, African tribesman, and a handful of other people from around the world. Some of the cages were empty, containing only large color photographs of their former occupants. Joshua noted that the men in the cages ignored him, not even acknowledging his existence. What Joshua didn't know was that the human specimens of the zoo had all, save one, long ago gone insane. As a result, they simply sat or mulled around their cages with blank expressions on their faces.

The last cage stood alone, separated from the others. It appeared to be an important exhibit given its larger size and row of viewing benches in front. Joshua looked at the man in the cage and immediately felt an emotional connection. He sat down on the bench in front of the cage to observe the man more closely.

The man had a long grey beard, and wore a ragged long black coat and prayer shawl. On his forehead he wore the black box known as *tefillin,* or phylacteries. The sign under the cage read: "Eastern European Jew. Born in Poland, 1915. Most Subhuman Species of *Homo sapiens.* Considered the most dangerous animal ever to exist."

As Joshua was staring at the cage, the man suddenly began speaking. "If you would like to know, I am a Jew."

Joshua was surprised. He thought to himself, "Impossible. No Jew can speak." He looked carefully at the man and was able to see that he had a red flap in his mouth like an Aryan.

The old man continued, "My name is Rabbi Gershon Cohen. I was once considered among the world's foremost authorities on the Talmud, the Jewish oral tradition."

This statement was true. Rabbi Cohen had been considered one of the leading experts in Jewish law prior to the outbreak of World War II. At an early age, Rabbi Cohen had been admitted to Etz Chaim, otherwise known as the Volozhin Yeshiva, the famous rabbinical academy in Lithuania. Its founder, Rabbi Chaim of Volozhin, was a student of the Vilna Gaon, and the yeshiva gained a reputation of being the world's top rabbinical academy under Rabbi Naftali Berlin, better known as the Netziv. After being closed down in 1892 by the Russian Government for failure to comply with requirements regarding secular studies, it reopened in 1899.

At that time, the Yeshiva recruited a young prodigy, Gershon Cohen. At age nine he became the youngest member of the most advanced class in Talmud that the Yeshiva had to offer. His photographic memory was so incredible that he was able to memorize the 2,711 pages of the Babylonian Talmud along with all of its commentaries.

In order to test the young *illui,* or genius, his teacher would perform what was known as the "pin test." He would stick a pin through a random volume of the Talmud. Then he would read Gershon the line, emphasizing the word which the pin passed through. With this information, young Gershon Cohen was able to state the tractate and page number of the line, as well as the line and word the pin passed through on all subsequent pages.

By the age of fourteen, Gershon Cohen was ordained by the heads of the Yeshiva. Upon graduating at age eighteen, he surprised his teachers by enrolling at the University of the Sorbonne in Paris. He explained that in order to deepen his understanding of some of the more enigmatic sections of the Talmud, he would need a solid basis in the natural sciences. By his twenty-first birthday, Rabbi Gershon Cohen had successfully completed doctoral degrees in both mathematics and biology.

Soon after World War II broke out. Rabbi Cohen was sent by the Nazis via cattle car to the infamous Auschwitz extermination camp. Initially he was given the job of scavenging gold teeth from the mouths of his fellow Jews who had just been murdered in the gas chambers.

Rabbi Cohen kept a low profile and somehow survived the weekly selections that the Nazis used both to terrorize the Jews and to weed out the weaker ones. Near the end of the war he was sent along with several hundred Jews to a temporary camp in Crete, and then on to Valhalla. While the other Jews were placed in the concentration camp, Rabbi Cohen was chosen to be separated and housed permanently in the Untermenschen section of the zoo because of his irritating tendency to comfort and encourage the other Jews though stories and prayer. While the other humans on display in the zoo eventually went insane, Rabbi Cohen was able to keep himself lucid by constantly reviewing the giant scope of Jewish and worldly knowledge that he had obtained.

He would often gain courage from remembering the Talmudic story of Rabbi Shimon bar Yochai, the most famous disciple of Rabbi Akiva and author of the central book of Jewish mysticism, the *Zohar*. Chased by Roman persecutors, Rabbi Shimon bar Yochai and his son Eleazer sought refuge in a cave where they survived miraculously by eating the fruit of a carob tree. Rabbi Shimon and his son studied Torah together in these conditions for thirteen years.

Rabbi Gershon would console himself by thinking, "I, too, have been confined to a cavern for a long period of time. I will use my time productively, as they did, for reviewing my knowledge. Perhaps the Master of the Universe has spared me, as he spared Rabbi Shimon bar Yochai, for some greater purpose."

"My son, are you Jewish?" The Rabbi called out to Joshua.

Joshua was incapable of answering verbally, but nodded his head. He then opened his mouth wide to show the Rabbi that he was missing the flap. It dawned on him how to prove that he was, in fact, Jewish. He lowered his pants and showed the startled Rabbi his Bar Mitzvah circumcision.

Rabbi Gershon began to weep. It had been a great many years since he saw a fellow Jew. The Human House, as the Rabbi called it, had not been serviced by Joshua's predecessors because there was a toilet in every cage. The only people the Rabbi encountered were Aryans touring the zoo and zookeepers who fed him once every two days. The visitors would sometimes throw him peanuts but more often would spit at him. On occasion, the more audacious Nazis would fling lit matches at him. For the past few years, Rabbi Cohen had mostly pretended that he, too, was insane, which he surmised would be safer.

The Rabbi gently wiped away his tears using his prayer shawl, and then addressed Joshua.

"You are a Jew. In spite of what the Nazis say, being a Jew is a something to be proud of." He continued in a calm, soothing voice. "They treat us like animals, but one thing is for sure, they are the beasts. We Jews are an upright and noble people. And Jews are not treated like dirt everywhere. I once heard a few Aryans talking in front of my cage. They said that the Jews now have their own country called Israel, with its own army. I'm sure you were never told that above these caverns there is a wonderful world of sunlight and fresh air."

The Rabbi observed a puzzled look on Joshua's face, then said. "I know, what I'm saying must be strange to you. Never mind, I will teach you everything. I'll tell you about the world, Judaism, and God. The Jewish God, the one true God, not the raving lunatic called the Reich Gott, may its name be erased forever. I will teach you the concepts of freedom, goodness and morality. I promise you that in a short time you will know what it means be a good human being and a proud Jew."

Joshua felt in his heart that this man, a talking Jew, was sincere. So he made up his mind to concentrate all his efforts to learn everything that the Rabbi had promised to teach him.

From that day on, as soon as Joshua arrived at the zoo, he would clean the animal cages as fast as he could to allow himself as much time with the Rabbi as possible. By rushing he was able to finish by 2:00 a.m., which allowed him six uninterrupted hours with his mentor. The Rabbi, an excellent teacher, instilled meaning into Joshua's life. Joshua first learned about God and then learned to pray. He prayed that someday he would take the Rabbi and Miriam to live in the Jewish nation, Israel. Although he knew that such a prayer was impossible, the Rabbi insisted that nothing was too difficult for the God of Israel.

14

After killing the last sentry, Ronald Fletcher carefully descended the hill leading to the PLGA base camp. The intelligence report Barnes had obtained for him, though somewhat dated, had indicated that there were no mines or booby traps on the hill directly facing the camp. Regardless, movement was difficult given the uneven ground, heavy rain, thick fog, and darkness.

Since all the guards had been eliminated, Fletcher entered unopposed by way of the main gate. While moving stealthily toward the center of the camp, he took mental notes on its layout. Finally, Fletcher stopped behind an open jeep which was parked in front of the row of barracks where PLGA terrorists were housed. He dumped the contents of his knapsack on to the front seat.

Fletcher glanced at his watch. He allowed himself five minutes to place and prime the C4 plastic charges around the barracks, power plant, and ammunition dump, taking care to strategically place the explosives where they would cause maximum damage.

Fletcher then returned to the jeep and removed the magnesium flares. He set them directly in front of the jeep in several rows. He then moved from the jeep to behind a row of empty oil barrels about fifty feet away. There he organized his weapons cache. When he was finished, he picked up the remote detonators, released the safeties, and, with a devious smile, pushed the button on the first detonator.

Explosions ripped through the entire base. The ammunition dump erupted like a volcano, causing the ground to shake while at the same time littering the base with debris and black smoke. The generator was destroyed completely, plunging the base into complete darkness. Simultaneously the roofs of all three barracks buildings collapsed, crushing many of the sleeping terrorists.

Fletcher pushed a second button, igniting the flares. The area in front of the barracks was suddenly illuminated with blinding light. Fletcher noticed a handful of surviving PLGA terrorists that had been awoken violently by the explosions stumbling out the front door. Concealed behind the oil barrels, he picked them off with automatic fire. He then fired a Willie Pete at a second group of terrorists that had gathered between the buildings, setting them ablaze.

Fletcher maintained the light by igniting the remaining magnesium flares at short intervals. The next group of surviving PLGA terrorists, having watched their comrades slaughtered, opened fire with assault rifles. However, the blinding light obscured Fletcher's position. He lobbed several M67 incendiary grenades and fired the remainder of the Willie Petes, turning the ruins of the barracks into a giant inferno. He then sprayed the remaining terrorists with hundreds of rounds from the Colt Commando.

Within minutes, all the terrorists that had been housed in the barracks had been neutralized. Dead silence enveloped the base. Still, Fletcher new from experience that there were probably a few terrorists around that were either playing dead or hiding. He put the Commando into semi-automatic mode and walked around the base, firing one shot into the head of each body he came across. When he was finished, he slung the rifle over his shoulder. He then picked up the Colt .45 pistol and held it in his right hand, and placed the Israeli air gun in his left.

As Fletcher approached the administrative buildings, he reviewed the accomplished objectives of his mission thus far. Hundreds of dead terrorists, and a nearly destroyed main base of operations. The PLGA was on the ropes but not down for the count, yet. Ron felt a sweet surge of satisfaction run through his veins. He had experienced this feeling many times before during his military career, and, though he hated to admit it, he still enjoyed it. However, Fletcher knew that his quest for vengeance had only just begun. The terrorist leaders who had orchestrated the death of his beloved Mary had yet to feel his wrath.

He entered the one structure on the base that he had purposely left undamaged. It was a long, single story administration building. Fletcher had refrained from destroying the building for two reasons.

First, he wanted to collect raw intelligence on PLGA from its higher-ups. Second, he wanted to get up close and personal with the terrorists that had most likely played a role in the planning of his wife's murder. These dredges of society deserved a special kind of justice that Ron savored the opportunity to dispense.

Fletcher entered the building and walked quickly down the main corridor, casually tossing into each room he passed a MK3 concussion grenade. When he approached the door at the end of the hallway, his intuition told him that this room was likely the office of the commander of the base. He also instinctively knew that any remaining PLGA terrorists were probably waiting behind the door to ambush him.

Drawing on his military experience in clearing Viet Cong tunnels, Fletcher carefully opened the warped wooden door a crack and introduced a mirror with an extendable arm attachment. With this device he was able to survey the room. He saw five terrorists spread across the office. Two of them he immediately recognized from the intelligence files: Abu Jihad and Mohamad Talabi, among the most wanted terrorists on the Interpol watchlist. Together they had been responsible of dozens of attacks and targeted assassinations.

The five terrorists were no match to Fletcher's hardened combat skills. He quickly determined his preferred order of elimination and proceeded in rapid sequence. Kicking in the door, he shot three of the terrorists in the dead center of their foreheads with the Colt .45 within five seconds. He then opened fire with the Israeli air gun, hitting the remaining two stunned terrorists in their necks. They immediately dropped to the ground but were far from dead. Their shrieks of pain caused even Fletcher to flinch.

Fletcher walked over the two terrorist leaders who were convulsing from pain. He addressed them in Arabic.

"I only have one proposition to you scum of the earth. Whoever tells me where I can find the documents I'm looking for, I'll mercifully put them out of their misery quickly. Then I'll get a chair and enjoy watching the other one die a slow, agonizing death that only gets worse from here. It might take hours, but I have all the time in the world."

After hearing the proposal, in their agony both simultaneously pointed to the long dark curtains covering part of the back wall. Fletcher walked up to the curtains and parted them at their center. He saw that they covered a heavy steel door with a large combination lock resembling a bank safe. He examined the lock on the door and concluded that there was no way of forcing it.

"What's the combination?" he growled at the two cowering terrorists. They shook their heads to indicate that they didn't know, and one was able to just barely squeak out, "Only Rajad."

Fletcher stood there for a moment assessing the problem, then decided that the best way to access the area behind the locked door would be from the outside. So he started toward the exit. As he was about to leave the room, he remembered that the two terrorists were awaiting his decision.

Fletcher stared coldly at the murderers on the floor. Finally he said, "Sorry, you were both so quick in pointing out that room. It was a tie. Since there was no winner, you must both be the losers."

With that, Fletcher exited the building and returned to his stash of weapons. He grabbed the M72 LAW rocket launcher and the knapsack with the rest of his munitions. He decided that his best chance of gaining entry to the area behind the steel door while preserving whatever intelligence could be recovered would be to blow off a corner of the building. After taking cover about twenty yards from the building, he fired an LAW rocket at the edge of the fortified concrete wall, creating a deep depression. He then aimed the second rocket at the same target. When the dust and smoke cleared, Fletcher saw a hole in the corner of the wall just large enough to step through.

Fletcher squeezed himself through the jagged edges of the opening and found that he was in the secured room. It was a large space that contained mostly shelves and boxes of files. His eyes became transfixed on a small desk that contained a locked filing cabinet. One shot from the Colt .45 was sufficient to destroy the small padlock. He then opened the drawer and dumped its contents into his now nearly empty knapsack. After exiting the room he tossed two remaining M67 incendiary grenades through the opening, just in case there was something inside that could be useful to terrorists in the future. The subsequent explosions caused flames to surge out of the blast hole.

As he left the PLGA base by way of the main gate, Fletcher was satisfied that he had successfully completed the first phase of his mission. He remembered back to the phrase that he and his fellow commandos in Vietnam had told themselves many times, "Revenge is a dish best served cold."

Fletcher was confident that the PLGA would be out of action for some time. He wondered about what possible information could be gleaned from the papers he had obtained from the locked filing cabinet. Perhaps some clues regarding those responsible for his wife's death? In any event, the next phase of his operation would focus on the leader of the PLGA, Ali Rajad.

For the next several hours, Fletcher hiked southeast toward a certain Christian village. The commander of the village militia, George "Daredevil" Franji, was an old friend of Fletcher's. The two had collaborated on anti-terrorist activities during his service as CIA liaison in Beirut. Fletcher knew that Franji would make sure he would be safely escorted back to Israel without asking any awkward questions.

15

Joshua 74575 was smiling broadly that Sunday as he made his way to see the Rabbi. He had finished his work even faster than usual, and was anxious to tell the Rabbi how much he had enjoyed the Sabbath. During the "lectures" of the SS education officers, Joshua had kept his eyes closed and dreamed of being free in Israel. The Rabbi had taught him sign language and how to read and write in basic Hebrew, and he was looking forward to using his new skills. Joshua had come to love the Rabbi in the way that a son loves his father.

Unfortunately, Joshua had no idea what it was like to be a son. His mother was killed soon after his birth, and his father was not allowed to have any connection with his offspring. Joshua had been raised in the only place a Jew could grow up in Valhalla, the concentration camp orphanage.

The Rabbi was also very fond of Joshua. He was encouraged that Joshua, in spite of having been brainwashed by the Nazis from birth, had a very Jewish soul. This had strengthened the Rabbi's belief in divine providence more than ever. The Rabbi was convinced that there was a heavenly plan in which Joshua would play a critical role.

When he spoke to Joshua, he remembered the Talmudic statement of Rabbi Chanina, "I have learned more from my colleagues than my teachers. But I have learned from my students most of all."

As Joshua approached the Rabbi's cage that Sunday, he was thinking of his recent conversation with the Rabbi in which he had expressed his feelings toward Miriam. The Rabbi told him that he was in love, and that that this feeling is a powerful force for good in the world. Joshua was pleased with the idea that, in spite of his dreadful situation in Valhalla, he was able to find meaning in life through his love of Miriam and the teachings of the Rabbi.

Then a dreadful thought entered his mind. In a few months, Miriam would give birth. She would be allowed to nurse the baby for a short period. Then she would be taken to the Broder Lab, never to be seen again. This thought filled him with great anxiety, however, he knew there was nothing he could do to stop it.

As he approached Rabbi Gershon's cage, he knew something was wrong. The Rabbi was sitting on the floor, mumbling prayers, tears flowing from his eyes. As Joshua drew closer, Rabbi Gershon caught sight of him. The great scholar rose and wiped the tears from his face.

Joshua, using sign language, asked, "My teacher, why are you crying?"

The Rabbi forced out his reply. "Trouble has once again befallen the Jewish people. This morning, I had a visitor. His name is Mueller. He is better known in this man-made hell as the High Priest. He approached my cage and began to shout, 'The hour of the Fuhrer's revenge is near! The Reich Gott has commanded that in one month, all the Jews of your precious State of Israel will be exterminated. Afterwards, we will destroy all the other nations, and begin repopulating the world with pure Aryans from Valhalla.' Then he burst out laughing like a madman, then abruptly turned and walked away."

The Rabbi paused for a moment before continuing. "Joshua, I'm a very good judge of people. I'm sure Mueller was speaking the truth. And, as I have taught you, it is our duty to help our fellow Jews as well as any person in need. You must escape and warn Israel and the nations of the world! I'm too old to make such a journey, but you, Joshua, are young and strong. You could make it to Israel and return with the Jewish army. Only they could stop this pagan god of destruction."

"But Rabbi," Joshua protested, "There is no way out of these caverns. The only exit is the elevator located in the center of the SS base."

Rabbi Gershon responded with a quiet voice. "There is another way out. Over thirty years ago, when they were building this terrible place, I was assigned to the rock quarry in the East Clover. I worked there before that section was closed off and used for storage."

"During my last days in the quarry, while swinging my pick, I broke through into an empty space. I managed to pick away at the edges and make an opening. It led to a long narrow shaft upwards. When I entered, I looked up and saw light at the top. That could only mean it reached the surface. The shaft was extremely narrow, but I was able to ascend by pressing my back against the wall and pushing up with my legs. After climbing up halfway, I lowered myself back down because I knew I would need food and water to survive the journey through the desert.

"I planned my escape for the next day. I carefully replaced the rocks to conceal the entrance and marked it with a wooden board. On the right upper corner of the board I scratched out a small symbol, a Star of David.

"The following morning, I was fully prepared for my escape. However, there was no roll call for my work detail that day. Soon after, I learned that the Nazis officially closed the quarry. I was reassigned to the coal mines, and, before long, I was transferred to the zoo. Here my chances for escape ended."

"Joshua, it is a dangerous journey. I cannot force you to go. But you are the only hope for the salvation of the world. Are you willing to attempt the impossible by escaping and warning mankind of their impending doom?" The Rabbi's eyes were filled with hope.

Without hesitation Joshua nodded and signaled in sign language, "Yes, of course."

The Rabbi was greatly moved. "You must leave right away. First, fill as many bottles as you can carry with water, and take food from the animal cages. Drink as much as you can before leaving. Then wrap everything for the trip in in that sheet." The Rabbi pointed to an old tarpaulin that had been discarded in the corner of the hall.

"Before you leave, make a small cut on your finger and drip blood on to your shirt. Then, throw your shirt into the lion's cage. That should fool the Nazis into thinking you were eaten. Afterwards, go to the far wall of the East Clover, There, search for the board with the Star of David."

"How will I find the Land of Israel?" Joshua asked.

The Rabbi handed him his Hebrew Bible, his only book. On the last page he had carefully etched out a map and star patterns using spent matches that Nazis had thrown at him.

"Use this map. During the day, when it is light, stay under the sheet to protect yourself from the sun. Travel only at night, when it becomes dark all around you.

"The dots on this map represent stars, which are tiny lights high above your head in the sky which you will see when it is dark. By following these stars you should reach a large body of water, called a sea, within four nights. When you reach the sea, you will turn right and continue walking. Remember, do not drink the water from the sea no matter how thirsty you may be. It is not for drinking. If you do, it will make you very sick."

"When you come upon people, if they are friendly, show them this book. If the people try to hurt you, run away! If they should catch you, don't tell them anything."

"I will miss you," Joshua said, sadly.

"And I will pray for you," The Rabbi answered.

The two stood silently for a moment. Then the young pupil left the great sage, fully aware of the critical importance of his mission. If he failed, the Jewish people and the nations of the world would be destroyed.

Joshua followed each of the Rabbi's instructions to the letter. He was able to make it from the zoo to the East Clover by way of Aryan neighborhoods that had not yet been populated. When Joshua reached the storage yard, there was only one guard at the main gate. Joshua found a hiding spot and waited for an opportunity. After about a half an hour, the guard hurried behind some large crates to relieve himself. That gave Joshua enough time to slip past him.

It took Joshua quite some time to find the board bearing the Star of David, which was now covered by a thick layer of dust. Working quickly, he cleared away the rocks, revealing the entrance of the shaft. He entered the shaft with his food and water wrapped in the tarp and moved the rocks back into place to avoid discovery. Joshua was surprised to see that even though there was no light coming from the caverns, he could still see. He looked around found that light was coming from the top of the shaft.

As the Rabbi had instructed, Joshua pressed his back to the shaft wall and pushed up with his legs. The process was slow, but he made steady progress toward the light above. When he was over a hundred feet up, the tarp opened, and the food and water bottles fell out. Joshua heard the glass shatter as it crashed to the ground. Joshua knew that he had to make a crucial decision. He could either descend to retrieve the food or continue. Remembering how the Rabbi's delay had prevented his escape, Joshua decided to continue toward the light.

It took Joshua another hour to reach the surface. He cleared away a few rotting boards that partially covered the top of the shaft and lifted himself to the surface. When he looked around, he couldn't believe what he saw. Joshua was first blinded by the dazzling light of the sun which he had never before experienced. His head was spinning trying to take in the sight of endless sand dunes, heat and fresh air. In his mind, he had entered a foreign and bewildering realm of existence. The Rabbi had tried to explain the outside world to Joshua, but he was totally unprepared for the overload of new stimuli.

Joshua felt he could stand and stare at this new world forever, but reality set in. He had on his shoulders the responsibility to save the lives of the Rabbi, Miriam, the Jews of Valhalla, Israel, and the people of the world. He covered himself with the tarp until the light around him began to dim.

While Joshua was waiting, sunset began. He watched the most unbelievable sight he had ever seen, day turning in to night. Then he saw the myriad of stars appear. Joshua remembered the Bible with its star map and removed it from his pocket. Unbelievably, the Rabbi had charted a course relying on his memory of those sections of the Talmud dealing with the Hebrew Lunar Calendar and combining it with his university-acquired knowledge of astronomy and mathematics.

Joshua lined up the stars with the map and starting walking in the direction of the arrow. He spent the first night crossing a salt marsh in the Sahara Desert. When the sun came up, the heat was unbearable. He unrolled the tarp, covered himself, and went to sleep. When he awoke, he found that he was a bit thirsty, but not more than he had by the end of a regular Sabbath in Valhalla after fasting for 24 hours. His many years of slavery had strengthened him to cope with almost any physical challenge.

At nightfall he again began walking at a steady pace. By the third day he was nearly completely dehydrated. The last two days had been marked by record temperatures reaching above 125 degrees Fahrenheit. He was in desperate need of water, and kept moving only by sheer willpower. His mind told him to move forward, so he went on. Still, the human body can take only so much abuse. He had no appetite and was beginning to fell giddy. Then he started stumbling. He remembered that in Valhalla, if a man started stumbling in the mines, he was close to his end. But he knew that if he stopped, he would have no chance to save Miriam or the Rabbi.

Suddenly, Joshua felt something being crushed under his foot. He looked down and saw a colony of white snails. He tried stepping on another one and saw fluid coming out. He suddenly had an epiphany. He took about a dozen snails and placed them in the tarp. He then squeezed the tarp and let the murky fluid flow into his mouth. After repeating this process several times he felt refreshed. The snails, of the species *Eremina ehrenbergi Roth*, had saved his life.

Joshua made camp that morning near the snail colony. He managed to tear a piece of the tarpaulin and fashion it into a makeshift receptacle to hold the precious snails.

Two nights later, Joshua reached the Mediterranean Sea. Again, he looked out and could not believe his eyes. The sea was lit up by a full moon. He thought to himself that Project Valhalla's river was nothing compared to the great sea on the surface of the world. Joshua bent down next to the shore and splashed himself until his body and clothes were drenched with the cool water. He heeded the Rabbi's warning and did not drink from the sea. Joshua stood there for some time, gazing in awe at the majestic view.

Joshua was happy. He loved this new world. He turned eastward and followed the coast. After walking for a few hours, he spotted a truck approaching from the opposite direction. The truck looked similar to those held in the storage area of Project Valhalla. As he moved closer, he observed that it was filled with soldiers. Joshua innocently waved at the driver to stop.

The Libyan army soldiers were shocked by the sight of a shirtless, bearded, disheveled man of ash-gray complexion wandering alone in a remote area of the coast. The driver stopped the truck and the soldiers disembarked. They began to approach Joshua menacingly. When he showed them the Hebrew Bible, they pointed their rifles at him. Joshua tried to run, but he was quickly apprehended. While the commanding officer taunted Joshua by setting the Bible on fire with his cigarette lighter, the soldiers beat him to a bloody pulp. When they were done, they tied Joshua up, loaded him into the back of the truck, and brought their prize back to their base.

Joshua was tortured continuously by Libyan agents in an effort to make him reveal what he was doing alone wandering along the seashore. Again he remembered the Rabbi's advice and refused to cooperate. Years of Nazi abuse had taught him how to endure pain. On the third day of torture, Joshua blacked out. The frustrated interrogators reluctantly called in their base physician. After a preliminary examination, the doctor pointed out to them that their prisoner was incapable of making a confession because he was lacking a tongue. He ordered that Joshua be sent to a hospital in in Tripoli given his critical condition.

After a few days in intensive care, Joshua miraculously regained consciousness. At that point, the Libyan government abandoned the idea of interrogating Joshua and opted to stage a show trial. Joshua was charged officially with spying for the State of Israel, a capital crime.

When the Prime Minister of Israel was informed of the upcoming trial, he ordered an investigation to find out who the man was. He was informed that no agent of Israel or even any Jew who had remained in Libya after 1948 matched the description of the alleged Israeli agent. The Prime Minister was dumbfounded. Nevertheless, he ordered that all efforts should be made to help this unfortunate victim of Arab hatred toward Israel.

An internationally renowned European lawyer was hired by friends of Israel, and attempts at diplomatic pressure were made. Despite this, Joshua, in a mockery of justice, was convicted of spying for the State of Israel after three days of trial and sentenced to be hanged. The execution would take place in two weeks in Tripoli's Martyrs' Square.

16

After throwing his cylinder into Lake Kinneret, Ali Rajad drove north toward the Lebanese border. By nightfall Rajad had reached a rendezvous point two miles east of the town of Metulla on the border of Israel and Lebanon. There he was met by Ishmael Kalem and three other PLGA terrorists. The group crossed the border through a break in the security fencing while Israeli border forces were dealing with heavy Katyusha rocket fire on Metulla.

This diversion had been planned by Rajad in advance in order to ease his crossing into Lebanon. He had ordered a group of his terrorists to infiltrate Christian-held Southern Lebanon and set up a mobile rocket battery in the hills outside Kafr Kila. From this position they bombarded the downtown business district of Metulla. Not long after the terrorists began firing their rockets, Christian militiamen were alerted to the source of the attack by radio from an Israeli military monitor. The battery was targeted by 135mm howitzers, killing the entire PLGA squadron. This did not concern Rajad in the least. His men wanted the glory of fighting the Israelis and he gave them the opportunity to die as martyrs. He would arrange an honorable funeral for the men once he made it back to his base.

Rajad, who loved danger, decided that he and his guards would use the opportunity to scout out Christian militia positions in Southern Lebanon between the Israeli border and PLGA headquarters. Rajad hated the Christians as much as he hated the Jews. As he and his men hiked the hills of Lebanon, Rajad daydreamed of becoming Prime Minister of Greater Palestine, which would include all of Israel, Lebanon, and Syria.

After a day of traversing the challenging rocky terrain they caught sight of smoke billowing from the PLGA base. As Rajad and his men cautiously entered the main gate in combat formation, they realized the battle was already over. The entire area reeked of burnt flesh and expended munitions. Hovering above the mutilated corpses was a swarm of black flies, and wandering packs of jackals where already picking away at the cadavers. Kalem opened fire with his assault weapon, scaring off the scavengers.

One of Rajad's bodyguards cried out, "How can this be? They are all dead, all of them!"

Kalem raised his arm and slapped him across the face, "Are you a woman? Get a grip on yourself!"

Then, turning to Rajad, he said, "It must have been Israeli commandos."

Ali Rajad showed no hint of shock or surprise. He knew that the price of the game they played was high. Perhaps Kalem was right, and the Israelis had finally decided to confront them directly. On the other hand, Rajad had many enemies capable of wreaking havoc, including local rivals. Therefore, it would be dangerous to jump to conclusions.

Rajad said, "I want a complete investigation. We must be absolutely positive in knowing who is responsible."

Kalem found a jeep that had sustained only minor damage, and they began to survey the base for clues. However, they discovered quickly that there was little information to be gleaned from the wreckage. Rajad's guards left the base to question local farmers and shepherds, who told them that they had not seen any helicopters or military vehicles. One elderly Lebanese olive grower said that he saw a lone man in full military gear walking away from the base.

Eventually Rajad was informed that a police station some distance away was holding an abandoned rental car. After handing the police chief the customary bribe, he was able to determine that the car was rented from Cedars of Lebanon Car Rental at the Beirut Airport, and that man who rented the car matched the description given by the olive grower and other witnesses. Rajad then gave the police chief an additional bribe to allow him to return the vehicle.

Rajad and his crew drove the Peugeot to the car rental agency and went directly to the counter. Rajad asked the manager a few questions, but he was uncooperative. Kalem, recognizing the need for more proactive persuasion, reached across the counter and began to squeeze the manager's hand. The awesome strength of the Palestinian giant brought the manager to tears. He quickly produced a photocopy of the renter's identification papers, a French passport bearing the name Claude Marchand. Appreciating the quality of the presumably forged passport, Rajad knew immediately that they were dealing with a professional. He would need to use his connections with KGB if he had any chance of determining the man's true identity. Rajad and his men booked a flight to Libya.

Upon arrival at Idris International Airport, about twenty miles outside the Libyan capital of Tripoli, Rajad and his men were greeted by a large contingent of his local security force. Rajad entered his armored Lincoln Continental Mark IV and ordered his driver to take him directly to the Soviet Embassy. Once inside, the terrorist chieftain was ushered into an office on the lower level. There he handed the photocopy of the French passport to KGB station chief Igor Chertkov, with whom Rajad had a strong working relationship. He promised Rajad that he would get back to him as soon as he had something.

The next day a courier from the Soviet Embassy arrived at Rajad's plush downtown office. He handed Kalem a thin yellow manila envelope which Kalem placed on Rajad's desk. Rajad opened the envelope and began to read.

The envelope contained a short summary and even shorter dossier. The KGB had determined that upon forensic examination the passport appeared to be authentic. Initially the KGB had difficulty identifying its owner, as there were currently at least 4,000 Claude Marchands living in France, of which more than two hundred fit the approximate age and height listed on the passport.

Providentially, however, a KGB analyst in Moscow had recognized the photograph to be that of an American intelligence officer by the name of Ronald Fletcher. The brief dossier stated that Fletcher had been in the Green Berets, fought in Vietnam, and was currently serving as an education officer at the United States Embassy in Israel. It was suspected that he was currently working as a military liaison coordinating joint activities and intelligence sharing between the United States National Security Council and the Israeli military.

Ronald Fletcher scored the KGB's highest ranking in all five categories used to evaluate foreign agents: natural intelligence, knowledge of espionage techniques, tactical weapons mastery, hand-to-hand combat skills, and the ability to kill. The report concluded that it was unlikely that one person acting alone could have caused the destruction of the PLGA base in Lebanon, however, if anyone was qualified to execute such an operation, it was Ronald Fletcher. His experience in different roles of the military and intelligence services, including training in the use of a wide range of weapons and explosives, made him a unique threat.

Rajad stood up and walked toward the window, deep in thought. The name Fletcher rang a bell. Suddenly he remembered that on the plane from Beirut to Tripoli he had read an article in the New York Times International Edition stating that the American killed during the Netanya beach attack had been identified as Mary Fletcher. The article had mentioned that her husband was a member of the U.S. diplomatic delegation in Tel Aviv.

Only once before had Rajad seen a KGB report listing someone with such perfect scores. That report had evaluated an international hit man that Rajad himself had employed several times in the past, always to complete satisfaction. This assassin was very expensive, but it was well known that once he accepted a contract, the victim could already be considered dead.

Rajad, an expert on the art of vengeance, had no desire to have an ex-special operations soldier burning with revenge for his wife's death stalking him for the rest of his life. He turned to Kalem.

"We need to call in Phillip John Hearns."

17

On a tiny island off the coast of Costa Rica, Phillip Hearns sat in his library carefully reading over the KGB's dossier on Fletcher. Ishmael Kalem had personally delivered it to Hearns' estate along with the non-refundable ten-thousand-dollar consideration fee. While awaiting Hearns' decision, Kalem sat next to the pool and stared at the vast Pacific Ocean. After several hours, Hearns informed Kalem that he would accept the contact. Kalem thanked him and began the long trip back to Tripoli.

Hearns had built up a reputation over the past few decades as the perfect contract killer. In the international underworld he was commonly referred to as the "Untouchable One." Originally a sniper for the South African Defense Forces, he had honed his skills fighting in counterinsurgency units in Namibia. Later on he changed sides when the Soviet Union began bankrolling the rebels, finding that training guerilla forces was a much more profitable endeavor.

Hearns then used his contacts in the KGB to create a lucrative business importing Soviet arms to local warlords in central Africa. But he ultimately found international arms dealing to be dull. He missed the thrill of wading in waist-high mud, drenched in sweat in the scorching heat, and scoring a perfect kill shot at 300 meters. Having fluency in several languages and an uncanny ability to mimic accents, a KGB contact joked to him that he might be useful as a contract killer.

Soon after, Hearns set up shop in Prague and quickly built up a clientele of dictators, drug lords, and mafia types, anyone who had an axe to grind between London and St. Petersburg. As his reputation grew, he became more and more picky about his contracts. A few years prior he had entered semi-retirement and moved permanently to his private island in Costa Rica. Since then he had limited himself to just one or two jobs a year.

Hearns returned to his library and reviewed the file. The contract stipulated that Ronald Fletcher must die within one month. Hearns felt it was a relatively short period of time to plan a hit against such a formidable opponent. On the other hand, he understood the need, given that Rajad was a great personal risk as long as Fletcher was still breathing. Therefore, there was no time to lose. Besides, it was worth it. Hearns' reward upon confirmation of the killing would be two million dollars in cash.

Hearns knew it would be downright foolish to try to kill Fletcher in Israel. Israel's security agencies would never rest if a member of the staff of the United States Embassy was murdered on their soil. And while there were ways of secretly getting out of Israel undetected, they were by no means foolproof. He predicted that in his quest for revenge Fletcher would soon leave Israel, and at that time he would strike. "Untouchable" Hearns credited his longevity in the highly volatile profession of contract killing to his determination not to leave anything to chance.

Since Rajad was in Libya, Hearns decided to focus his initial efforts there. He descended to the lower level of the villa where his wine cellar was located. Pressing a button hidden concealed behind a behind a fine burgundy, the wine rack shifted to the right. He then flipped the light switch, illuminating a vast arsenal of rifles, handguns, machine pistols, and ammunition.

Hearns pondered thoughtfully for a moment. Then he reached for a Dragunov rifle and scope. This was the standard sniper rifle of the Soviet Army, and Hearns had learned to appreciate its value against both Namibian rebels and South African Special Forces. Its reliability and accuracy made it Hearns' favorite weapon. Next, he pulled out an Ingram MAC-10 submachine gun. It was compact and featured a built-in sound suppressor. Unlike a silencer, the sound suppressor kept noise to a minimum without slowing down the firing rate. Most effective at close quarters, the MAC-10's ability to spit out bullets at over 1,000 rounds per minute made it almost impossible to miss, even when the operator was under extreme pressure. Finally, he selected a German Walther P38 automatic pistol and silencer.

Hearns had already ruled out employing his vast array of remote-controlled explosive devices and booby traps. Ronald Fletcher was too sophisticated an adversary. After reading about Fletcher's impressive solo attack on the PLGA base, Phillip Hearns was not going to take the chance of being discovered and thus becoming a target himself. Fletcher was destined to die by perfectly aimed bullet in which there was no possibility of failure.

18

Fletcher spent a peaceful evening with Captain Franji at the militia command post in the village of Marjayoun, sipping Turkish coffee and tasting an assortment of baklava. The following morning, Ronald was escorted to the "Good Fence." This was the unofficial border crossing between Christian-controlled South Lebanon and Israel. The Good Fence was used by Israel to transfer supplies to its allies in Lebanon, as well as to allow sick and injured Christians passage into Israel to access its medical system.

As Fletcher passed through security, he asked the Israeli Druze border guard to take him to Brigadier General Ofer Kahan, commander of the Good Fence program. Fletcher considered him to be an outstanding officer and a loyal friend. When the General saw Fletcher, he greeted him warmly and invited him for breakfast in the mess tent. The pair wolfed down scrambled eggs and toast, washing it all down with thick Israeli Army coffee known as "*botz*," which literally means mud.

During the meal, the two warriors reminisced on old times. The General told Fletcher how sorry he was for what happened. He tactfully avoided the subject of what Ron was doing in Lebanon in the first place. When the meal was over, Kahan offered Fletcher the use of his personal car and driver, and Fletcher gratefully accepted. He slept most of the long drive back to Tel Aviv.

When he arrived at his apartment, Fletcher went directly to the bathroom and took a long, cold shower. He had become accustomed to taking only cold showers since his time in the Special Forces, and felt invigorated by the freezing jets of water. While he showered, he remembered the events of the previous day with some satisfaction. The violence he had perpetrated against the PLGA had been a positive act for society. Fletcher thought to himself, "Those terrorists were responsible not just for killing my Mary, but for the murder of hundreds of innocent lives. Someone needed to stop them. Because of my quest for revenge, many others will live."

Fletcher got dressed and brought the knapsack laden with PLGA files to the kitchen table. He filled a mug with steaming hot black coffee and began rummaging through the documents.

Near the bottom of the pile was a disorganized folder containing handwritten notes. Ron noted that the writing matched a letter than he had spotted in the intelligence file Barnes had delivered to the airport. He remembered that it was the handwriting of Ali Rajad. Attached to the notepad was a cassette tape and a still image from a closed-circuit security camera of three men meeting with Rajad.

Browsing the notes, Fletcher quickly realized that he was holding the operational plan for the Netanya terror attack. In the folder there was also a map of Israel which indicated where the three cylinders were to be planted. He then walked over to his son's bedroom and found a tape player. He popped the cassette in and pressed play. Recorded was the actual conversation between Rajad and the men in the photograph. Fletcher noted that only one of the men spoke while the others remained silent. The man spoke in Arabic with a distinct German accent. Fletcher looked again at the photograph. The men looked not just German, but actually stereotypically German. He was also struck by the sickly pale skin tone shared by all three men.

The entire meeting didn't seem to make sense. Why would these men hire a Palestinian to smuggle cylinders into Israel? The German stated that Rajad was hired because he was the most reliable option. But judging by the placement of the cylinders, any tourist could have successfully executed the mission.

Moreover, if these three men were in fact German, they were probably East Germans. Fletcher was well acquainted with East German intelligence. The Stasi had a reputation as being one the most effective intelligence agencies in the world. They never would never have trusted a Palestinian to perform such an operation. And even if they did, it was impossible to imagine that they would cough up a hundredth of what Rajad was offered. Maybe Odessa, the organization that helped Nazis escape after World War II, had that kind of money. But as far as Fletcher knew, they hadn't been active for decades.

Fletcher turned his attention to the cylinders. He had assumed they contained some sort of poison. But conventional poisons would be diluted to harmlessness in a major body of water. They were also too small to contain any sort of nuclear device. Polonium-210? That was about a billion times more lethal than cyanide. But creating Polonium-210 in significant quantities requires enormous resources and a nuclear reactor, and could probably only be achieved by a major superpower. Perhaps some sort of novel biological weapon?

Fletcher's gut feeling was that these three men, who also bore responsibility for his wife's death, were representing some person or entity even more sinister than Ali Rajad.

Suddenly, Fletcher's need for vengeance returned in a fury. His blood began to boil. He had become a drug addict whose "fix" was revenge. He slammed the table, causing the mug of coffee to spill all over the papers and on to the floor. He thought to himself. "I don't care who these people are, they must pay for killing my Mary!"

Suddenly Fletcher noticed the picture of Bobby and Jane playing in a park taped to the fridge. It suddenly dawned on him that he hadn't seen his children in three days. He dropped everything and rushed out of his apartment. Exiting to the street he spotted his white Ford Fairmont sedan with its embassy plates. He assumed it was brought for him from Jerusalem where he left it on the day of the attack.

Fletcher did a routine check for planted explosives. When he finished, he reached behind the auto's left front tire well and removed a magnetic box which held the car keys. He hopped in and within minutes he was on the highway. Soon he arrived at Tel Hashomer Hospital, just outside of Tel Aviv.

As Fletcher parked the car next to the entrance of the hospital grounds, he saw a young recruit reporting to the nearby military base. The recruit looked like he was barely eighteen years old. Given his crisp new combat boots and the fact that he wore his beret straight like a European cab driver, Fletcher assumed he had been in the Israeli Army for less than a week.

Fletcher thought about the new reality the young man was facing. He knew that the army base next to the hospital was called Bakum, short for *Basis Klita u'Miyun*, the Army Base for Induction and Classification. He had been briefed by his Israeli colleagues and toured Bakum within the first month of his arrival as the new Education Officer for the United States Embassy.

As he walked, Fletcher thought about the briefing he had gotten from his Israeli colleagues regarding the draft processes. "Less than a year ago the boy received his *Tzav Hityatzvut*, or Order to Report, to Bakum. When he reported he was given an aptitude test, a medical examination, and an interview. He was then assigned a profile based on those tests. A composite score of 81 or above was needed for him to become *kravi*, a combat soldier. Israel Defense Forces selection officers reviewed his file and tentatively decided to which branch of military service he would be assigned. Several months later, he received a letter from the *Lishkat HaGius*, the Army Draft Induction Board, to report to Bakum. At the base, he was fingerprinted, photographed, and then issued his *pinkas choger*, army identity card, which contained his *mispar ishi*, or army serial number, his new identity for life.

"Then he and the other new recruits joined something of an assembly line. First, he received his uniform and gear. Then he received a buzz cut, a haircut even shorter than a crewcut. After saying goodbye to his hair, which represented to him his former civilian life, he walked between medics who injected him with a number of different vaccinations and booster shots. He was then given eight minutes to dress in his new uniform. This was the first time he used *gummiot*, rubber bands, to tuck in his pant legs above his boots.

"After filling out a number of forms, he was interviewed again by a selection officer, assigned a tent number, and given a postcard so he could write his family. Minutes later, a sergeant yelled at him that his hair was way too long and ordered him to report to the barber shop and get another haircut. Perplexed, since he just got a buzz cut, he went to the barber station. He was probably approached by a professional photographer who would offer, for a nominal price, to take his picture so the recruit and his family could remember what he looked like on his first day in *Tzahal*, the Israel Defense Forces.

"That evening he and his fellow recruits were taken to a special ceremony where he swore his oath of loyalty to the State of Israel, shouting at the end, *Ani Nishbah*, meaning, "I swear," three times. Within a week he would be transferred from Bakum to one of the basic training bases for the Israeli Army, Navy, Air Force, Tanks, Artillery, or Paratroopers.

Fletcher thought, "For the first eighteen years of his life, this kid was pampered by doting parents. They shielded him from the grim reality that the entire Arab world would like nothing better than seeing Israel wiped off the map. He was probably convinced that the reason that they don't act is because of the strength of the Israel Defense Forces. Now he's going to become part of it. He'll be made to run the gauntlet, including hellish training that will ravage his body and mind. At the end he will become a warrior ready to face the hordes of Israel's enemies that want him and his family dead."

Fletcher walked through the main gate of the sprawling hospital campus and found a map. He had been told that Bobby and Jane were being housed in the Children's Ward of the Department of Psychiatry. When he arrived, he saw that the ward was a one-story building in a park-like setting, surrounded by trees and bushes.

Fletcher walked directly to the main desk and asked the receptionist, "Do you know in where Bobby and Jane Fletcher are staying?"

She answered, "You must be Mr. Fletcher. Hold on, let me get the doctor."

A few moments later a tall psychiatrist arrived.

"I'm Dr. Yonah Katz, chief psychiatrist in the Children's Ward. Your children are under my supervision."

"How are they doing?"

"Jane is doing wonderfully. She has responded very positively to our treatment program. I can assure you, aside from the expected period of grief, she will completely recover," Dr. Katz answered confidently.

"Bobby is an entirely different case," he continued. "It appears that he is having a major identity crisis. He has withdrawn from his surroundings and is not responding to outside contacts.

"In my opinion, he feels responsible for his mother's death. Growing up in a family of military men and war heroes, Bobby apparently feels he has failed to live up to the standards of his male role models in the Fletcher family."

Fletcher was taken aback. "That's ridiculous," he protested. "Bobby is only twelve years old! What could have he have done?"

"Age is not the essential issue here. It's his understanding of the situation. Bobby is convinced that if you had been there, his mother would still be alive. Perhaps he feels that in your absence it was his responsibility to act in your place."

Dr. Katz paused. "What do you think? If you had been there, could you have done something?"

The psychiatrist's words hit Fletcher like a bombshell. He felt like his head was going to explode. He thought to himself, "Damn right, I would done something. I would have pounded those murdering bastards faster than they could say the word 'Jihad!'" The thought gave him a fuzzy feeling.

Instead of responding, however, Fletcher regained control of himself and just stared back with a non-committal expression.

"Mr. Fletcher, your friend Mike Barnes had informed me that you would be away for at least another week."

"That's true. I still have some pressing matters to attend to."

"In that case, I would strongly advise you not to see your children. It has taken them some time to accept that they wouldn't be seeing you in the short term. It might even be harmful to have a brief visit today, only to leave them again. Why don't you wait until you can give them your full attention?"

Fletcher understood Dr. Katz's concern and reluctantly agreed. "I'll come back in a few days. Thank you for all of your efforts. If anything should come up, please contact Mike Barnes. Do you have his phone number?"

"Oh yes, he's been wonderful. He stops by every day with gifts for your children. Even Bobby seems to be listening to him when he visits."

Fletcher was about to leave when he was stopped by a nurse.

"Mr. Fletcher, I 'm sorry to disturb you, but I have a request from Mrs. Zelda Steiner. She's in the intensive care ward. Mrs. Steiner asked that when you came to visit your children, she would like to speak to you."

Fletcher paused for a moment, trying to recall the name. Then he realized the nurse was referring to the woman who shot and killed his wife's murderer. He thanked her and asked for directions.

In the corridor leading to the intensive care unit there was a man in a wheelchair selling flowers. He had undergone above-the-knee amputations of both legs, and his face looked like it had undergone several surgeries for burns. Judging by his IDF uniform and relatively young age, Fletcher guessed that he had probably been in a tank or armored transport vehicle which had been hit by a missile. He had seen similar wounds on other Israeli war veterans. Fletcher picked out the most expensive flowers he had for sale for Zelda, and a copy of Newsweek Magazine for himself.

Fletcher entered the ward and went to the front desk. Spotting an intern, he asked how Zelda Steiner was doing. The intern shook his head, saying that it was only a matter of time. He escorted Fletcher to her room.

Fletcher looked at Zelda lying on her bed. She had an extensive array of tubes and wires attached to her frail body. Monitors above her bed were beeping away furiously. She looked up and saw him.

"Shalom," Zelda said in a weak voice, "You're the father of the children on the beach. I'm sure of it, the boy looks just like you."

Fletcher placed the flowers in an empty vase on the nightstand next to her bed. Then he mustered a courteous response in Hebrew. "There is no way I can express my enormous gratitude to you for saving my children," he said.

Zelda smiled. "Thank you for the lovely flowers. I'm happy that I had the opportunity to trade my life for those of your lovely children. Still, I'm so very sorry that I couldn't help your wife, Mr. Fletcher."

Fletcher interjected, "Please, call me Ron."

"O.K., Ron it is. Things happened so quickly. Especially for an old lady like myself."

"You're not so old." Fletcher teased.

"Oh, really, you are too kind. I know it will be difficult for you to raise your children alone. They will demand twice as much from you."

Fletcher felt ashamed. His real responsibility was to help his children through this horrible tragedy. Instead, his burning desire for revenge had completely warped his priorities. After hearing from Dr. Katz about the mental anguish his son was experiencing, he knew that, from a rational perspective, he should drop everything and stay with him. But Fletcher was no longer acting rationally.

Fletcher knew he should leave and let Zelda rest, but he couldn't help to ask the question that had been bothering him. "Why did you risk your life to save my children?"

"If you must know, I did it for selfish reasons."

Zelda Steiner began to cough uncontrollably. Fletcher went to the door to call for help when she suddenly stopped.

"Don't leave," Zelda called out, "I want to answer you!"

Fletcher turned and saw Zelda reaching toward him.

"I won't leave," he said.

"You are a good soul. I must tell you my rather tragic story. Please sit down."

Fletcher took a seat next to Zelda's hospital bed.

"Before World War II, I was happily married to a young lawyer. We lived in a large house in Warsaw and had two wonderful children, Paulina and Michael.

"When the Germans invaded Poland, my life collapsed around me. One day, I went with my children to buy some food. A group of Nazi soldiers stopped me. They knew that we were Jewish by the yellow Stars of David we were forced to wear. They handed me a toothbrush and ordered me to polish their shoes. My children had no choice but to watch the cruel act while a crowd of Poles gathered and had a good laugh.

"Later we were forced to live in the Ghetto. I suffered as my family was systematically starved to death by the Germans. My husband gave us most of his rations and, as a result, he became deathly ill from pneumonia and died. I was alone, and I barely managed to scrape enough food together to keep my children alive. I didn't know what I could do to save my family.

"One day, I was walking down the main street in the Ghetto when I passed a large poster that was just being put up. It stated that anyone who reported to the railway station by noon would receive a loaf of bread and a bottle of milk. I rushed home and told my neighbors. My friends warned me not to trust the Nazis, and I knew they were right. But I was crazed by hunger. I grabbed my two children and went to the train station. There were hundreds of others waiting for rations, just like us. Then the Nazis appeared with their vicious dogs. We were herded into the cattle cars like animals.

"We stood for hours in the packed train. My children were crying the entire time. Then the train stopped. I looked through a crack in a wall and saw a sign that read 'Auschwitz.' When the door slid open, we were pushed into a line by vicious Nazi soldiers. When we finally got to the front of the line, there was a man sitting at a table who was dressed like a doctor. He looked at me and pointed with his baton to the right. Then he looked at my children and pointed to the left. I begged the doctor to let me go with my children. He didn't even look at me. I was whipped by the guards and forced to the right. That was the last time I saw my little Michael and Paulina.

"I was forced into a delousing chamber. One of the Jewish workers, a kindhearted soul, congratulated me. He told me that I was lucky. Then my heart broke when he said that all those sent to the left were taken to the gas chambers and murdered. I went hysterical. My children were sent to be killed and I couldn't even comfort them. They had to face death alone. I felt totally lost and helpless. There was nothing I could do to save my children.

"Only one thing kept me going for the two terrible years I spent at Auschwitz. I prayed for the day that I could see with my own eyes the Germans suffering for their crimes against humanity. Near the end of the war, as the Germans retreated, I was put on a forced march to Dachau concentration camp. When the American soldiers came in to liberate us, my prayer for vengeance was answered. I watched with joy as the Americans made our Nazi tormentors bury thousands of Jewish bodies. The Germans were treated like the scum of the earth, as they deserved.

"With my wish fulfilled, I felt that there was no reason to go on. I found a discarded razorblade and went behind the building that housed the crematoria. I was about to slash my wrists when a young American officer grabbed my hand.

"He said, 'Don't add another tragedy to the list of Nazi horrors.'

"I broke down and cried. I poured my heart out to him, telling how helpless I had been to save my two children. He patiently listened to my ranting, not leaving my side.

"Finally, I finished. All the pain had left my soul. I was now ready to listen myself.

"The soldier said to me in a soft voice, 'You must go to Palestine, and find peace for yourself.' He said that the Jews there were making progress in establishing their own country. They had pledged that never again would they allow such a tragedy befall their people.

"He took me to the hospital and arranged for my needs. He even visited me several times over the next few weeks while I recovered. He was truly a good man. I am sorry to say that over the years I have forgotten his name.

"Slowly, I grew stronger. I made friends among the other survivors. I even went to Zionist gatherings. Finally, I decided that I would take the American soldier's advice and build a new life in the Jewish State.

"A representative of the Jewish Council gathered a group together to go to Palestine. I was the first to volunteer. We travelled by train through post-war Europe, eventually making our way to a small port in Greece. The British were not allowing Jews to immigrate to Israel at that time, so we had to be smuggled in. Our boat ran the British blockade surrounding Palestine and landed on the beach, where I was taken and hidden by members of a nearby kibbutz. I later married one of the men that had helped hide me and became a member of his kibbutz. We fought for the Haganah during the War of Independence. When it was over, we returned to the kibbutz and had a normal life. A safe life. A life filled with happiness. We had many children. Two of them became officers in the IDF.

Zelda paused for a moment. Fletcher looked at her curiously. He felt as if he had a spiritual connection to this elderly woman.

"When I was on the beach and saw the terrorists running towards your children, the feeling of hopelessness that I felt when I had arrived at Auschwitz suddenly came back. I felt as if my children were being taken away again. However, this time I was in my own country. It was as if I had a second chance to save my dear Michael and Paulina. I took my gun out of my purse and, this time, I was not going to allow these killers to harm your children.

"Now you know my selfish motive for what I did. By explaining this to you I have finally found peace with myself. I hope you too will someday find the same peace.

Fletcher had the feeling that he had heard Zelda's story before. He was racking his brain trying to remember, but couldn't place it. Finally he said, "Whatever your reason was for saving my children, I am forever grateful."

Zelda look at him. "You may think this is strange, but when I saw your son, I was amazed by the resemblance he bore to that young American officer. Now looking at you, I see that very same officer. I suppose both my mind and eyes are failing."

With those words Zelda closed her eyes. The alarm on the monitor went off and a team of doctors and nurses entered. But it didn't matter. Zelda died with a smile on her face.

Finally, Fletcher remembered where had heard the story. When he was a young boy, some of his friends had teased a classmate because he was Jewish. When he came home, he asked his father about it. His father sat with him for over an hour trying to explain about differences between people and while some people choose to hate. He told him about his own experiences during World War II serving in Patton's Eighth Army. His regiment was among the first to enter the Dachau concentration camp. Among the tragic stories Fletcher's father told him was one of a woman who he had saved from committing suicide.

19

On the Twenty-fifth Anniversary of the Glorious Fourth Reich, a special Sunday service was held at the Reich Temple. In attendance were Valhalla's over twenty-five thousand residents. The complex's two newspapers, Der Sturmer and the Volkisch, had been announcing for weeks that there would be a special announcement at the ceremony delivered personally by the Reich Gott. All of Valhalla's residents waited with great anticipation for the announcement.

On the main stage, Heinrich Mueller, the High Priest, stood the right of Das Maschine containing the Reich Gott. To the left was the reclusive Dr. Josef Schreiber. With the exception of those who worked at the Schreiber Institute and the few remaining original inhabitants of Valhalla, barely any of the attendees recognized him. For years he had restricted himself to the confines of the institute, performing endless diabolical experiments on Jewish victims in his surgical laboratory. Thousands had died under his scalpel, and yet the goals of his experiments remained obscure even to his closest colleagues. For the past few weeks, however, Dr. Schreiber had been emerging from the Institute on a daily basis, meeting privately with the Reich Gott for hours.

The ceremony began as a regular Sunday service. Near the end of the service, however, Dr. Schreiber lifted up a black cloth to reveal that several new modules had been attached to Das Maschine. After a short pause of complete silence, to everyone's astonishment, a voice was heard over the Reich Temple's loudspeaker system. It had a somewhat mechanical quality, but it was unmistakably the voice of Hitler.

Dr. Schreiber had finally fulfilled his promise by having successfully added the modules to Das Maschine that would let Hitler hear and speak. He was also near completion of a third module which would allow vision. However, after discussions with Hitler via the teletype, he had been ordered to install the two working modules and save the visual module for a later ceremony upon its completion.

Hitler addressed his people as if he was back on stage in 1930s Nuremberg.

"Using my power as the Reich Gott, the beginning of a new era in the history of the world is about to begin. In just three days, I will unleash my vengeance against the peoples of the upper world."

"The first country to feel my wrath will be the so-called State of Israel. This country made up of subhuman mongrels, untermenschen, is polluting the hallowed ground of our planet. They believe they are the chosen people. I will expose this lie. Israel will be the first country that I will destroy. On that day I will kill all the Jews, including those living in Valhalla."

"I will then proceed to kill the remainder of mankind. When this holy work is complete, I will send you, my children of pure Aryan blood, out of the Halls of Valhalla to repopulate the world. The coming Fourth Reich will encompass all of Earth. For I will rule the world forever."

Tears flowed down the jubilant faces of the congregants. Heinrich Mueller and Professor Broder couldn't believe their ears. It was, without a doubt, the same Hitler they had known and loved, speaking to them once again in his own voice. They were so overwhelmed that they began to repeatedly shout at the top of their lungs, "Heil the Reich Gott! Heil the Reich Gott!"

Soon, all of the citizens of Valhalla were on their feet, shouting "Heil the Reich Gott!" The deafening noise shook the air of the caverns for over fifteen minutes.

Finally, Mueller called upon the crowd to be quiet, motioning with his hands. Silence fell over the Reich Temple.

Again Hitler's voice came in over the loudspeaker. "Professor Broder, come stand with me."

Broder, in emotional ecstasy having heard the Reich Gott address him directly, immediately jumped to attention. Even though he had grown old in the sunless caverns, he sprang up with the energy of his youth and raced to the stage, remembering the exuberance he had felt at the numerous Hitler rallies he had attended before the War. He proudly stood next to Mueller in a state of euphoria.

Hitler continued, "Professor Broder, you have served me with total devotion. You have fulfilled your solemn vow not to rest until you achieved success. Now you have fulfilled your purpose in the world, providing the Fourth Reich the ultimate weapon which we will use against our manifold enemies."

"I will now bestow upon you the highest honor possible. You will have the glorious distinction of being the first human sacrifice to me, the Reich Gott."

Broder, upon hearing Hitler's proclamation, became confused. He thought to himself, "After all these years of locking myself up in the laboratory, have I forgotten the difference between reward and punishment?"

Looking at the smiling, envious faces of the thousands of residents of Valhalla, he resigned himself to his fate. With a mighty thrust of his arm, he gave a final Nazi salute, shouting repeatedly, "Heil the Reich Gott!" He then bent over and placed his head on the altar.

High Priest Mueller walked over to the altar and raised the ceremonial silver sword. In one swift motion he brought the razor-sharp blade down onto Professor Broder's neck. Broder's head rolled off the block into a gold basket. Mueller then lifted Broder's head out of the regal basket by its hair and displayed it high in the air as blood flowed out of its severed neck. The congregation broke out in wild jubilation. They chanted together, "Heil the Reich Gott" with sublime intensity.

Afterwards, the remainder of Broder's team were called up and one by one sacrificed to the Reich Gott. When the ceremony ended, Hitler instructed Mueller to destroy all of the research concerning the Strain. Hitler had a practical reason for doing this. In Hitler's mind, thee Strain was to be a one-time weapon of mass destruction comparable to Noah's Flood. Once the world had been emptied of its current inhabitants, there would be no more need for the Strain. Additionally, Hitler was concerned that one of the scientists would have second thoughts about their role in the mass murder of billions and somehow leak word to the outside.

That same day the Messengers gathered in Bonn, Germany for their own ceremony marking the successful placement of twenty thousand cylinders across the globe. Only for Israel had Mueller used an outside agency to place the cylinders, because Hitler had felt that it was inappropriate to send an Aryan to the cursed ground of a Jewish country.

At the end of the ceremony, the Messengers were ordered to open a small pendant hanging from their necks. They each removed the small brown cyanide tablet within and swallowed it. Then they raised their arms high and declared, "Heil the Reich Gott!" Seconds later they were dead.

With this final act of obedience to the Reich Gott, there was no longer any evidence of the existence of Valhalla or the Strain Project outside of the complex. All that remained were the bodies of the Messengers and letters by Adolf Hitler send to the leaders of all the countries of the world informing them of their imminent destruction.

The following day, West German police were alerted to the discovery of dozens of bodies in an abandoned industrial facility in what appeared to be a mass suicide. Unfortunately, the investigators had no idea of its significance.

The only hope for the world that remained was Joshua 74575. However, Joshua was locked in solitary confinement in a sub-basement of a prison in Tripoli. Moreover, he was about to be executed in just two short days.

20

Upon leaving Tel Hashomer Hospital, Ronald Fletcher drove directly to the United States Embassy in Tel Aviv. He knew there was hell to be paid for going AWOL. Furthermore, he was sure that his higher-ups had realized that the unusual activity at the PLGA base in Lebanon was somehow linked to his absence. Fletcher just didn't give a damn. He had warrior blood in his veins, and the commando attitude of "I just don't really care what you think." Still, he was somewhat concerned about the valuable time he might have to waste dealing with his superiors.

Being Sunday, there was only a skeleton crew in the building. That suited Fletcher just fine, as he was in no mood to answer questions. As he entered the Embassy building, he passed the American Marine guard. It gave him a warm feeling to know that he was entering a secure haven for Americans in a foreign country.

Fletcher rode the elevator to the third floor and used his key to open his locked office. There was a stack of memos on his desk, mostly copies of reports that had been forwarded from other intelligence services.

A CIA memo regarding an unusual letter received by the White House mail office caught his eye. Attached to the memo was a copy of the letter. It read:

To the President of the United States of America,

Soon your country will fear the wrath of the Reich Gott. Behold, I will unleash a second Holocaust against the Jews that will begin on the twenty-fifth of June. You will observe in horror as my cylinders of justice bring me my long-awaited revenge. The following day it will be your country's turn to experience my vengeance.

Adolf Hitler

The memo concluded with a report from the Federal Bureau of Investigation's Forensic Laboratory. It stated that the letter, which had been mailed from a public post office box at Chicago's O'Hare International Airport, was printed on a German teletype machine made between the years 1942 and 1944. The paper was similar to teletype paper that was found in a bombed-out factory in Dresden in 1945.

After carefully reviewing the memo, Fletcher was certain that the "cylinders" mentioned in the letter referred to those brought by Ali Rajad into Israel. He also was sure that the three Germans who had met with Rajad were connected to "Adolf Hitler."

Fletcher sat down his chair to think. Unconsciously, he picked up the Newsweek Magazine he had bought at the hospital. Thumbing through the pages he noticed the feature story of the week. It concerned the trial of an alleged Israeli spy who had been sentenced to death in Libya. The article included some color pictures of the accused individual. Fletcher stared at the picture and suddenly made a connection. The alleged spy had the same ghostly skin tone as the three Germans who had met with Rajad.

Fletcher rushed out of his office and drove to the only person that he felt could provide him with some answers, Rachel Bronot. The offices of her anti-terrorist organization, Nekama, were located at the national military headquarters, HaKirya. Ron was grateful that in Israel, all government offices were open on Sunday.

Fletcher parked his car and walked over to HaKirya's main gate. Handing his U.S. Embassy identification card to one of guards, he said that he would like to speak with Rachel Bronot. The guard scrutinized the photograph on the card and then asked him to wait, disappearing into the complex.

Five minutes later he returned with Bronot.

"Hello, Ron! I thought you Americans didn't work on Sundays. Did you come to visit?"

Fletcher was not in the mood for banter. "This is strictly business."

They walked through the park-like area leading to the office building where Nekama was located and took the elevator to Bronot's office. Fletcher sat down opposite Bronot in front of her desk. His body language screamed that he had something important to tell her.

Fletcher began. He systematically reviewed all of the information he had gathered from the PLGA base, leaving out the details of just how exactly it had been obtained. He then described the letter that had been received from "Adolf Hitler." Fletcher knew the only way to get intelligence from the Israelis was to show as much of one's hand that was permissible. Once they were convinced of your sincerity, they usually opened up.

Rachel smiled. "You haven't been to Rajad's base by any chance? I've received several reports that the base, along with hundreds of PLGA terrorists, has been mysteriously wiped out. And as much as we Israelis would love to take credit, it wasn't us. In fact, there is a rumor circulating that the base was destroyed by one man. Do you know anything about it?"

Fletcher gave a cold stare at the beautiful spy chief and replied, "Maybe. Are you going to cooperate or not?"

Rachel knew Fletcher had given Israel at least a fighting chance against Rajad and his cylinders of death. Her question about the PLGA was rhetorical, as she had confirmatory evidence that the man responsible was Fletcher. He had done Israel a great service in destroying the PLGA base of terror.

"Ron, I'm going to let you know what we found. First, we received a similar letter warning us of our impeding destruction. Also, while you were away, we recovered two of the three cylinders. Our forces are scouring the country in search of the third cylinder.

"Our scientists discovered the hard way that the cylinders contain some sort of deadly biological material. It is so dangerous that the missing cylinder contains enough of the material to wipe out the whole country. We are still trying to determine how the cylinders are activated. Unfortunately, I understand this will take some time."

Fletcher tried to digest the new information. "I have some information concerning the approximate location of the third cylinder. I would be more than glad to share it with you. What I need is your permission to have one of our experts examine the cylinders you have."

Bronot thought for a moment. "If I can arrange for your expert to examine the cylinders, it will have to done here in Israel. They cannot be moved from their present location, which is a contaminated laboratory."

"Deal," Ron replied. "Next question: Who is that guy in Libya?"

Bronot was taken aback. "Honestly, we have no idea who that man is. And not for lack of trying to find out."

"I think he's the key to stopping Rajad. I've got to speak to him."

Bronot was confused. "I'm not sure where you're coming from, but I'll take your word for it. So far, you've been spot on."

"The problem is, I can't get to him."

"We've actually been working on that, however, for a totally different reason. Apparently, when he was captured by the Libyan army, he handed the soldiers on patrol a Hebrew bible.

"I'm sure you're aware that our Prime Minister is devoutly religious. When the Chief of the Mossad told this information to the Prime Minister, he was livid. He said that the man must be Jewish, and, according to our tradition, saving a Jewish soul is equivalent to saving an entire world. He demanded that we find a way to rescue him before the execution."

"Is it possible?"

"Logic says it's not. The prison is impregnable. Also, the route to the execution in Martyrs' square is supposed to be lined by practically every soldier in the Libyan army."

"Since when did you Israelis become so logical?" asked Fletcher.

"Ah, Ron, I see you're on to our game. Very good. Well, I spoke to the Mossad Chief today and he presented a plan that defies logic."

Bronot summarized the details of the plan with Fletcher. "What do you think?"

"I like it." Ron smirked.

"Are you with us?"

"I can't answer for my government. As you probably have already gathered, I have my own agenda in this matter. But I'm with you personally if you agree to one condition."

"What's that?"

"I choose the stand-in."

Rachel smiled at Ron. "Deal."

After meeting with Bronot, Fletcher drove directly to the United States Ambassador to Israel's villa in Herzliya, just north of Tel Aviv.

The Ambassador, Wendell J. Cranston III, was a self-made billionaire. He had founded the most cutthroat and universally despised law firm on Wall Street, but had given it all up to pursue his dream of becoming the United States Ambassador to England. As a self-identified bigwig, all he wanted to do was spend his days hobnobbing with kindred souls. And as a top donor to the President's campaign, Cranston had been high on the list of candidates. Unfortunately, an unintentional snub of the Secretary of State's wife at a state dinner doomed his short-term prospects. Still, the President assured him that if he did a good job in Israel, he had an excellent chance of getting the post when it opened up after the next elections.

Fletcher knew that Cranston, despite his pretentiousness, was a man of action. In fact, that is precisely why the President gave him the toughest assignment in the diplomatic corps. Fletcher knocked on the door and was greeted by Cranston's imported English butler who showed him into the Ambassador's study.

Cranston then entered the room. "Ronald, please let me express my deepest sympathy to you and your children. Mary was a remarkable woman, and we will deeply miss her."

He then gave Fletcher a castigating look. "You know, it wasn't very professional for to send your assistant to inform me of your leave of absence. Where were you?"

Ron wasn't about to tell the Ambassador about his unauthorized raid on the PLGA. Instead, he ducked the question. "Well, I was depressed about my wife's murder. I had to get away for a few days."

"Of course, how insensitive of me," Cranston sighed unconvincingly.

"You have a big responsibility on our team. I'm sure you realize the Israel military establishment has a great deal of respect for you. You represent the United States that the free world so much wants to believe in: strong, soft-spoken, and always ready for action."

Fletcher thought to himself, "Cranston could deliver a two-hour speech praising a mannequin."

He decided to jump into the purpose of his visit. "Sir, did you read that unusual CIA memo about the threat to destroy Israel and the United States?"

"Yes, nasty business that. I believe the madman signed the letter as Adolf Hitler. Well, what about it?"

"I've received some evidence supporting the claim. In fact, I believe the threat is real." He filled in the Ambassador regarding Rajad's meeting with the Germans and the smuggling of the cylinders into Israel.

Cranston listened carefully. When Ron finished, the Ambassador walked to the window facing the garden and stared out for a long moment. Then he turned to Fletcher.

"I'm afraid to admit it, but what you say is quite concerning. If your conclusions are correct, we are facing a serious threat. On the other hand, you realize, some of this is mere conjecture. How am I to convince the Secretary of State that pale men with German accents are prancing around the desert? We need real evidence. And secondly, we need to determine whether these cylinders are really as dangerous as the Israelis claim."

Fletcher nodded. "I have permission from the Israelis to have our scientists verify their findings. But it has to be done at their facility."

Cranston thought for a moment. "I want you to track down Professor John Carlson. He's a friend of mine who's in the country on sabbatical from Harvard. I believe he's lecturing at the Weizmann Institute. Ask him to help out as a favor to the State Department. John is an expert on biological warfare and has top security clearances. If he substantiates the claims of the Israelis, then I'll fly to Washington tonight and take this matter up directly with the President.

"Regarding Libya, just get that man out of there. I don't care how you do it. As a matter of fact, don't tell me. Libya is not under my jurisdiction and I can't promise any assistance. You're better off working with the Israelis and thereby avoiding our own protocols. I'm going to take responsibility and authorize your full participation in any and all Israeli actions."

Fletcher was surprised. Cranston was taking a big risk allowing him to operate outside the borders of Israel. As Fletcher left the Ambassador's villa, he wondered whether Cranston was building political capital for his own future ambitions or simply acting out of concern for the welfare of the United States and the world. He preferred to think it was the latter.

21

The next morning, June 23rd, at 9:00 a.m., a top-secret meeting was held in the Oval Office of the White House. The goal of the meeting was to decide whether the United States should act on the information provided by Ronald Fletcher. In attendance were the President of the United States, Ambassador Cranston, Professor Carlson, the Secretaries of State and Defense, the Director of the CIA, and the Presidential Advisor on Military Affairs, former Chief of Staff General George Smith.

The previous evening, Ambassador Cranston and Professor Carlson had flown to Washington D.C. on the only plane available for immediate transit, a Boeing 747. The flight for the two lone passengers cost the United States Government almost a quarter of a million dollars. Upon hearing this, the Secretary of State had a fit. He threatened to fire Cranston or, even worse, transfer him to the Ambassadorship of Nauru. Cranston responded that he would simply resign and turn over the information to the Secretary of Defense. Not wanting to lose face if the intelligence turned out to be critical, the Secretary of State relented. With a few hours a meeting was arranged with the President and senior members of the National Security Council.

The President opened up the conference.

"The Secretary of State has briefed me on a problem of the greatest urgency. I want everyone to listen carefully so we can come up with a strategy to thwart what appears to be a very real and imminent threat to the United States. Let's start with our Ambassador to Israel."

Cranston spoke slowly. "Mr. President, evidence has come to my attention by way of embassy liaison Ronald Fletcher that quick action is necessary to avoid a catastrophe of unparalleled destruction to our country as well as the rest of the world."

"Professor Carlson," the Secretary of State interrupted, "Please tell the President about the biological agent shown to you by the Israelis."

"Well, it's quite involved," Carlson said.

"Take all the time you need."

"Yesterday, in the late afternoon, Ronald Fletcher approached me with an urgent request from Ambassador Cranston to look over some evidence of a biological nature. Of course I agreed. We travelled to a rendezvous point in the Dead Sea region and were transferred by means of a helicopter with blacked-out windows to a top-secret Israeli laboratory at an unknown location. From the helicopter we were transported by van to a large, underground complex.

"In the complex there was a large laboratory that was sealed off due to contamination. Outside of this laboratory was a smaller makeshift lab that was set up in order to access the contaminated one.

"We were greeted by five scientists, Israel's top experts in the field of biological warfare. Two are members of the faculty of the Weizmann Institute of Science, where I'm on sabbatical. They briefed me on the background of the organic material and the accidental contamination of the lab.

"I then reviewed all the physical evidence and notes. What was discovered is that the cylinders contained a previously unknown prion."

"A what?" asked the Director of the CIA.

"A prion. A protein, one of the building blocks of cellular material, that is misfolded in such a way that when it meets another similar protein it bends it until it is misfolded in the same way. Then the two proteins go out and do the same to other proteins until the tissue is completely destroyed. This is the origin of some rare diseases such as Kuru among cannibals in Papua New Guinea, as well as mad cow disease and its human equivalent, Creutzfeldt–Jakob disease.

"What makes this prion different is that it contains a region that induces cell surface proteins to rapidly incorporate it into the cell, as if it were invited. The victims die without warning and their bodies turn rapidly into a fine, gray, dust-like material. Not only that, it is of very low molecular weight and spreads quickly through the environment with just a small amount of force, such as that which is produced when the cylinder opens. Because it interacts with proteins that exist only in humans, it has no effect on animal or plant life.

"The cylinder in which it was held contains an unusual soil bacteria that stabilizes the prions. When the prions are removed from this bacteria, they only last about twenty-four hours before they naturally break down. In fact, just a day after the original contamination, the Israeli scientists were able to reenter the contaminated area without any special precautions.

"I have concluded that this prion is a danger to the very survival of mankind."

"Is there way of fighting it? Perhaps can a vaccine be made?" asked General Smith.

"As a protein, it is not affected by any known antibiotics or anti-viral agents. In any case, its method of lethality is too rapid to allow such an approach. Nor would a vaccine be effective, as the protein targeted is ubiquitous in all humans.

"If it were to be targeted prior to release, the only method of destroying it is heating to approximately one million degrees Kelvin. That is nearly 1.8 million degrees Fahrenheit."

"I only know of one weapon that creates that kind of heat, a nuclear bomb. Are you saying that to destroy this 'prion' we would have to explode a nuclear bomb?" said General Smith.

"Well, the heat produced by a nuclear bomb would definitely produce sufficient heat to kill the prion," answered Professor Carlson.

At this point, the Secretary of State rose to his feet. "This discussion is pure madness! We have confirmed so far that at least ninety-two countries have gotten the same letters. Within those countries, we haven't a clue where the cylinders are! We're not going to start dropping nuclear bombs randomly!"

"Hold on, no one is dropping any bombs yet," interjected the President.

"How is this agent released from the cylinder?" asked the CIA Director.

"By means of a coded radio signal. There does not seem to be a way to neutralize the mechanism without releasing the contents of the cylinder," said Carlson.

"Well, if we could locate the transmitter, we could stop it from being released," said the CIA Director.

The Secretary of Defense spoke up. "We don't know who is responsible or where they are. But in any case, we can't leave those cylinders around. What if one somehow broke open by natural causes?"

Professor Carlson responded, "The cylinders are extremely well constructed and resistant to changes in temperature and moisture, and even capable of sustaining enormous physical forces. They should remain intact for an indefinite period of time, hundreds if not thousands of years."

"We still can't leave those cylinders around. Anyone who attempts to investigate them could end up opening a Pandora's box," the Secretary of Defense protested.

"I suppose you prefer bombing the world out of existence to solve the problem," said the CIA Director.

General Smith, noticing the friction, decided that it was best to change the course of the discussion. "Surely those responsible have records of the locations of the cylinders at their base of operations. We must target them."

"But we have no idea where this base is located!" pointed out the CIA Director.

Now it was Ambassador Cranston's turn. "Right now, under my authority, Ronald Fletcher is working with the Israelis on a possible lead. He is convinced the alleged spy that is scheduled to be executed by the Libyans tomorrow is connected to the cylinders. And the Mossad agrees."

The President responded with some confusion. "Just last week I spoke to the Prime Minister of Israel, who called for help on the matter. He said they had really had no idea who that man is!"

"Mr. President," Cranston interrupted. "Ronald Fletcher has been on my staff for over two years. I have yet to meet a man as capable as him. My instincts tell me if he feels strongly that this man in Libya is the key to breaking the case, I back his conclusion one hundred percent."

"Let's suppose Fletcher is correct," the Secretary of State said in a condescending tone, "How can we interview a man who is in prison in a country ruled by a lunatic and about to be executed? It's not like we can send a diplomatic request by cable!"

The Ambassador responded with a sneer, "I have already given Fletcher permission to work with the Israelis to free this man by any means necessary."

The Secretary of State shot a cold stare at Cranston for not consulting him, while the CIA Director prepared to protest the blatant infringement of protocol. But the President beat them to the punch. "Good work, Cranston. Finally, a man with initiative!"

Then he turned to General Smith. "O.K. George, enough talk. How do we get out of this mess in one piece?"

General Smith sat silent for a moment, preparing his response. He then stood up. "I feel that our chances for success are based on eliminating three factors. First, the conspirators. Second, the transmitter. Third, the lab and storage facility where this biological weapon was produced. I assume all three are located in Libya. We must act decisively and remove all three factors before the deadline noted in the letters."

Ambassador Cranston opened a folder and removed two photographs, along with a report prepared by Rachel Bronot. He handed them to the President.

Scrutinizing the photographs, the President asked, "What are these?"

Cranston explained, "These photographs were obtained by Ronald Fletcher. The first depicts a meeting between four men. The three men, Germans, hired the fourth man, Ali Rajad, an international terrorist, to smuggle three cylinders containing the deadly agent into Israel. The other photograph is of the man to be executed tomorrow in Libya."

The President commented, "Funny. The Germans and the condemned man look so, well, white!"

162

Cranston said, "The report you hold in your hand discusses that very phenomenon. We have consulted with physicians who believe that all four men have not been exposed to sunlight for a very long time. The report also discusses a theory conceived by Rachel Bronot, head of an Israeli anti-terrorist organization. She has suggested they may have come from an underground facility within walking distance from the place where the condemned man was apprehended by the Libyan army. That would be somewhere under the Sahara Desert."

"If she is correct, a small nuclear device exploded in the Sahara would be much more acceptable than blowing up Tripoli," said the Secretary of State.

"Indeed. If the base is located underground, there would only be negligible radioactive fallout," commented Professor Carlson.

George, how would we handle it militarily?" the President asked.

"I suggest we have one of our portable nuclear devices, a backpack-sized one, sent to the Sixth Fleet in the Mediterranean Sea. The fleet is currently on NATO maneuvers off the coast of Algeria, and could be at the Gulf of Sirte within 24 hours. One of the *Iwo Jima*-class amphibious assault ships participating has on board a company of Black Berets. They are the Navy's best commandos and are well-versed in this kind of operation."

The Secretary of Defense then spoke up. "I suggest we invite the Israelis to participate."

"Why?" the President asked.

"First of all, they are not going to fully depend on us to handle this alone when their very existence is at stake. They'll probably try to run their own operation."

"Why not let the Israelis do whatever they want? It might be a good failsafe in case something goes wrong with our operation. The Prime Minister of Israel seems fairly oblivious to world opinion when his country's welfare is at stake in any case," the President remarked.

"That's quite true, Sir," said the Secretary of State. "But I must point out that a major Israeli operation on Libyan soil may have its own consequences. Libya might be pushed to call in the Soviets, and I think

163

we would all agree it's better that they're not given an opportunity to get their hands on one of the cylinders. Moreover, the Islamic world might not take an operation by the Israelis sitting down. They could use it as an excuse for launching a new Jihad."

All eyes fell on the President. His decision would affect the fate of mankind. The President closed his eyes and thought for a moment before he spoke. "I'm ordering a joint operation with the Israelis. What do we name it?"

"Since the conspirators signed their letter 'Adolf Hitler,' perhaps we should call it Operation Nemesis," said General Smith.

"That's fitting. From this moment, I want all of you to coordinate your work on Operation Nemesis. None of you are to leave the operation center until we successfully thwart the danger or, God forbid..." he trailed off. "I don't even want to think of the other possibility. Meeting closed."

22

As the deliberations at the White House were wrapping up, Ronald Fletcher and Rachel Bronot boarded SAS flight 487 from Copenhagen, Denmark to Tripoli. Both were using British passports, presenting themselves as a vacationing couple excited to explore Tripoli's famous antiquities bazaar. After passing through customs at Idris Field, Ron hailed a taxi to their hotel near the Medina, Tripoli's historic district. What they did not know was that a man who had recently arrived with a forged Italian passport was following their cab in a rented BMW. That man was Phillip Hearns.

Fletcher and Bronot checked into the two-star, inappropriately named Castle Garden Hotel which was located a few hundred yards away from the gate known as Bab Al-Bahr. The hotel was a two-story walk-up. They registered at the small desk at the bottom of the stairway under the names printed on their passports, Mr. Richard and Lisa Nelson. Bronot noticed the clerk was a bit nervous when he handed Fletcher the key to their room. Her sixth sense was ringing five-alarm bells. She was right to be nervous, as Hearns had been investigating all new bookings of Tripoli hotels from foreigners for the past few days. Just a few hours earlier, he had given the clerk three one-hundred-dollar bills to ensure that the Nelson party would be given suite 204.

The porter, a bent-over gentleman at least seventy years old, was barely able to carry their two pieces of luggage to the second floor. Fletcher asked him repeatedly if he needed any help, but the porter stubbornly refused. Opening the creaky door, they saw a sparsely furnished room with a worn carpet, aging king-sized bed, and rusty light fixtures. Ron tipped the grateful porter and walked over to the large open window facing the city wall, gazing at the traffic.

At that moment, Phillip Hearns was kneeling on the ramparts of the old city wall directly opposite the Castle Garden Hotel. He held the Soviet-made Dragunov sniper rifle in his hands and lined up the crosshairs of the PSO-1 scope with the center of Fletcher's chest. Hearns was calm. As he began to pull the trigger, he thought to himself, "It's so easy to kill a man. Even a dangerous man like Fletcher can eliminated without much difficulty."

Bronot suddenly shouted, "Ron, hit the floor!"

Fletcher reacted instantly and dropped to the ground. His ability to react on a dime had been fine-tuned in Vietnam.

At the exact same time, Hearns squeezed the trigger, releasing the bullet. Seeing Fletcher fall, he was perplexed. Hearns asked himself, "Did I hit him, or did he fall on his own?" The timing seemed a hairsbreadth off. Hearns picked up a pair of binoculars to check.

The bullet had pierced the wall above the headboard of the bed, Both Bronot and Fletcher lay flat on the floor.

"How did you know?" Fletcher asked.

"Just call it women's intuition," Bronot answered.

Bronot's experience as the chief of security for the Prime Minister had served them well. She had been perturbed from the moment they checked in. The desk clerk had the look of a man who had been compromised. Bronot was familiar with this look as she herself had bribed clerks in a half-dozen Middle Eastern countries. It was also unusual that when they entered the room the window was wide open, and the shades were not drawn to keep out the sizzling mid-day sun. These two facts would not have alarmed a regular person, but, lucky for Fletcher, Bronot was not a regular person.

"I guess our cover's been blown. Back to square one," Fletcher said, disappointed.

Bronot contemplated Fletcher's statement. Then she replied, "Not necessarily. It couldn't have been the Libyans; they would have come in through the door. My guess someone is out to get you. Do you have any enemies we should know about?" asked Bronot.

"Only about a million. What makes you sure this was a hit?"

"We had some low-level intel that Rajad ordered one."

"You're only telling me this now?"

"We couldn't confirm it. Anyways, it wouldn't have changed your plans."

"But that means Rajad knows we're in Libya!"

"Not necessarily, if he farmed it out. Professional killers usually don't keep their employers in the loop on their location and methods. They just call in "it's done" at the end."

Fletcher crawled to his bag. He pulled out a walkie-talkie. "Barnes, someone took a shot at me from the wall across the street. Meet you at the rendezvous point in three minutes."

Bronot remarked, "You are full of surprises."

"Mike Barnes is my personal bodyguard for this mission. Cranston's orders. You wait here."

 I'm a big girl, I can handle myself."

Fletcher looked at her. "Fine, let's go."

They ran down the stairs and exited through the hotel's back door. Fletcher signaled that he would go left and pointed to Bronot to go right. The plan was to cover the wall across the street from both sides to maximize their chances of spotting the shooter.

The problem was that both were unarmed. As per protocol, Fletcher and Bronot had arrived in the country without firearms in order to avoid detection by airport security, and would receive weapons from local operatives at a later time if needed. For the time being, though, they would have to rely on their cunning and natural resources.

Bronot ran along the wall until she found a set of stairs that led to the ramparts. When she reached the top, she arrived at an extremely narrow path without a parapet. The path led to a wider observation deck with its own set of stairs leading to street level. It was complete with benches, allowing tourists excellent views of both the city of Tripoli and the Medina bazaar below. Here Bronot spotted the assassin. He was in the process of packing his gear. The rifle he used was leaning against the wall a few feet behind him.

Seeing that Hearns was facing in the opposite direction of his rifle, Bronot silently crawled in its direction. She was quickly approaching the rifle when Hearns suddenly swung around. Their eyes met. Bronot was too far from the rifle so she leaped for cover behind a large garbage can.

Hearns opened his black leather suitcase and removed the MAC-10 submachine gun with two clips. He inserted the first and fired a quick burst of rounds. The sound suppressor reduced the noise to the sound of tapping. Bronot knew he was testing to see her reaction. When no fire was returned, Hearns assumed she was unarmed.

On the one hand, Hearns knew he had to kill Bronot. If he let her live, she would surely report the situation to the CIA. They would be relentless in tracking down any party responsible for the death of a member of the American intelligence community. On the other hand, if he killed her, the Mossad would never rest until they had found and eliminated the culprit. And there was no way he could rely on Rajad's organization, or whatever was left of it, not to leak his name.

As Bronot knelt behind the garbage can, she knew that she was about to die. She recognized that the hitman was the infamous Phillip John Hearns. She did not fear death, in fact, she welcomed it. Finally she would join her fiancée, the only man that she had ever loved. Bronot's only regret was that she would no longer be able work to protect Israel, especially in this critical hour.

Hearns cautiously approached her position until he had a clear shot. He knew the game was over. In a moment of unique sentiment, he broke his personal rule of not speaking to victims. He said, "I' m really sorry, but I have no choice." With that, he lifted the MAC-10 and took aim.

In a blur, Fletcher sprang on to Hearns from behind. Rachel was stunned, as she had not heard anything aside from the assassin's voice. Fletcher jumped onto Hearns' back, pulling him back by his shoulders, while at the same time buckling his legs by pushing with both feet at the backs of his knees.

Fletcher landed on his back with Hearns on top of him. He put Hearns in a headlock and wrapped his legs around the front of his legs, putting him in an inescapable stranglehold.

At that moment, Mike Barnes, who had also come out of nowhere, pulled out a curved jambiya dagger with an ivory hilt. He stabbed Hearns in a rapid manner along the sides of his ribs and then slit his throat. Fletcher pushed off Hearns' dead body, and Barnes stretched out his hand to help him stand up.

"Are you O.K.?" Fletcher asked Bronot.

Rachel was not sure whether to thank Fletcher for saving her or to be angry for his stealing her opportunity for final peace. She looked at him for a moment.

"Yes, I'm fine. Ron, thank you so much. Mike, you can be my bodyguard anytime."

Fletcher turned to Barnes. "Yeah, thanks, Mike!"

"Just doing my job, boss." Mike said, smiling.

"Where'd you get the knife?" asked Bronot.

"Oh, this?" Barnes said, holding up the dagger. "Just thirty dinars, not bad, right? The guy in the bazaar swore it was Damascus steel. Hey, I paid with my embassy credit card. Can I keep it, or is it United States property?"

Fletcher and Bronot smirked.

Walking over to Hearns' lifeless body, Fletcher said, "Rachel, do you know who this guy is?"

"His name is Phillip Hearns. A very high-priced assassin. I would say that he is the top contract killer on the international market."

"Now that he's dead, is the operation still on?" Fletcher asked hopefully.

"Yes. We are still good to go. By the way, what do you suggest we do with the body?" Rachel asked.

Fletcher turned to Barnes. "You know what to do."

Barnes replied, "You got it, boss."

Fletcher retorted, "Enough with the 'boss.' That's an order!"

"You got it." Then a fraction of a second later Barnes added, "Boss."

All three started to laugh.

When Fletcher and Bronot returned to the hotel room, there was an awkward moment when they both looked at the one bed. Over the years, on every mission in which Bronot had participated with a cover as the "wife," the "husband" would without exception spend the night on the couch. But this was no an ordinary mission. She was still jittery about her brush with death, and having waking dreams about her former fiancée.

Fletcher was similarly distracted. He laid down on the bed and closed his eyes, thinking about the terror attack on the beach, his frightened children huddled behind the boat. He could see the terrorist approach his beloved Mary, and in a moment of rage bludgeon her face with the stock of his rifle. He felt chills running up his back, and was overcome with a feeling of loneliness and fright, like a lost child with nowhere to run to.

Rachel turned off the lights and lay down next to Ron fully clothed, cuddling up to him. Ron realized he needed her warmth. With their eyes closed, they dreamed about their deceased loved ones. There was no passion in the embrace. They spent the night in each other's arms, using each other's warmth to replenish their souls.

23

The following morning at 6:30 a.m., Muhamad Hassin, a prison cook, prepared Joshua 74575's last meal. In most civilized countries, a condemned man is given his choice of last meal. Not in Libya. Hassin placed a small moldy piece of bread called *khubzit howsh* and a cup of water on a metal tray.

Hassin's hands began to shake as he removed from his shirt pocket a crumbled piece of newspaper. He looked around the empty kitchen, several times, and then unwrapped the paper. Inside was a small tablet. For a moment, he hesitated.

Yesterday, a Mossad agent had visited him in his one-room apartment in the dilapidated neighborhood of Ain Zara. The agent had handed Hassin twenty-five one hundred-dollar bills.

"What's this for?" Hassin asked. It was the first time he had ever seen such a large sum of money at one time.

"This is the first payment for a favor you're going to do for me tomorrow," the agent replied.

"Anything you wish," Hassin said with a smile.

"All you have to do is place this pill in a cup of water that you're going to give to the Israeli spy before the execution."

Hassin turned pale. "The man is too well guarded. If I get caught, they will cut off my head." Hassin tried to return the money to the agent.

The Mossad agent, a powerful man, grabbed the frail Hassin by the neck and whispered, "You will do as I say, or I will return and make you wish those guards had slit your throat to put you out of your misery."

Then the agent released his grip and continued in a calm voice. "After you do me this small favor, you will be delivered five hundred dollars in cash every month for the next five years." Then he walked out.

Hassin held the tablet over the water and thought to himself, "Is it not a good thing to give the Yahood something to make his last moments on earth a little less painful?" He was sure the tablet contained some kind of narcotic. He pleasantly reflected on the money he would be receiving, the house he would buy, and the weddings he would arrange for his three daughters. Then he remembered his benefactor's not-so-subtle threat. Hassin quickly dropped the tablet into the water.

At 7:00 am, Ronald Fletcher and Rachel Bronot ate breakfast in the cramped dining area on the hotel's first floor. Then they stepped out for a walk. The pair walked down a series of colorful side streets packed with artisans and craftsmen until they reached a small garage about a half-mile from their hotel. Bronot took a key from her purse and unlocked the side door. Inside was a brand-new Red Crescent ambulance with two pairs of white hospital scrubs in the back. Fletcher and Bronot changed into the scrubs and entered the ambulance. In order to avoid unwanted attention in a Muslim country, Fletcher took the wheel while Bronot sat in the back.

At 8:00 a.m., three cars pulled up in front of Bomgaar's Cafe in downtown Tripoli. Easily spotted by its royal purple canopy, the restaurant was popular among Tripoli's elites. From the front and back cars, both Audi sedans, emerged eight bodyguards. The middle car was Rajad's armored Mark IV Lincoln Continental. Rajad, Kalem, and two senior bodyguards exited the Lincoln and led the group into the restaurant. It was a ritual that every Sunday and Tuesday when Rajad was in Tripoli, he and his entourage would eat breakfast at Bomgaar's.

The restaurant's management always had a table prepared for Rajad and his crew in the far corner of the large, ornate dining room. At 8:15 am, Bronot's ambulance parked in the alley behind the restaurant next to an emergency exit. Fletcher stepped out of the ambulance and, using a key provided to him by Bronot, unlocked the door.

Fletcher entered a small dining area in the back used for private events. There were two phone booths about twenty feet apart in an adjacent corridor. He entered the more distant phone booth and dialed the number of the other booth. The phone rang for over a minute until a waiter heard it and came running from main dining area to answer.

"Bomgaar's Restaurant. May I be of service?" the waiter answered.

"Yes," replied Fletcher, speaking Arabic with an inflection of a German accent, "I believe a Mr. Ali Rajad is at your restaurant dining. Please tell him that his new business associate would like to speak with him."

"Right away, sir."

The waiter approached Rajad's table. "You have a phone call, sir."

"Did the caller give a name?" Rajad asked.

"No. He said he was a new business associate. I believe he sounded German. Let me show you to the phone."

Rajad turned to Kalem, "I'll be just a few minutes."

Kalem started to rise. "Do you want me to come along?"

"No, just enjoy your breakfast."

Rajad followed the waiter. When he arrived at the phone booth, he handed the waiter a large tip. The waiter then returned to the main dining room.

Rajad stepped into the booth and picked up the receiver. Before he could say "hello," Fletcher clubbed him in the head from behind with a homemade blackjack. He slumped unconscious into Fletcher's arms. Fletcher quickly lifted him onto his shoulders and darted out the back door.

Kalem was having second thoughts of not going with Rajad. He had a feeling that something was wrong. He got up and ordered his two lieutenants to accompany him. When they reached the corridor, Kalem spotted Fletcher carrying the unconscious Rajad out the back door. They made a dash toward Fletcher.

Fletcher was laying Rajad onto the stretcher in the back of the ambulance when he turned and saw Kalem and the two bodyguards exiting the back door brandishing automatic rifles.

Fletcher was unarmed. It looked like the end.

Suddenly, three shots rang out in short succession. As Fletcher watched, first Kalem's head then the heads of the two bodyguards exploded with blood as they dropped to the ground.

Fletcher looked up in the direction of the fire and spotted Barnes about one hundred meters away holding Hearns' sniper rifle. He waved his thanks, and received what appeared to be a semi-sarcastic salute in return from Barnes.

Fletcher finished securing Rajad's stretcher in the back of the ambulance and then rifled through his pockets. He removed an eight-round 9mm Italian Beretta, eight thousand dollars in cash, a half-dozen credit cards, a key, and a letter. Looking at Rajad, Fletcher wanted to strangle him as he lay in the stretcher, but he had a much more fitting end planned.

At 9:15 a.m., about two hours after Joshua finished eating his last meal, he began to feel stomach cramps. He walked over to the corner of his cell and relieved himself, filling the provided bucket with a large amount of watery diarrhea. Thereafter, every thirty minutes like clockwork, Joshua experienced the same sudden, desperate urge to evacuate his bowels. No matter how hard he tried to resist, he had to relieve himself immediately.

At 10:30 a.m., an hour and a half before his scheduled execution, five guards entered Joshua's cell and escorted him up the stairs to the prison courtyard. There, a convoy of eleven armored jeeps with mounted heavy machine guns were waiting. Joshua was placed in the center jeep and the column began to move. At precisely 10:45 a.m., Joshua again had the urge to relieve himself. There was no bucket in the jeep, so, as he had done every Sabbath in Valhalla, he relieved himself in his pants to the disgust of his guards. He received a terrible beating; however, this did not stop him from doing it again at 11:15 am. Neither Joshua nor his guards knew that the cause of his malady was the medication Hassin had placed in his water that morning. It was a powerful laxative in a pulse-release preparation designed to induce uncontrollable diarrhea at specific intervals.

As the convoy made its way towards Martyrs' square, Fletcher and Bronot made an unscheduled stop at Umma Bank. Fletcher entered the bank and returned about ten minutes later. Then they continued toward the center of town, where the ambulance was waved through an army roadblock. Fletcher noticed that the closer they got to Martyrs' square, the more soldiers, tanks, and armored personnel carriers they passed. The mad dictator ruling Libya, excited by the international attention attracted by the execution, had decided to take advantage of the publicity and make a display of his regime's military might. Over 15,000 troops had been brought in to line the streets surrounding Martyrs' square.

While Fletcher drove, Bronot was busy preparing Rajad in the back. She first injected a paralytic blocking agent into Rajad's facial nerves on both sides, and a second medication into his thigh muscle. She then removed a battery-operated hair clipper from a drawer in the ambulance and gave Rajad something akin to a crew cut. Afterwards, she sprayed Rajad's face, neck, arms, and lower legs with an aerosol spray developed by a team of Israeli dermatologists, turning his skin a dusky pale white. Finally she dressed Rajad with a different set of clothing from a bag next to the stretcher.

At 11:20 a.m., Bronot's ambulance approached another check post. Fletcher handed the guard a forged pass. The confused soldier scurried off with the document to show to his superior. An argument erupted as the officer in charge accused the guard of wasting his time as he was trying to enjoy the pre-execution festivities on a portable television. With barely a glance at the pass he waved the ambulance through.

Fletcher proceeded in the direction of Martyrs' square. When he was about fifty feet from the gallows, he turned into an empty alleyway behind a small wooden structure. It was a public restroom consisting of a broom closet, two stalls, and a sink. The prior day, a team of Mossad agents dressed as workmen had made a few alterations to the restroom's interior. They first removed the wall that divided the left stall from the broom closet and replaced it with a sliding wooden panel. Then the divider separating the two stalls was replaced with another sliding panel. An exit hatch was constructed in the back wall of the broom closet. Both the right stall and broom closet doors were nailed shut. Finally, a spring lock mechanism was installed on the left stall door.

At 11:30 a.m., the convoy parked in front of the ceremonial dais next to the gallows. Joshua was brought before the Libyan Army's chief of staff, General Abu al-Kalib, for inspection. The General was disgusted by the prisoner's smell and appearance. He shouted at the officer in charge of the convoy, "Are you a fool? This execution is being broadcasted on live international television!"

"But, sir," The officer protested.

"You are hereby demoted. Get out of my sight!" yelled the General with indignation. He turned to the captain of the honor guard.

"You are now officially promoted. Get this Yahood cleaned up, fast!"

Delighted with his promotion, the officer took Joshua along with a few of his honor guards to the public restroom. He ordered two of the guards to get a prison uniform from a nearby detention center and meet him at the restroom.

When Joshua and the honor guards arrived, there was an old man standing at the sink, washing his hands. One of the guards angrily ordered him to leave. The guards looked around the restroom and saw nothing suspicious. As they examined the nailed shut door of the right stall, the two guards sent to obtain a clean uniform for Joshua arrived.

Fletcher and Rajad were in the broom closet. Rajad had by this time regained consciousness, but his facial muscles were completely paralyzed by Bronot's injections and he was unable to open his mouth to shout for help. The second drug Bronot had injected was a powerful muscle relaxant which had caused Rajad severe weakness, as if his arms and legs were made of rubber.

The officer in charge of the honor guard ordered Joshua into the working left stall, and instructed the guard holding the clean uniform to hand it to him. Joshua took the clean prison garb and placed it on the floor next to the toilet. Then Joshua removed the soiled uniform and pushed it towards the guard. The guard felt nauseous as he picked up the clothes. As he left the stall to dispose of the soiled uniform, Fletcher pushed a button in the broom closet that caused the left stall door to swing shut and lock.

Fletcher slid open the panel and saw Joshua sitting on the toilet. He quickly covered Joshua's surprised face with a cloth which had been soaked with a powerful sedative, causing Joshua to pass out immediately. Fletcher moved Joshua into the broom closet, then grabbed Rajad, lowered his pants, and sat him on the toilet with his back leaning against the wall. The guards were not able to hear anything because the noise from the tens of thousands of shouting spectators in Martyrs' square was deafening within the thin-walled bathroom.

Rajad looked around at his unfamiliar surroundings. His head was still spinning from the effects of the multiple injections he had received. He noticed his prison clothing and his pale white hands. He tried in vain to scream out, but his vocal cords had been completely paralyzed. This caused him to become even more frightened, so he began to weakly pound on the door.

The honor guards interpreted the sound as a signal that the mute prisoner was finished changing. They opened the door and pulled out Rajad. A close examination might have revealed the switch; however, the flow of events gave no reason for suspicion. To the guards, the man who entered the stall was obviously the same man who came out. Rajad tried to flail his arms to signal the guards, but the only responses he received were prods from the bayonets on the guards' rifles to stop.

The honor guard returned to the ceremonial dais to present their detainee to General Abu al-Kalib. He looked the terrified Rajad over and said, "Good job. Now we can have a proper execution."

As soon as the soldiers had left the restroom, Fletcher lifted Joshua and exited through the hatch in the back of the broom closet. He placed Joshua in the rear of the ambulance and laid him on to the stretcher. He closed the back of the ambulance and returned to the driver's seat, started the engine, and drove slowly through the throng of spectators. While they drove, Bronot helped the now stirring Joshua into clean clothes and gave him a cup of water with an antidote to the laxative he had received.

Fletcher returned along the same route. When they arrived at the check post, the road was blocked but there were no soldiers. He knew it would be unwise to drive around the barricade without permission, so he got out of the ambulance and began to look for a guard. He found all the soldiers standing around the small black-and-white television set of the officer in charge. He looked over one of the guard's shoulders at the screen and felt a warm surge of satisfaction surge flow through his body.

Ali Rajad was being led to the gallows by the Libyan honor guard. After climbing the steps to the platform, a man dressed in black placed a barbed wire noose around Rajad's neck. The wire was passed through a steel loop on a scaffold and the other end was held by five husky soldiers with special gloves. The President of Libya gave a signal and the soldiers lifted Rajad until his toes barely touched the platform. He struggled to stop the strangulation by stretching his feet like a ballerina, but to no avail. The guards simply continued to lift him another inch off the ground. After several long minutes, Rajad, with his eyes bulging out, slowly and painfully strangled to death.

Fletcher watched with glee as his moment of revenge had finally arrived. After four and a half minutes, Rajad's fight for survival ended. Fletcher, fully satisfied, asked the commanding officer if someone could open the gate. The officer ordered one of his men to allow the ambulance to pass. When he returned, Fletcher found that the path was blocked with a crowd of pedestrians, so he turned on the siren and proceeded slowly out of the cordoned area.

The ambulance headed east and eventually made its way on to the coastal highway. About an hour later, Fletcher exited the highway and drove along a dirt road next to the shore of the Mediterranean Sea. There he spotted a waiting car. When Fletcher and Bronot stepped out of the ambulance, two Nekama agents approached and carried Joshua out of the back. A third took Fletcher's place in the driver's seat and drove the ambulance off road to an overhanging cliff. He put the ambulance into neutral and then pushed it off the cliff into the sea, where it immediately sank.

Fletcher, Bronot, Joshua, and the Nekama agents then entered a large inflatable rubber boat with an outboard motor. When all were on board, one of the agents started the motor and they made their way out to sea. A second agent began navigating with a compass. After thirty minutes, they cut the engine and dropped small iron anchors at the four corners of the raft.

Minutes later, the boat rocked from side to side and then the entire craft was abruptly lifted out of the sea. The group found themselves on the port deck of a submarine. A hatch opened and the captain of the submarine, along with several Israeli Navy crew members, emerged.

"Shalom, Rachel. How was your sightseeing tour of Tripoli?" asked the captain.

"Not what I expected. It's a shame I didn't have a chance to buy you anything," Rachel joked.

"Maybe next time. And you, Mr. Fletcher, how did you like our little submarine trick?"

"Not bad," said Fletcher. "It reminded me of a plane landing on an aircraft carrier. Except instead of the plane maneuvering to land, the carrier adjusts to catch the plane."

"Very good. Then I take it you approve," the captain smiled.

Within minutes all were safely aboard the Israeli vessel. It was an ex-British Royal Navy Triton-class diesel-electric submarine. It submerged and it headed northwest, toward the United States Sixth Fleet.

24

The Prime Minister of Israel spoke with some trepidation into the secure telephone connected to the White House.

"Mr. President?"

"Speaking. How are you, old friend?" the President asked.

"Looking forward to better days!"

"Was the mission successful? We watched the execution on television, but I bet General Smith here a dollar the man hanged wasn't our boy."

"You can collect your money from General Smith. We did manage to switch prisoners."

"Well, I hope it was someone deserving of the honor." The President had a gut feeling it was some enemy of the Jewish people.

"I'm sure he was delighted to have been selected to do this service for our country. I must tell you, by the way, we are most impressed with your attaché, Mr. Ronald Fletcher. He was an enormous help. The man is simply remarkable. Are you sure he isn't at least part Jewish?" the Prime Minister asked.

"He is as much a Baptist as I am," the President answered.

"That's a pity. You know we Jews have a tradition of not proselytizing. However, I must admit we are truly tempted in the case of Mr. Fletcher."

The President and the Prime Minister shared a laugh. Then the President was ready to get down to business.

"Do you know the location of the source of the cylinders?"

"Yes, Mr. President. I'm going to play for you now a recording of the transcript of an interview Mr. Fletcher conducted of Joshua 74575, the man who was meant to be executed."

"74575? What kind of name is that?" the President asked, curious.

"You will soon find out," the Prime Minister answered. "The reason we are playing a recording of the transcript is that Joshua was interviewed in German."

"I'm fluent in German," said the President.

"Ah, that's right. I did know that. Well, there's another reason. Joshua 74575 is only able to communicate in sign language. It pains me to tell you that the Nazis long ago cut his tongue out."

The President leaned back in his chair. A cold sweat appeared on his forehead. He had had a premonition that episode of the cylinders was only a preview to an even greater horror.

The Prime Minister of Israel switched on a tape player. There was a short introduction explaining that Joshua 74575 was initially unwilling to cooperate with the Israeli psychologist. Then he was given a pen and paper and asked if he wanted to write or draw out his thoughts. Joshua took the pen and paper and wrote in child-like letters, "Ani Yehudi," "I am a Jew" in Hebrew. One of the naval officers then showed him the Jewish Star hanging on his neck, to Joshua's great excitement. He started waving around his arms in an attempt to communicate. Fletcher recognized his movement as sign language. Knowing how to sign himself, Fletcher began to ask questions.

"What is your name?" he asked.

"Joshua 74575."

"Why 74575?"

"This is the name I was given at birth."

"By your parents?"

"I have no parents."

"Then how did you acquire your name?"

"All the Jews are given numbers at birth by the Nazis."

"Where are you from? You seem far too young to have lived under the Nazis."

"I come from a place called Project Valhalla. There the Nazis rule and we Jews are their slaves."

"What is this project?"

"It is a community, deep under the ground."

"Does this community have a leader?"'

"Yes, he is called the Reich Gott."

"Who is the Reich Gott?"

"The Rabbi says his real name is Adolf Hitler."

"Joshua, Adolf Hitler died many years ago. Have you ever seen this Reich Gott? What does he look like?"

"I only saw him once, when I was ordered to clean the Temple."

"What does he look like?

"He is a box with lights and switches. On the top of the box there a device that the Rabbi called a typewriter. The Rabbi said that Hitler communicates by receiving and sending messages through the typewriter."

"Why do you call him the Reich Gott?"

"That is his name. All the Aryans worship him."

"Do you worship him?"

"Of course not. I am a Jew. I believe in the one and only God. The God of Israel."

"The Aryans allow you to believe in your God?"

"We Jews are not allowed to worship the Reich Gott. Instead, the Aryans teach us a false version of Judaism."

"How do you know that what they are teaching is not real Judaism?"

"At first I just felt it couldn't be true. Later, the Rabbi taught me what real Judaism is."

"Who is this Rabbi?"

"He is a Jew who lives in a cage in the zoo."

"Does he have a name?"

"His name is Rabbi Gershon Cohen."

"Why is he in a cage in a zoo?"

"He is an exhibit in the Untermenschen section of the zoo. There is a row of cages with humans from different countries."

"Where did you live?"

"In Hell, with all the Jews."

"What is Hell?"

"The Rabbi told me it is a concentration camp."

"Why do the Jews live there?"

"Because the High Priest says all Jews belong in Hell."

"Who is this High Priest?"

"The Rabbi says his real name is Heinrich Mueller."

"What does he do as High Priest?"

"He reads the communications of the Reich Gott and executes his orders."

"Why did you leave Project Valhalla?"

"The Rabbi told me that I must escape."

"Why?"

"He said that the Nazis are planning to destroy the State of Israel on the twenty-fifth of June at noon. He told me I must escape and bring back the Jewish Army to stop Hitler."

At this point a dubbed-in voice announced, "End of Tape One."

"Well, Mr. President, any thoughts?" the Prime Minister asked.

The President was thinking maybe he was asleep and in the middle of a nightmare. "Valhalla, Hitler, a human zoo? This must be the Nazi version of Alice in Wonderland," he thought to himself.

"I have a feeling this is only getting worse," the President replied.

"You are correct. Did you hear Joshua mentioning Heinrich Mueller?" asked the Prime Minister.

"Yes, what about him?"

"Heinrich Mueller was the head of the Gestapo in Nazi Germany. He was last seen in the Fuhrerbunker the night before Hitler's suicide, and was never seen again."

"Are you saying that Mueller is running the show at Project Valhalla?" The President asked.

"Maybe. And perhaps he is using this machine called the 'Reich Gott' to assert his authority in Hitler's name. In any case we have located the origin of the cylinders, which were probably developed using the last resources of Nazi Germany."

"Where is this place located?"

"I'm sorry, Mr. President. I must withhold this information unless you are prepared to agree to certain conditions," said the Prime Minister assertively.

"What do you mean, conditions?" the President said in an exasperated tone. "You do understand that the base must be destroyed by tomorrow!"

"That's exactly the problem," said the Prime Minister.

"What do you mean?"

"Well, Mr. President, it's obvious. Hundreds, maybe thousands of Jews are living in this man-made Hell as if the Holocaust never ended. The State of Israel was created in order to ensure that Jews would never again suffer so terribly at the hands of anti-Semites. I will not allow one more Jew to die because of the evil actions of a Nazi!" declared the Prime Minister in a trembling voice.

The President was slow to answer. He knew the Prime Minister of Israel had spoken from the depths of his soul.

"I understand your feelings. But your country, along with the rest of the world, is in grave danger. Furthermore, you must be aware that a boots-on-the-ground military operation would likely result in the deaths of many combatants."

The Prime Minister responded with confidence. "The soldiers of the Israel Defense Forces are fully prepared to risk their lives to protect the Jewish people. This is our mandate from the Creator of the World, our national identity, and the reason for our country's existence."

"I'm sure you're aware that even if you are successful, if Israeli violates Libyan sovereignty war will likely break out in the Middle East," the President pointed out.

"We are a small country that only wants peace with our neighbors. Our army is called the Israel Defense Forces for a reason. The emphasis is on the word 'defense.' And there is no room for compromise when the very lives of our people are at stake. The Jews of Valhalla are no less citizens of the State of Israel then the Jews of Tel Aviv," the Prime Minister stated emphatically.

The President was silent for a moment. He thought to himself, "This Israeli is as stubborn as he is proud. In any case, they know where

184

the base is and therefore, they are holding all the cards. We can't let them trigger world war by going in alone."

Finally, the President spoke. "I suppose you have a plan?"

"Of course. We have many plans," the Prime Minister replied with some relief.

"Do any one of those plans include a joint operation, by any chance?"

"As a matter of fact, that is the one I was going to propose. We have formulated our strategy with Ronald Fletcher's expert assistance."

The Prime Minister paused. "Before I share it with you, do I have the United States' commitment to the safe evacuation of the Jewish prisoners of Project Valhalla?"

"You have my word," the President answered.

"Thank you, Mr. President."

The President was now ready for business. "Please place your chief of operations on the line. I'll call in General Smith and they can go over the details," he said. "I just hope to God that this plan works."

The Prime Minister answered sincerely, "If we put our faith of the God of the Jews and the Christians, and not in the abomination called the Reich Gott, I'm sure we'll be successful."

25

On June 25th, at 4:30 a.m., Ronald Fletcher, Mike Barnes, Rachel Bronot, and Joshua 74575 were lowered by harnesses into the same drilling hole Joshua had used to make his escape. By comparing the information Joshua provided with the estimated location of his capture, a team of Israeli geographers and geologists were able to determine the approximate location of Project Valhalla. A unit of U.S. Marines from the U.S. Sixth Fleet, now twenty-five miles off the Libyan coast, had accompanied them on a CH-46 Sea Knight transport helicopter that cruised less then forty feet above the waters of the Gulf of Sidra at an average speed of one hundred and fifty miles an hour to avoid detection by Libyan radar. After about forty minutes of flying, they arrived at the large salt marsh where the caverns were believed to be located. Joshua remembered every detail of the first views he had experienced of the above-ground world, and thus able to guide the pilot to their destination with remarkable precision.

The reconnaissance sortie led by Fletcher constituted the first phase of Operation Nemesis. Their job was critical. They were tasked with scouting Valhalla and gathering enough information to guide the second stage of the operation. Though Joshua had demonstrated a remarkable memory for details, the strategists in the Pentagon and HaKirya were lacking vital information regarding internal security systems and the location of the transmitter designed to send coded signals to the cylinders. A number of elaborate attack strategies had already been chalked out; however, it was still unknown which was the most likely to achieve total success.

Fletcher was the first to be lowered down into the shaft. Once at the bottom, he carefully removed the pile of rocks Joshua had placed to conceal the entrance. Peering into the cavern, he was shocked by what he witnessed. At the far end of the cavern, a giant circular light fixture was being lifted up mechanically. He watched with awe as successive rings of lights were illuminated, the artificial sunrise slowly turning night into day within the cavern complex.

Fletcher was located at the end of an aisle within a seemingly endless maze of twenty-foot high stacks of wooden crates. Each crate was marked with a series of letters and numbers preceded by a swastika. Close to his position, a map marked out the locations of various stored items. As Fletcher was relaying the information to Bronot by walkie-talkie, he spotted a soldier apparently on guard duty about two hundred yards away. Fletcher felt that this soldier could be a valuable source of intelligence and decided to seize the opportunity.

The guard, an SS private, was a perfect example of the results of Dr. Josef Schreiber's Aryan Breeding Program. He was approximately eighteen years old, well over six feet tall, and had a squarish muscular build that made him appear as if he was shaped out of block of granite. The light blond hair and blue eyes framing his unnaturally white skin made him look to Fletcher like a visiting alien who had not yet become accustomed to life on Earth.

Fletcher quickly determined the guard's route. He waited for him behind a pile of crates marked "blankets." As the guard approached the crates, Fletcher sprang from his position, blocking the path of the startled soldier. The two were separated by less than a yard. The guard's reflexes reacted instantly and he raised his rifle, but it was too late. Fletcher unleashed a flawless Hapkido heel stomp on to his knee. The German superman crumbled to the ground, just like any ordinary soldier.

Fletcher thrusted at the soldier with the Vu Khi, driving it deep into his chest. He then pressed a button at the base of the long needle releasing four microhooks from the tip. The soldier winced in agony as Fletcher twisted the needle, locking the hooks into the pericardial tissue surrounding his heart. The pain was so great that the soldier immediately emptied his bowels. Fletcher had stuffed a piece of cloth in the guard's mouth, so all that could be heard was muffled screams.

Fletcher addressed the guard in slow, methodical German. "I know this is very painful. I can absolutely guarantee that in the next few moments, you will experience ten times the agony. I am offering you an alternative. If you answer my questions fully, the pain will stop. If not, you have only yourself to blame."

The German soldier looked down and saw his own blood oozing from the wound onto Fletcher's hand. The excruciating pain, combined with the fear of what could come next, was too much for anyone to bear. At this point, death would be a welcome alternative.

The soldier nodded his head. Fletcher removed the gag from his mouth, while at the same time partially retracting the microhooks, drastically lowering the level of inflicted pain to allow the guard to respond coherently. Fletcher held the walkie-talkie next to the soldier's mouth so that their conversation would immediately be transmitted to his team and then relayed to the Pentagon and HaKirya.

"Where is the Broder Laboratory?" Fletcher demanded.

"In the far corner of the North Clover." The guard coughed out the words. He was somewhat relieved that his pain was now at least bearable.

"How many soldiers are guarding the lab?"

"At least one hundred and fifty SS and another fifty Gestapo."

"What kinds of defenses protect it?"

"Two machine gun nests and three cannon platforms. The door itself is made of fortified steel." Then he added, "Even if you get past the guards, the doors can only be opened from inside the laboratory."

"Where is the location of the elevator that is used to go up to the surface?"

"In the center of the SS base in South Clover."

"How many soldiers are on the base today?"

"About six hundred."

"How many are guarding the Reich Temple?"

"Five hundred, including two hundred Gestapo."

"Why so many?"

"There is a special ceremony today. The Reich Gott is going to destroy the Jewish State during the service."

Fletcher was now convinced that the transmitter was located within the Reich Temple.

"How many people will attend the ceremony?"

"Everyone except on-duty soldiers. About twenty-five thousand people."

"Where is the electricity produced for the Project?"

"In the West Clover, near the entrance."

"How many guards?"

"At least fifty, with another hundred guards nearby in Hell watching the Jews."

Fletcher looked at the dying Aryan and decided to end his suffering. He pressed a second button on the base of the needle which released concentrated Russel's viper venom, killing the soldier almost instantly. Then he retracted the microhooks and wiped clean the Vu Khi on the dead soldier's shirt.

Fletcher returned to the drilling hole entrance. There Bronot was busy activating a field telephone. He grabbed the phone, which was connected via the CH-46 Sea Knight's radio scrambler to the USS *Arlington*, a former light aircraft carrier which had been converted into a communications ship. The ship had direct linkups with the United States and Israel by way of the U.S. Navy Fleet Satellite Communication System.

Within seconds, the War Rooms in both the Pentagon and HaKirya were bombarding Fletcher with a flurry of questions. After much discussion, an operations model was selected. General Smith relayed the information to the President in the Presidential Emergency Operations Center below the White House. When he was finished, the President gave his final approval.

Now it was the President's turn. Gathering his thoughts, he asked an aide to activate the Washington-Moscow Direct Communications Link. Though it was widely assumed that a "red phone" connected the leaders of the two superpowers, oral communication had been considered too risky to be used to prevent nuclear conflict, lest there be a miscommunication. Rather, a teletype machine was employed for this type of diplomacy when needed. If the

President was unable to convince the leader of the Soviet Union of the viability of his operation, a nuclear war could potentially break out between the United States and the Soviet Union. Then it would not be a matter of survival, but merely a choice of how one preferred to die, by radioactivity or biological agent.

26

A presidential aide called the Pentagon officer in charge of the communication system which linked the United States and the Soviet Union. At the same time, the United States Ambassador to the Soviet Union contacted the Soviet Foreign Ministry to notify the Kremlin that the President of the United States had an urgent communication for the Soviet Premier.

The messages were sent in each leader's own language, with translations performed in the Pentagon and the Kremlin. Multiple U.S. Intelsat and Soviet Moiniya satellites transmitted the encrypted messages for redundancy and confirmation purposes.

"Mr. Secretary," the President wrote, "I must inform you of a situation of the utmost urgency."

"Is this related to your naval movements off the Libyan coast?" wrote the General Secretary of the Communist Party, leader of the Soviet Union.

"Yes. Recently my country received a letter threatening the destruction of the United States as well as the rest of the world."

"We also received such a letter."

"Our intelligence services have tracked the source to an underground base in Libya. They have confirmed that the threat is real. The conspirators have a biological weapon capable of destroying all of mankind. Our scientists have determined that the only safe way of stopping the implementation of the threat is with a nuclear explosion.

"We are currently carrying out a military operation to place a small nuclear device in position to destroy the threat. The base is well guarded, so we have no alternative other than to employ a substantial military force to accomplish this. If all goes well, the nuclear explosion should take place around noon. The location is far from any populated area, so we do not expect any civilian casualties. I want to make it perfectly clear that as soon as our mission is accomplished, we will immediately withdraw from Libyan soil."

The President began to perspire. He knew that if the Secretary didn't believe him, it could precipitate a nuclear conflagration. The President was under a great deal of pressure. First and foremost in his mind, he felt that the future of the United States was on his shoulders. Many American soldiers might be also killed in the military assault on the base. He was also feeling the weight of his having approved a nuclear explosion which would kill tens of thousands of people living in Project Valhalla.

The leader of the Soviet Union was experiencing a similar dilemma. He too feared a nuclear holocaust. The Secretary wanted to inquire further regarding the nature of the biological weapon and the conspirators, but he didn't want to show weakness. Why hadn't the KGB investigated this threat? The report he received regarding the letter had dismissed it as a prank. He thought to himself, "If we survive until the morning, heads will roll in my so-called intelligence service. They have proven themselves again to be a gaggle of incompetent fools."

Finally, the Secretary answered. "I'm well aware of the situation. We were also planning a similar military operation. However, when I received the report that the United States was moving into position, I ordered my military to stand down. If you fail, we are ready to act."

The President sighed with enormous relief. He thought to himself, "Like hell you knew, you sly old dog!"

Then the President responded, "There is only one problem. The Libyans have no connection with the threat; however, the base is located on their territory. My advisors have warned me that trying to deal with the Libyan government in an official capacity would hamper our mission and increase the risk unnecessarily. However, our action may be interpreted as an infringement on Libyan sovereignty. We are hoping that your country could persuade the Libyans not to interfere with our operation. If the Libyans get involved, we will have no alternative but to protect our men and their mission."

The Secretary was under no delusions about his ability to control the madman in charge of Libya. Although the Soviet Union and Libya were officially allied in the struggle against capitalist imperialism, they had virtually no influence over the lunatic who ran his country with an iron fist.

"I believe it is too late to work through diplomatic channels. Your country will have to make the best of the situation," the Secretary wrote. "We will of course be monitoring your operation closely. It would be most regrettable if your country deviates in any manner from what we have discussed. Also, if it becomes public that the United States is conducting military operations on Libyan soil, you can anticipate my country's official condemnation."

"Again, you have my personal assurance. What we have discussed is the absolute extent of this operation," the President replied.

The Secretary was convinced that the President of the United States had been truthful, despite the frigid relationship between the two countries. He concluded, "As you Americans say, good luck."

"Thank you, Mr. Secretary." the President answered, knowing they would need more than just luck to prevent a catastrophe of epic proportions.

27

With the fear of nuclear confrontation with the Soviet Union out of the way, the president turned to his Advisor on Military Affairs, General George Smith.

"OK, Georgie boy, it's all clear. The big bad bear is in the bag!" the President joked.

"That's just great," replied General Smith. "I can honestly say I was sweating bullets. I'll inform the Chief of Staff that we have the green light."

"Now, just make it work, please!"

Smith made a few calls and the machinery in the Pentagon began churning. Within minutes, the command center in the USS *Arlington* was coordinating hundreds of real-time photos sent by Fletcher and incorporating the information into charts and models of the cavern complex. Officers were even holding mock sand table battles to simulate different potential scenarios.

The staff in the command center radioed their orders to the three *Iwo Jima*-class helicopter assault ships: *Inchon*, *New Orleans* and *Tripoli*. Each was carrying a marine battalion. The marines were to be transported to Valhalla by way of CH-53 Sea Stallion heavy transport helicopters. To protect the mission, two nuclear-powered aircraft carriers, *Nimitz* and *Enterprise*, along with two *Forrestal*-class supercarriers, *Saratoga* and *Independence*, made up the armada. Together they contained over three hundred of the most advanced fighting aircraft available, including F-14 Tomcats, F-15 Eagles, and nine Grumman EA-6B electronic warfare aircraft.

The crews and soldiers aboard the CH-53 Sea Stallions waited impatiently for the signal to take off. On the *Inchon*, forty commandos of the Black Berets were also waiting for the go-ahead. They were charged with the awesome responsibility of planting the portable nuclear device at the target site. The bomb was being held by one of the Black Berets in a large, specially designed backpack.

A few days earlier, two United States transport submarines, the USS *Grayback* and the USS *Growler*, had been sent to Israel. The submarines came to a stop about ten miles off the coast of the port city of Ashdod. There, they released underwater landing crafts which resembled submersible motorboats. These mini submarines made their way to the Port of Ashdod where Israeli frogmen boarded. These elite commandos were considered to be the best trained fighters in Israel, comparable to American Navy Seals. From there, the underwater transport crafts returned to the submarines, which rendezvoused with the task force off the coast of Libya. The Israeli commandos boarded the *Inchon,* and, within a few hours, they were sitting in helicopters also waiting for the green light.

Once the President's order was received, scores of helicopters with fighter jet escorts took to the sky. First to approach the Libyan radar umbrella were the EA-6B electronic warfare aircraft. These planes were tasked with rendering the Libyan radar useless. Assisting these aircraft were F-14s carrying AGM-45 Shrike radar-bursting missiles and loads of electronic countermeasure packages.

The Libyan soldiers manning their radar scopes saw thousands of unidentified flying objects. They were not sure if they were experiencing a mass invasion or the radar equipment was again malfunctioning. As per protocol, the General in charge of coastal defense ordered Libyan Air Command to send up aircraft to investigate. A squadron of Soviet-made MiG 25 Foxbats were given the task.

Fleet Radar immediately picked up the Libyan response and relayed the information to the *Arlington.* As the Commander on the *Arlington* was not authorized to make any decisions concerning Libyan intervention, he passed the information on to the Pentagon. Confusion broke out in the War Room. The President took notice of the chaos as watched it unfold on the screen of his video link-up from the Presidential Emergency Operations Center.

He asked, "George, what's going on?"

"The Libyans sent up some fighters. Some of the boys in Air Force Intelligence believe they're Foxbats. They look damn worried. The *Arlington* is waiting for orders on how to respond," General Smith said sullenly.

"Can't anyone make a decision?" The President shouted, exasperated. "Those helicopters are carrying our boys; our top priority is to protect them! We can't let the Libyans get close enough to see them! Am I perfectly clear?"

"Yes, Sir," General Smith replied. "I'll see to it immediately."

General Smith passed on the President's directive to the Head of the Joint Chiefs of Staff, who relayed the order to the Commander of Operation Nemesis on the *Arlington* to stop the Libyans. Seven F-15 Eagles were scrambled from the aircraft carriers along with five F-14A Tomcats with orders to take out the Foxbats.

Each of the U.S. pilots proudly wore a patch on their sleeve with the image of a jet fighter and the words, "United States Navy Fighter Weapons School." That meant that they were graduates of the elite "top gun" program at Naval Air Station Miramar in San Diego, California. As a final test, the pilots had simulated air sorties against course instructors utilizing the most advanced Soviet air tactics.

Within minutes of the initial order from the *Arlington*, an epic battle of tactics and technology ensued. Computers on the U.S. jet fighters determined optimum firing conditions at Mach speeds. The Tomcats launched their AIM-9 Sidewinder air-to-air missiles while at the same time the F-15s from the *Nimitz* fired their AIM-7 Sparrows. The battle was over in less than thirty seconds, a total success with all Foxbats downed. Upon hearing the results, cheers went up in command centers at both HaKirya and the Pentagon. American technology and excellent pilot training had been the decisive factors.

When they reached ten miles inland, the air convoy of helicopters and their fighter jet escorts split up. Twenty helicopters and a squadron of Tomcats continued heading southwest while the bulk of helicopters and fighters turned southeast towards the coordinates of Project Valhalla.

The first group of choppers landed twelve miles northeast of the project, at the site of an abandoned World War II-era Italian airfield. As the spy satellites had indicated, the airstrip was in excellent condition. The runway was too short for larger planes, but it was just long enough for the needs of Operation Nemesis. Marines secured the perimeter of the airfield while engineering crews made quick repairs of any large cracks in the runway.

One hour later, several Lockheed C-130 Hercules transport airplanes from Morón Air Base in Southern Spain landed on the short airstrip. One of the planes was a mobile hospital. They were escorted by F-16 fighters equipped with supplemental fuel tanks.

At the Valhalla site, the main body of the air convoy had already landed. The soldiers were in the process of unloading tons of equipment. Hundreds of U.S. Marines were fanning out to secure the area.

Out of one of the Sea Stallions emerged a top-secret unit of twenty men. They were called "the Edge" by the few privileged to know of their existence. This was the most advanced unit that would be entering Valhalla, equipped with unusual "space age" technology. The Edge consisted a squadron of Air Force commandos wearing movement-enhancing rocket boosters and armed with automated laser firing systems. Each soldier had a helmet-based microcomputer with optical sensors that controlled laser weapons mounted on their shoulders able to fire at up to three targets simultaneously. The strategists of Operation Nemesis were depending on the Edge to help overcome the many defense fortifications and manpower advantages of the Aryans. They were the first group to be lowered into the complex.

The Edge unit was followed by ninety Israeli frogmen with full underwater tactical gear. They were organized at the jump-off point into three lines, and briefed by Rachel Bronot regarding their specific objectives. The first two lines entered the waters of the river which passed just one hundred yards from the drilling hole entrance in East Clover. They were to swim the length of the river to West Clover, where the concentration camp and power plant were located, then wait submerged until the official mission execution time, 10:40 a.m.

The third line was led by Ronald Fletcher and Mike Barnes. After they donned underwater gear and selected weapons, they swam to the center of the river near where it passed the Reich Temple. As they remained submerged, Fletcher's team could hear the loud, rhythmic chanting of the thousands of Aryans that packed the Temple, causing the water to vibrate.

During this time, a battalion of 450 marines from the USS *Inchon* descended the shaft and organized into three companies. The first company's objective was to secure the Reich Temple. The second company was tasked to break through SS defenses in South Clover and capture the elevator control room. The third company was to march to North Clover and demolish its defenses, however, they were not to enter the laboratory or destroy any of its infrastructure.

Accompanying the third company were the forty Navy Black Berets carrying the nuclear device. They were under strict orders that in the case of mission failure, or if they were unable to properly place the bomb before the 12:00 noon deadline, they would detonate it. The nuclear bomb would eradicate any stores of the agent as well as the transmitter believed to be located in the Reich Temple.

At 10:39, the Israeli frogmen prepared to emerge from their position in the river in West Clover. They were primed for action. Some looked at the mission as their opportunity for revenge against the accursed Nazis. Others thought about the Jewish prisoners of Valhalla, some of whom might even be their relatives. Every one took a short time to whisper a personal prayer to the One Above for success.

Only one minute remained before the official launch. The President of the United States and the Prime Minister of Israel had just finished their fifth telephone conversation. Both were on the edge of their seats. The next hour would decide the success or failure of Operation Nemesis and the future of mankind. In the Pentagon, HaKirya, the Sixth Fleet, and the Sahara Desert, tension had risen to a fever's pitch. They had reached the point of no return. There was no going back now.

28

As the minute hand on his diver's watch reached 10:40, Lieutenant Commander Yitzhak Sofer ordered both units of Israeli frogmen under his command to emerge from the water and remove their wetsuits. It took them less than sixty seconds to don black fatigues, the official uniform of both Americans and Israelis taking part in the operation. Along with the uniforms, the water-tight polyurethane bags they had brought contained prototype Mini Uzis weighing only six pounds and capable of firing up to 950 rounds per minute, as well as a variety of weapons and explosive equipment.

The area along the river's edge was deserted. The commandos stood among towering mounds of freshly mined coal. Usually this section of the river was bustling with activity, with Jewish prisoners unloading barges of coal pulled by teams of fellow slaves from the mine. But as per Hitler's decree, all Jews in Valhalla were confined to the concentration camp during today's special service in the Reich Temple.

A team of Sofer's frogmen carrying a modern automatic version of the medieval crossbow positioned themselves behind a mound of coal near the main gate of the electric power station. At 10:50 am, a loud collective thump was heard as the archers pulled the triggers on their crossbows and released their lethal arrows, causing the Gestapo guards at the gate to fall to the cavern floor. Four commandos who were trained demolitions experts ran at full speed toward the generators. When a spotter alerted them that a patrol of SS soldiers was approaching, they immediately dropped to a prone position. A hail of crossbow arrows rained out from behind the coal piles. When the four looked up, an additional ten Nazis were lying dead.

The demolition team arrived at the generators at 10:58 a.m. Each commando emptied his heavy backpack laden with C-4 plastic explosives and leaned the charges against a generator. They set their timers for 11:02 a.m. and then ran at full sprint back to the coal mounds. As the demolition experts dove for cover, a tremendous explosion ripped through the entire clover. Instantly all of Project Valhalla was thrown into total darkness.

The commandos in the first unit emerged from behind the coal mounds wearing a helmet with a special visor made of light amplifying glass. Small amounts of light, barely detectable by the naked eye, were being produced by devices placed by specialists in every unit participating in Operation Nemesis. This miniscule amount of light, amplified by the visor, allowed the frogmen as well as other participants in the operation to see clearly.

In West Clover, the elite Israeli frogmen split up into small groups and engaged the Nazis in several skirmishes. The minimal amount of light created by ineffectual Nazi automatic rifle fire was inadequate to remove the distinct advantage held by the Israeli forces due to their superior vision, preparation, and modern fire and movement tactics, such as "leapfrogging" in fire team formations. In less than fifteen minutes, over two hundred Aryan supermen stationed in West Clover were dead without a single casualty among the Israeli frogmen.

When the Israeli commandos opened the doors to the barracks of Hell Camp, the Jewish prisoners were initially petrified. Lieutenant Commander Sofer, himself the son of concentration camp survivors, had tears in his eyes as he spoke in German over a portable megaphone.

"Do not be afraid. We are fellow Jews from the Jewish nation, Israel. We have come to free you."

These words had an immediate calming effect on the prisoners. Although they were in total darkness, their eyes strained to see the source of the words of someone claiming to be a talking Jew. The frogmen fanned out and placed light-enhancing goggles over every inmate's eyes. Then small group of frogmen organized the Jews into groups of fifty. The rest left to tackle their next objective, a strike on the SS base in South Clover.

When the lights went out in the cavern complex, Rachel Bronot, Joshua, a company of marines, and the Black Berets carrying the

200

nuclear device headed through North Clover toward the Broder Laboratory. When they reached the walkway that led toward the Reich Zoo, Joshua broke off from the group and ran toward the Human House. Rachel had expected this and told Major Carl Brenner to take over temporary command as she and a contingent of Marines accompanied Joshua.

Bronot followed Joshua to the Human House. She was in shock as she pointed her flashlight at the many cells, which featured life-size photographs of each of the former inhabitants. Yesterday they had all been shot save for Rabbi Cohen, who had been taken to the Reich Temple for today's service. Joshua stood before the empty cell of his teacher and cried. Bronot did her best to comfort him. Then she led him and her unit towards the Broder Laboratory.

At the same time, a company of Marines joined the frogmen in their attack on the SS base in South Clover. During the battle, SS engineers were successful in initiating backup generators, flooding Valhalla with red emergency lights. During the battle, a unit of US Army engineers above ground set off explosives at the surface entrance of the elevator, blowing off its hinges. Cables were then attached to the mangled door, allowing a Sikorsky CH-53K King Stallion cargo helicopter to drag it off the elevator shaft. Giant chain ladders were then unrolled into the shaft, and a battalion of Marines descended to assist in the battle. A short time later the entire SS base was captured, with all defending SS soldiers eliminated.

With the elevator shaft captured, the Israeli frogmen led their fellow Jews through the SS base's main gate and to the elevator shaft. The commandos wished them luck as the Jewish prisoners were lifted to the surface. Dozens of helicopters above ground were waiting to transport them to the abandoned airfield, where C-130 Hercules transport aircraft would fly them directly to Israel.

When the lights went out in the cavern complex, Ronald Fletcher and his group of frogmen emerged for their assault on the Reich Temple. Though they initially found themselves in total darkness as expected, disaster soon struck. Unknown to the planners of Operation Nemesis, the attendees of the special service at the Reich

Temple had been given prayer candles that were to be lit as Hitler broadcasted the code to release the Strain from its cylinders in Israel.

Soon after the Reich Temple was engulfed in darkness, a few congregants began to light their candles to see what was happening. The orange glow of the candles quickly exposed Fletcher and the frogmen, who had stealthily made their way into the Temple and were approaching the central podium. Gestapo honor guards alerted to the threat entered the Temple and opened fire with their StG 44 assault rifles. Eight frogmen were immediately hit before they were able to react. Fletcher and the frogmen were in an area without cover about fifty yards from the main stage.

High Priest Heinrich Mueller had just finished sealing Rabbi Gershon Cohen into the glass booth next to the sacrificial altar when the cavern was plunged into darkness. The booth had been specially constructed for this ceremony. Mueller had planned to press a large white button releasing the Strain into the booth at the same time the codes were transmitted as a demonstration of the Reich Gott's power. When the cavern was plunged into darkness and gunfire erupted throughout the complex, Mueller took cover behind the sacrificial altar. He crawled over to Das Maschine and asked Hitler what should be done. Hitler responded by saying, "We will see who will get the last laugh! I will now release the Strain all over the world. Bring me my codes!"

Hitler, thanks to Schreiber, was able to hear the transpiring events. Already in a state of euphoria due to the current setting on Das Maschine, Hitler now took the greatest pleasure as the leader in charge of defending Valhalla. Free of his ailments that hampered him during his command of German Forces during the Defense of Berlin in April 1945, he would make sure this time the results would be in his favor.

Hitler barked out directions by way of a direct patch into the radio system of all SS and Gestapo units. He ordered them to make their way immediately to the Reich Temple. The attendees hearing the Reich Gott's orders were inspired. With the Reich Gott in command, victory was assured. And they appeared justified in their beliefs, as the candles had created a major setback for Operation Nemesis.

Mueller scrambled down the steps and under the stage where the Reich Temple office was located. The code book for the Strain program, containing the precise location and the individual release code for every cylinder on Earth, was located in a safe in the office.

Reinforcements streamed into the Reich Temple as a result of Hitler's orders. Fletcher, seeing the hopelessness of his unit's present position, shouted out to the Israeli commandos in Hebrew. "Hold your fire! I repeat, do not fire! I'm calling in support."

The disciplined commandos obeyed their American commander, despite the seemingly nonsensical command. Incoming fire was getting more intense.

He then picked up the walkie-talkie. "Unit One to Command Center One, over."

"Command Center reads you, over."

"We are pinned down by enemy fire, Send Edge! Repeat, send Edge! Over."

"Message received. Edge squadron to be dispatched immediately. Over and out."

In less than forty seconds, the twenty rocket-enhanced members of the elite Edge unit cruised over the walls of open-air Reich Temple. They adjusted their computer-controlled target finders to small arms fire. As the Gestapo honor guards, along with reinforcements of Gestapo and SS soldiers, continued to press their attack, edge helmet-based sensors detected their firing rifles and unleashed laser pulsations from the shoulder-mounted automated firing systems, melting the German weapons. Many of the magazines on the StG 44 rifles exploded as the intense heat of the lasers reached the gunpowder in the cartridges. Within minutes, the entire force of Gestapo security and SS reserves were either dead or disarmed. The shocked and unarmed attendees in the Temple fled to the exits of the stadium.

Fletcher spotted Mueller out of the corner of his eye as he emerged from beneath the stage with the code book. He looked exactly as Joshua had described. Seeing the book in Mueller's hands, Fletcher immediately realized he was carrying the release codes for the transmitter. He ordered the frogmen to secure the stage area as he headed in Mueller's direction.

When Mueller passed the Rabbi in the glass booth, he couldn't resist the urge to see for himself the destructive power of the Strain. He reached for the white button that would release the deadly agent. The Rabbi stared at Mueller coldly. In a clear voice, he began to recite the most sacred of Jewish prayers, which as per tradition is declared before one's death: "Hear O' Israel, the Lord is our God, the Lord is One."

Mueller watched the rabbi praying with some amusement. It brought back pleasant memories of the countless occasions in Nazi Germany when he had witnessed Jews uttering similar supplications before their death. He was about to press the white button when he felt a crash come down on his hand. The attacker grabbed Mueller's arm and spun him one hundred and eighty degrees and on to the ground on his back. Mueller looked up and saw the face of Ronald Fletcher. He felt the steel needle of the Vu Khi thrust into his nose and entering his brain. Fletcher released the microhooks and twisted with all his strength, decimating Mueller's frontal lobe. He then removed the needle and wiped it clean on Mueller's white satin robe. Fletcher then opened the door to the booth and released the Rabbi.

Fletcher asked, "Are you Rabbi Gershon Cohen?"

"I am Rabbi Cohen. How did you know?"

"From your friend, Joshua. He brought soldiers from the State of Israel and the United States of America to save you."

The Rabbi burst out in tears, saying, "Thank God!"

Suddenly from behind the far side of the stage, Dr. Josef Schreiber jumped out of his hiding place wielding a MP40, better known as a Schmeisser. He aimed the gun at the Rabbi and Fletcher. But before he was able to fire, Barnes came out of nowhere and slapped him on the side of his face so hard that Dr. Schreiber slumped to the floor, dropping the gun.

Fletcher turned to Barnes. "How many times are you going to save me?"

Barnes chuckled. "As long as you're my boss, you can be sure I'll be there to protect your behind!"

Barnes then turned to the Rabbi. "Are you O.K.?"

Rabbi Cohen responded, "Yes, thanks to you. May God bless both of you all the days of your lives."

Rabbi Cohen then turned towards Das Maschine. Looking at Fletcher and Barnes, he said, "You must destroy this evil apparatus. I know it is hard to believe, but I assure you that inside is the madman Adolf Hitler. May his name be erased forever."

The three approached the undefended Das Maschine. Fletcher signaled to a pair of Israeli frogmen to drag Dr. Schreiber to them.

The Rabbi said, "This is Dr. Josef Schreiber. He is the man who made the machine that keeps Hitler alive. He is a wicked man who murdered thousands of Jews in his nefarious experiments."

Fletcher turned towards Schreiber and hit him in the stomach with all of his strength. The Nazi immediately fell to the floor, clutching his abdomen. As he gasped for air, Fletcher ordered the two frogmen to pick him up. Fletcher motioned with hands that he was going to repeat the blow.

The terrified German gasped out, "Please, no!"

"Fine, I'll give you a chance. How do you speak with this thing? Tell him it's over, he's been totally defeated."

Before Schreiber could answer, Hitler, who had been listening, spoke up in his mechanical voice.

"How dare you defy the will of the Reich Gott?"

Fletcher, Barnes, and the two frogmen were amazed that the apparatus was actually talking to them through a speaker at the side of Das Maschine.

Fletcher responded. "Look, Mr. Reich Gott, or whatever you want to call yourself. It's over. You're finished."

Hitler responded. "Insolent fool. You have no idea who you are speaking to. I am the all-powerful Reich Gott. You should know that I have already won. My true vengeance is complete. I have already sent the code to release the Strain in Israel. The Jewish State is no more."

The three gasped. Rabbi Gershon approached Das Maschine. It looked like he was about to smash it to the ground. Fletcher felt destroyed that he was helpless to stop this new Holocaust.

Suddenly Fletcher shouted, "Wait!"

The Rabbi stopped in his tracks. Fletcher grabbed Schreiber by the collar. "How is it that this device hears and speaks?"

"By way of these two boxes."

Fletcher then looked at the panel at the front of the box. There was a dial conspicuously marked "Himmel." "What does this do?" he asked Schreiber.

Schreiber said, "This dial maintains the Fuhrer in a state of euphoria."

"You mean Hitler can experience feelings?"

"That's correct. It's set right now to the highest level of pleasure. He is currently at a level of perfect bliss not achievable by mortal man."

Fletcher turned the dial counterclockwise to lower the level but found it wouldn't turn more than 30 degrees. "I think it's stuck," he said. He pried the metal panel surrounding the dial off of Das Maschine. "I see the problem, there's this metal tab here." Fletcher bent back the tab, removing the dial's only safeguard. He could now turn it to the lowest setting. Hitler cursed Fletcher through the speaker of Das Maschine.

"What are you doing?" yelled Dr. Schreiber. He lunged for the machine and turned the dial back up. "You don't understand! The lowest setting is ultimate pain! No living being should experience such pain!"

"Really, Dr. Death?" Fletcher's blood was boiling. "What about all the Jews you experimented on, huh?" He hit Dr. Schreiber with a double upset punch and the German slumped to the ground.

Fletcher said, "Sorry, I couldn't help myself. That guy was like a walking plague."

Barnes replied, "No big loss. He was getting on my nerves, too." Rabbi Gershon nodded in agreement.

Fletcher turned towards Das Maschine. This device represented the source of Fletcher's burning desire for revenge. It was controlled by Adolf Hitler, whose order set off the chain of events that led to his beloved Mary's death. This evil machine was the reason

Fletcher's children would be growing up without their mother. Now, it says that it killed everyone in Israel. Destroying it would be too small a punishment.

Fletcher approached Das Maschine and addressed it. "Well, it's time for me to judge the Reich Gott. I find you guilty. Any last words?"

Hitler spoke, "You American Jew lover. I curse you and your country."

Fletcher said. "Your first punishment will be that I rip out these two boxes so you can never hear or speak again. Your second punishment will be excruciating pain. How do you like that?"

Fletcher tore the two small boxes from the wires connecting them to Das Maschine and smashed them on to the concrete floor of the stage. Then he reached for the dial and turned it slowly toward the lowest setting. A string of threats and expletives in German exploded from the teletype printer. Fletcher yanked out the cord connecting Das Maschine to the teletype, stopping the output. He then completed turning the dial to the level of ultimate pain.

Examining Das Maschine, Fletcher looked for its power source. There was an electrical cord that ran to a battery on the floor. A note in German attached to the battery stated that it had been connected the previous day and had enough power for one week.

Fletcher turned to the frogmen. "You two are in charge of this box. We're taking it with us." He then walked over to Mueller's body and picked up the book of codes, placing it in his bag.

Yitzhak Sofer, commander of the Israeli frogmen, arrived. "All opposition outside the Reich Temple has been eliminated. We have a clear corridor to South Clover."

"Got it. Let's move the men out. We need two guys to assist Rabbi Cohen. Also, get a group of your boys to help transport this machine here. Don't tell the Americans what it is, just get it to your government."

"I'll take that as an order," said Sofer, saluting Fletcher.

Outside the Reich Temple, the complex was ablaze with tracer bullets and laser beams as the Edge squadrons and Marine units mopped up the remaining Gestapo and SS resistance.

At the Broder Laboratory, opposition was fierce. Already a dozen Marines had been killed by cannon fire from the fortified platforms around the lab entrance. Bronot and Joshua joined the large force taking cover behind nearby buildings.

Joshua instinctively understood the solution was to eliminate the cannon platforms. He went up to one of the Black Beret sergeants who had earlier communicated with him in sign language and signed that he knew where the entrance to the cannon platforms was located. The Sergeant took five of his men and followed Joshua.

When the Black Berets arrived, they noticed that the door had been left unguarded. The Sergeant and his men shot the lock off the door and climbed the ladder. The SS gunners at the cannon were taken completely by surprise as the Black Beret commandos eliminated them without sustaining any casualties. A short time later, the Marines and Black Berets secured the area surrounding the lab facility. The Marines were then ordered to go to South Clover for evacuation.

The Edge unit then cruised to the fortified steel laboratory door. Focusing their laser weapons at the door, they burned through a man-sized hole. The Black Berets then entered the area. The lab was deserted. The commando carrying the atomic device placed it next to a sealed door with multiple biohazard warning signs. He set the device for 12:00 noon. Their mission was now complete. The Edge and Black Berets headed toward the elevator entrance in South Clover. When they arrived, they found that the area was protected by a handful of remaining Marines.

The last troops were lifted to the surface, where a few remaining helicopters were waiting. At 11:50 a.m., they took off. They were twenty miles out when a tremendous explosion rocked the sands of the Sahara. Project Valhalla and the Fourth Reich were no more.

29

Just prior to Operation Nemesis, about forty thousand Israeli soldiers, both reservists and those on active duty, had been called up to the North of Israel. They cordoned off Lake Kinneret and evacuated the City of Tiberias and all of the surrounding villages and towns. No one was allowed within a 20-mile radius. Additionally, all water pipes and canals leading from the Kinneret were shut off. The Jordan River was dammed in both directions, with giant portable pumps set up to collect runoff water and recycle it to the lake. This operation effectively isolated the cylinder.

Since Israeli scientists at the secret biological warfare complex near the Dead Sea had observed that once separated from its bacterial host the prion contained in the cylinder was inactive after 24 hours, it was decided that the best course of action would be to allow the cylinder to open and let it run its course. Fletcher's discovery that the third cylinder had been placed in the Kinneret allowed the Israeli authorities to formulate a plan that would protect Israel's citizens without any effort to jam the signal or recover the cylinder. Thus, the coded signal sent sadistically by Hitler led to the release of the agent but did not cause any harm.

Two weeks after Operation Nemesis, Ronald Fletcher drove from Ben Gurion Airport to Kibbutz Galuyot, translated as the Gathering of the Exiles, in the center of the Galilee region. During those two weeks, Fletcher had been quite busy, He had originally returned to Israel on one of the Hercules transport planes carrying the Jews of Project Valhalla. The President of the United States ordered Air Force One to be placed at Fletcher's disposal. He used the plane to take his family back home to the United States. Mary's body was placed in a stainless-steel coffin for the flight. The plane landed at Chicago's O'Hare Airport and the Fletcher family received a military escort to Kenosha,

Wisconsin. Two days later, Mary Fletcher was buried in a private ceremony at a small cemetery near the shores of Lake Michigan.

Fletcher spent the next eight days with his children in a large log cabin he had built by hand some years earlier near the Dells resort area in central Wisconsin. There the three began the painful process of adjustment without Mary. Afterwards, the three returned to Kenosha. Fletcher left the children in their grandparents' care as he prepared to finally bring a close to this tragic period of his life. When Fletcher arrived at the main gate of Kibbutz Galuyot, he was stopped by two Shin Bet guards. When they saw that it was Ronald Fletcher, they gave him a salute and waived him through.

Fletcher was pleased with the natural beauty of the newly founded agricultural settlement. It was a lush paradise. Fletcher drove to the Director's Office. There, he entered to find Rachel Bronot and Rabbi Gershon Cohen.

"It's so good to see you, Ron!" Bronot said.

"How are you, Mr. Fletcher?" asked the Rabbi.

"I'm doing just fine. How is it to be living in Israel?"

"It's a dream come true. The land is even more beautiful than I ever imagined, Also the people. What can say? It's like coming home to family. They have opened their hearts to us."

"How is Joshua?"

"Well, tonight he's going to marry Miriam according to Jewish Law. I will be preforming my first wedding ceremony in over forty years. Joshua has asked if you could be his best man."

"Of course. I'm honored."

"Ron," Rachel said. "I don't know if you heard. Last week, Miriam gave birth to Joshua's son. He's very cute. You'll get to see him tonight!"

A warm feeling overcame Fletcher. Then he turned to Rabbi Cohen. "What are your future plans?"

"Well, the government has been very helpful to us. They have sent doctors, teachers, psychologists, dieticians, just about every kind of expert they have to help us adjust to a life of freedom in the modern world. They say we will be much better off in a year or two. Those who

210

wish to stay here will become part of the Kibbutz, and anyone who does not will be given assistance to settle anywhere in Israel that they choose.

"As for me, I will remain here as their spiritual advisor. These poor souls are born Jews, but they have no idea what that means."

"Don't be so modest, Rabbi Cohen," Bronot interrupted. "When word leaked out that the great Rabbi Gershon Cohen survived the Holocaust and was now living in Israel, the country's rabbinical leaders demanded that he be immediately appointed Chief Rabbi of Israel. You see, Rabbi Cohen is considered the world's foremost authority on Jewish Law. Even our present Chief Rabbi was pushing for his own replacement. He said that he was just a child in his scholarship next to Rabbi Cohen."

"I should only have such children!" Rabbi Cohen said, laughing. "In any case, I have decided for the time being to stay here and take care of my people. We already have plans to build a yeshiva."

Fletcher said, "I would like to let you know I didn't come empty-handed. I have a gift for the new immigrants from Project Valhalla."

Rabbi Cohen looked at Fletcher. You shouldn't feel obligated to give us anything. You've already given us the greatest gift, our freedom."

"Well," said Fletcher, "The gift isn't exactly from me. Let's call it war reparations from Nazi Germany."

"What are you talking about?" Bronot said, perplexed.

"Do you remember when I asked you to make that short stop in Tripoli on the way to Martyrs' square?"

"You mean in front of the Umma Bank?" Bronot recalled vaguely.

"That's right. When I rifled through Rajad's pockets, I found an envelope with a safety deposit key and a note that said "Umma Bank." So I decided to make a pickup. I practiced copying Rajad's signature from his driver's license a few times, and I showed his I.D. to the clerk, telling him Rajad sent me. In his safety deposit box I found ten packets filled with diamonds."

Bronot asked, "You didn't want to just keep them?"

"Well, you might say it just didn't feel kosher," said Fletcher, eliciting laughs from Bronot and Rabbi Cohen.

Fletcher continued, "Yesterday I was in Switzerland and sold the diamonds. With the money, I opened up an account in the Kibbutz's name. I figure that even at slave labor rates, the Jews at Valhalla definitely earned it."

"How much money are we talking about?" Bronot inquired.

A little over fifteen million dollars." Fletcher answered. "If you are looking for ideas about what to do with the money, let me make a suggestion. I was speaking to an old friend of mine from the University of Chicago. He's now the head of ear, nose, and throat surgery at the medical school. He's been working with a biomedical engineering company to help out patients who needed to have their tongues removed because of cancer surgery.

"His team has designed a prosthetic tongue that can be implanted and is capable or replacing all the functions of a natural tongue. He assured me that the operation is safe. Moreover, he is willing to send a team to perform the surgery. All you would have to pay for would be the production of the artificial tongues. I did a rough estimate and it came out to about ten million dollars for all of the survivors. That will leave enough over to help build schools, yeshivas, whatever you want."

"That's fantastic!" Bronot said.

"You are truly a friend," said Rabbi Gershon Cohen, teary-eyed.

"Ron, let me show you around the kibbutz," said Bronot.

"Sounds great. Best of luck, Rabbi Cohen!"

The two walked down a dirt road lined by citrus trees. Bronot spoke first. "There was a big controversy regarding the man in the box. There were cabinet meetings about it all week long. They voted to put Hitler on trial in front of the entire world."

"Another Eichmann affair?" Fletcher asked.

"Exactly. However, the Supreme Court ruled in a private session that a machine cannot be considered a human. Therefore, no trial. In fact, they ruled the Israeli Government must maintain the apparatus at its present level until the brain stops functioning."

Bronot grinned and added, "The Prime Minister was particularly delighted with this decision."

"Why?" asked Fletcher.

"Simple. Thanks to you, the dial is currently set at ultimate pain. The Prime Minister considers this worse than any death penalty. He ordered that Das Maschine be sealed within a steel box without any door. The box is in a room underneath the Knesset building.

"A hole was drilled through the bottom of the box to allow an electric cord to feed power to Das Maschine. Our scientists believe that as long as the flow of electricity remains constant, Das Maschine should function indefinitely, perhaps, forever."

Fletcher remarked, "Isn't it ironic that Hitler's journey started in the Fuhrerbunker underneath the Reich Chancellery, and ended in a bunker under Israel's Knesset?"

Fletcher stopped walking. He turned to Bronot. "I have a gift for you."

"Another gift?"

"Well, this is really a gift to the State of Israel and the Jewish People." Fletcher reached into his sport coat's inner pocket and removed a yellow envelope. He handed it to Bronot.

Bronot opened the envelope. Inside was a copy of the book of codes Fletcher had taken from Mueller. She was astounded.

Fletcher explained, "This list contains the codes for all of the cylinders around the world, except for those planted in the United States and its protectorates."

"Why on earth would you give me this?" Bronot asked.

Fletcher said, "We both know that it's only a matter of time before Israel is confronted with a threat for which there is no solution. One day your country will be pressed against a wall and even your military won't be able to bail you out. I for one don't want to see another Holocaust befall your people. Let's just call this your 'Get out of jail' card."

Bronot was not satisfied. "Ron, what's your real reason?"

Fletcher sighed. "I am a man who always pays his debts. I'm paying back a private debt to three wonderful human beings that saved the lives of my children: Shlomo Mizrachi, Yoram Cohen, and of course Zelda Steiner. Zelda, in particular, killed the man that murdered my wife. I will always remember them for their courage and self-sacrifice."

Bronot asked, "What are your plans, now that all this is behind you?"

"After the wedding I'm going back to the States. The President has offered me a job as his personal intelligence advisor. I'll be looking for a place near Washington, D.C. What about you?"

"I've handed in my resignation. It's time for me to move on. An old friend of mine has a small political party. He offered me the number three position on his party's ticket in the next election. The party's platform is strong defense and economic freedom. And, you know what? I always wanted to try my hand at politics."

"Rachel, I'm going to miss you," Fletcher said, sincerely.

"I'm going to miss you more than you'll ever know," Bronot replied.

The two turned and walked silently down a tractor path through a field of strawberries.

30

At 4:00 am, the orders of the Prime Minister of Israel were executed. A coded signal was broadcast, releasing the contents of the cylinder located in Tehran. The deadly Strain spread, quickly turning the population of the city, including the Grand Ayatollah, the Iranian government, and the delegations of all 185 countries that had joined the New United Nations, to dust.

At the same time, a letter was delivered to the Chief of Staff of the New United Nations Freedom Expeditionary Force.

"The People of Israel have cried out to God beseeching him to save the offspring of Jacob from the evil forces of the world. Our Lord, Protector of Israel, has answered our prayers and has promised to destroy any nation that holds evil intentions against the Children of the Covenant. Behold the power of the God of Israel. Turn your eyes toward Tehran to witness the wrath of the Lord of the Universe."

At 8:00 a.m., the Prime Minister of Israel accepted a phone call from the Director of the United States Central Intelligence Agency.

"Hi, Mrs. Bronot. It's Bobby, Ronald Fletcher's son."

"So good to hear your voice, Bobby. It's been a long time. Please send my regards to your father. With all the excitement, I haven't had a chance to call him yet."

"I'm sure he would be happy to hear from you. You know he retired to Alaska last year. He's running a reindeer ranch now, and he's not always so easy to reach. I think he's enjoying himself too much."

"Well, what do you think?"

"As far as your response, I'd say you played your part perfectly. I just finished speaking to President Michael Barnes and showed him the code book. It's been sitting in the back of some Pentagon filing cabinet for all of those years.

"The President was greatly relieved that the crisis is over. He received almost a hundred phone calls from different countries asking him to relay to you their regret and beg for forgiveness. Or, as one so-called leader said, 'We wished we had come to Israel's defense and not played along with those nasty anti-Semites.'"

"I talked to President Barnes earlier. I'm sure you know he and your father saved me from certain death on more than one occasion. How both Barnes and I ended up becoming the leaders of our respective nations, only God knows. Anyway, he mentioned that he's developed Ambassador Cranston's penchant for visiting England as often as he can."

They both began to laugh. Bobby Fletcher said, "He's not kidding, next month will make his third official visit to England this year. Anyway, he told me to tell you that the United States unofficially congratulates your boys in winning the psychological warfare game. I'll tell you, I got goosebumps from reading your letter."

The Prime Minister of Israel then became serious. "You know, Israel owes its existence today to your father. As an old lady who has met some of the biggest personalities in the world over the years, I can tell you that your father is the best of the best. I don't know how to even begin thanking him."

"I spoke to him this morning," responded Bobby Fletcher. "He doesn't want any credit. He just reminded me of what happened on the beach so many years ago, and how Jane and I were saved. My father said that what he did back then was just payback for the courage of two retirees and an ice cream vendor!"

About the Author

Scott M. Neuman grew up in Chicago, Illinois. He holds a degree in criminal justice from the University of Illinois at Chicago Circle, as well as a J.D. from Thomas M. Cooley Law School of Western Michigan University.

He is a veteran of the Israel Defense Forces, where he served as a combat medic and fought in Operation Peace for the Galilee, otherwise known as the 1982 Lebanon War. He is also a black belt in Tae Kwon Do.

In 2018, Scott Neuman published "The Nazi, the Princess, and the Shoemaker," a historical work describing his father's experiences surviving the Holocaust. He is currently a practicing attorney in Michigan.

Printed in the USA
CPSIA information can be obtained
at www.ICGtesting.com
LVHW091049120524
780058LV00007B/383

9 780578 585369